Reichsführer Heinrich Himmler (second from left) touring the IG Farben plant under construction at Auschwitz III Monowitz

Channing Way Publications

Ryan, James, author
The Himmler Gambits / James Ryan – 1ˢᵗ ed.
Library of Congress Control Number 2025909939
(eBook) ISBN 979-8-9879213-8-8
(Trade) ISBN 979-8-9879213-6-4
(Hardcover) ISBN 979-8-9879213-7-1
Printed in the United States of America

THE

HIMMLER

GAMBITS

A NOVEL

JAMES RYAN

Other books by James Ryan

Temple Legacy

For my sister and brother
Kathleen and Michael

*"Those who cannot remember the past
are condemned to repeat it."*

— GEORGE SANTAYANA

Contents

Prologue

August 31, 1939, Gleiwitz, Upper Silesia, Germany

FRANEK OPENED HIS eyes, but his vision was blurred. Even as he slowly managed to focus, the room and its contents spun before him. After a while, his surroundings began to stabilize. He looked to his left to see a man standing beside him who seemed monstrously tall and towered over him. However, Franek soon realized he was lying on the floor.

Where am I? How did I get here?

He fought hard to remember. But try as he might, he couldn't recall anything before waking thirty seconds ago.

Then, ever so slowly, bits and pieces came to mind. He remembered being served his second Pils.

Yes, I was in Pohlom, at the Gasthaus.

Franciszek (Franek) Honiok, forty-three, was a typical citizen of German Silesia. Specific to himself, he was unmarried, a Catholic, an ethnic Pole, and, like many in this part of Silesia, he spoke both Polish and German. He made his living working the small family farm he'd inherited. Because the farm, by itself, wasn't enough to cover expenses, he also held a part-time job selling agricultural equipment.

He had come to the Gasthaus to celebrate. It had been a hard week on the farm, but he'd finally finished harvesting all twenty-seven acres of wheat. He was late getting it in, but that was because there had been only he and the hired boy from the village doing the work.

Then it came back to him—the three German police-men entering the Gasthaus. They stood by the door for a moment, then moved to the center of the room and stopped, looking from side to side. One of them loudly called out a name—"Franciszek Honiok!" His name.

Bewildered, Franek stood and said, "I am Franciszek Honiok."

Hearing that, they turned and walked over to him. "You will come with us," one of the policemen said. "We'd like to ask you some questions."

"Why? What have I done?"

"You'll know soon enough," said another policeman, taking him by the arm.

Then the three of them led him to the door and out to a waiting car.

They drove him northeast through the countryside until they reached the police barracks in *Beuthen*, twelve kilome-ters away on the Polish border. Throughout the entire drive, not a word was spoken by the policemen. Franek continued to ponder what they wanted him for. As far as he knew, he had committed no crime.

As they drove, Franek hit on one possibility, something in his distant past. *Could this all be because of that? It was so long ago.*

After the war, in 1921, he had participated in the last of the three uprisings by ethnic Poles living in the once-Prussian province of Upper Silesia. Polish speakers and nationalists wanted an end to the discrimination they'd suf-fered and felt that certain parts of German Silesia should join the newly formed Polish Second Republic.

The Treaty of Versailles had mandated a plebiscite to

determine the postwar partitioning of Upper Silesia between Weimar Germany and the Second Polish Republic. Though scheduled for 1918, the League of Nations didn't organize it until March 1921, after the first two uprisings had already occurred in 1919 and 1920.

Based on the referendum results, the British, French, and Italian governments, along with members of the Inter-Allied Commission, debated partitioning Upper Silesia, focusing on the industrial centers in the east, which were rich in coal and iron deposits. The French, wanting to weaken Germany, supported ceding the area to Poland. The British and Italians disagreed, sympathetic to Germany's claim that losing the area would hamper their ability to pay war reparations.

The third uprising—Franek's uprising—began in May 1921 after rumors spread that the Anglo-Italian option would be adopted. Allied troops ended it in July of that year with a cease-fire and a general amnesty for both sides.

The League of Nations finally settled the issue with the Geneva Accord in 1922, allowing Germany to retain two-thirds of the land, while awarding Poland most of the east's natural resources, mines, and industrial capability.

Despite the amnesty, Franek moved to Poland to live with relatives after the uprising. When he returned to his hometown of Hohenlieben in German Silesia in 1925, the government did not welcome him. With his checkered past and continued vocal support of Poland, he had fought deportation to remain in the country and work his family farm.

The uprising was eighteen years ago, and involvement was no secret to his friends and neighbors. Still, he knew he was on file as a rabble-rouser.

By all that's Holy, that was so long ago, and I have been a good citizen. I've done nothing wrong.

When they arrived at the police barracks in Beuthen, Franek asked again what he had done, but they remained quiet. After escorting him into the building through a side door, they led him to an office and sat him in a chair, where they seemed to forget about him for a while. People came and went, and he grew curious about why he wasn't being charged, questioned, or interrogated. Hours passed, and the men continued with their business, paying him no attention whatsoever.

Franek's spine ached from sitting in the stiff-backed chair for so long. He began to believe a mistake had been made, and maybe he wasn't the man they were looking for. However, when he asked if that was the case, he was told to remain quiet and that someone would speak with him soon.

It grew dark, and the men became more animated. One seemed to be giving orders, but he kept his voice low, and Franek couldn't hear what he was saying. Then, all at once, they crowded around him. He looked up at them, and they looked down at him, their faces expressionless and their cold, dark eyes meeting his gaze. He felt a slight sting as the man standing behind him pushed a hypodermic needle into his neck.

"What the hell?" Franek said, startled.

A warm rush came over him, and his vision began to blur. He struggled to keep his eyes open and found that he couldn't. That was the last that he remembered. He had no memory of passing out or falling to the floor. No one attempted to catch him as he did.

Franek's senses restored, he saw that he was no longer

in the same room at the police barracks, but a strange place filled with electronic equipment. The walls were covered in dozens of illuminated panels, each with scores of knobs and switches.

He felt a wave of nausea come over him, and the room started to swim around him. Pushing himself up with his arms, he discovered he couldn't move his legs. Frustrated, he looked down at them and saw that his clothes were different. The suit he had been wearing when he left the house that morning had been replaced with a Polish military uniform.

This confused Franek even further. *I am not a soldier, and I'm German, not Polish.*

He heard one of the men speak to another, saying, "Are we ready?" and turned his head in time to see an officer nodding his confirmation.

The nodding man held what looked to be a microphone. He cleared his throat, paused, and pressed a button on the side of the microphone. "Attention! This is Gliwice. This broadcasting station is now in Polish hands."

Another man, whom Franek recognized as one of the men in the police barracks, approached. He smiled at Franek, who smiled back. The man unholstered his automatic pistol, walked a few paces behind him, then stopped, turned, and shot Franek once in the back of the head.

He holstered his gun and said to the others, "We're finished here. Let's go." Then, looking down, he spoke to Franek's lifeless body. "I'm sorry, my friend, but your personal history made you the perfect candidate for the role."

The men departed the broadcasting station, stepping over several equally lifeless bodies, also dressed in Polish uniforms, their faces disfigured and unrecognizable. These were men taken from the Dachau concentration camp earlier, also drugged, brought here, and shot to reinforce the appearance and impression of a Polish assault on the station.

The next day, a significantly different version of the events in Gleiwitz on August 31 was reported in German newspapers and soon spread throughout Europe and the world.

Kroll Opera House, Berlin, 11:00 A.M., September 1

"This night, for the first time, Polish regular soldiers fired on our territory. Since 5:45 A.M., we have been returning the fire; from now on, bombs will be met by bombs.

"I am, from now on, just the first soldier of the German Reich. I have once more put on that coat that was the most sacred and dear to me. I will not take it off again until victory is secured, or I will not survive the outcome."

EXCERPT FROM ADOLPH HITLER'S SPEECH TO THE REICHSTAG. SETTING ASIDE HIS FAMILIAR BROWN NAZI PARTY ATTIRE, HE WORE INSTEAD THE GRAY MILITARY UNIFORM OF A GENERALISSIMO.

Although flawed, the false flag attacks staged by the Schutzstaffel (SS) along the Polish border inside Germany, of which the Gleiwitz radio transmitter was one, served as the casus belli Hitler needed to invade and occupy Poland.

And so it was that Franciszek Honiok, just a simple

farmer dressed as a Polish soldier, played his tragic role and entered the history books as the first man to die in the Second World War.

By the end of 1941, SS Obersturmbannführer Rainer Heydrich, Franek's executioner, would find himself on a U-boat destined for the United States.

ONE

"Just a reminder, boss. The board meeting you called for starts in one hour," Sophie Campbell said as she tidied piles of papers on the desk of J. Leland Wilson (J.L.), CEO (Chief Executive Officer) and Chairman of the Board of Union Chemical, a midcap multinational conglomerate.

"Yes, I'm only too aware," said Wilson, taking a deep breath and not looking up as he paced his office floor. Halting momentarily, he said, "Sophie, do me a favor and get Anthony on the phone. Ask him to come here for a minute."

"Right, boss."

Wilson thought about how it used to annoy him when Sophie referred to him as *boss*. He'd admonished her several times, but when she persisted, he finally gave up, realizing it wasn't much to put up with for such an excellent assistant.

Anthony Scrivner was Union's president and Chief Operating Officer, with an office located down the hall. Sophie pressed a button on the intercom on her boss's desk and said, "Mr. Scrivner, J.L. asks that you please join him in his office."

Wilson walked back behind the desk, reached into his pocket, pulled out a comb, and ran it through his graying but still full head of hair. He was healthy and in reasonably good shape for a man of forty-eight.

He picked up the report marked "Confidential Company

Private" that lay in front of him on his desk. He'd commissioned it a month ago from his finance department. It fell open to the page he'd read many times since receiving it last week. Once more, he reread this page that summarized the nearly two-hundred-page document.

It concerned one of the company's subsidiaries, a chemical plant in Blechhammer, Germany, producing adhesives. Ever since the Germans had launched the war by invading Poland, he'd paid close attention to the situation. Thus far, the subsidiary had remained independent and was showing a good profit—in fact, an excellent profit. When the States entered the war last December, he decided he needed facts to support a course of action that he might need to put before the board.

Although trade with Germany was prohibited, American-owned subsidiaries continued to operate, and the Blechhammer plant was technically a US operation. Nonetheless, Wilson was deeply troubled that the plant could potentially aid Adolf Hitler, a thug and a warmonger in his eyes.

The buzzer on his intercom sounded, and Sophie announced, "Mr. Scrivner to see you." Scrivner was already walking through the door as Sophie bleated the announcement.

Wilson motioned him to a chair. "Anthony, sit down. I want to discuss something with you before we meet with the board."

"And good morning to you, J.L. Yes, I'm fine, and yourself?"

"Cut it out, Anthony. This is important, and I feel we should be of like mind before we talk to the board."

"Is it about the report you requested regarding our German subsidiary?"

"Yes, but how did you know about it?"

"I'm president of the company, J.L., if you remember. That bit of noodling you had the finance and engineering boys do took eight of our best minds, four weeks, and ten thousand dollars to put together."

"Next time, I'll be more precise in my instructions regarding confidentiality. Nevertheless, we have to be very specific regarding how we're going to handle this, along with considering the financial impact on the company."

"What exactly is your concern?"

"I'm worried our plant could produce materials that could contribute to Germany's war effort. That's why I asked for the report. Germany has plenty of coal but lacks oil as a natural resource. Eventually, they'll run out of their oil reserves, which bothers me."

Scrivner raised his hands dismissively. "Good God! How can producing adhesives contribute to the German military's goals?"

"It's spelled out in this report. According to our engineers, with some reengineering, the plant could produce other materials much more vital to Hitler's ability to wage war."

"And what exactly does the report say about that?"

"It outlines two possibilities," said J.L., "both of which could be achieved at the Blechhammer plant. It discusses synthetic fuels and rubber, using hydrogenated coal for synthetic fuel production, as well as rubbers made from coal and limestone.

"Both options would require considerable plant

conversions, but the fundamental liquefaction processes are already in place. They have other facilities that produce synthetic rubber in the north. Given the plant's proximity to the coal fields in Eastern Silesia, I bet they'll use our facility to produce synthetic fuel."

Scrivner thought for a moment, then said, "What do you propose we do?"

"Abandon our operations there immediately. Bring our scientists and engineers home and whatever staff wish to emigrate, if we can get them out of the country. If necessary, we'll destroy key equipment and ensure we don't leave any trade secrets behind."

"Wait a minute, J.L. We're talking about a hundred and fifty million dollars in business. Some board members may not want to do what you're suggesting. Look at the American automotive and oil companies with subsidiaries in Germany. You don't see them shuttering their doors."

"You don't understand, Anthony. If we don't play ball with Herr Hitler, he'll just take over. Inevitably, he'll commandeer Blechhammer and convert it to fit his purposes. How do you think that will affect business?"

"I can see why you wanted to chat before the meeting. But we can't go in with this proposal. What you're suggesting will result in a huge revenue loss. At least give me a day or two to think over some alternatives. Then we'll speak to the board together."

"That's reasonable, although I honestly can't think of another way."

"Today is Monday. Give me until the end of the week to see what I can come up with."

"Okay, the end of the week. Then we go see the board together."

Scrivner stood and, as he walked to the door, said, "Who else have you talked to about this?"

"No one. Just you."

"Good. We don't want word of this getting out until we've prepared something."

Wilson went back to his desk. Though he liked Anthony, he had some reservations. *He's smart and capable and thinks he should be in charge once I retire. That's a problem, and I have to address that somehow.*

He understood the gravity of his proposed action. The German and Polish plants tied up twenty percent of Union's revenue. It would play hell with the stock valuation. But what could he do? Hitler and Nazi Germany now occupied nearly all of Europe, and thousands of people were imprisoned, displaced, or dead. He had to do whatever he could do within his power.

He pressed a button on the intercom. "Sophie, please get my daughter on the line. No, wait a minute. Get me Tobias Bach."

❧

Adam Wilson liked to go fast, and he was pushing his Plymouth P12 Special Deluxe convertible to its limits. The stylish red roadster, with its twin inline six-cylinder engine, was capable of reaching one hundred ten miles per hour, and he was clocking ninety-eight. He was on the last stretch leading up to his family's estate in western New Jersey.

"Adam, slow down," pleaded Julie Warren, Adam's

girlfriend of six months, sitting next to him on the front bench seat. "You know I don't like it when you go so fast."

"Damn it, Adam, ease up," said his sister, Barbara, who was in the back seat. "You'll get us all killed."

"Almost there. Hang on," said Adam, ignoring their appeals as they sped through the gate marking the property's boundary. The house was ahead, and he was fast approaching the horseshoe driveway out front.

Barely decelerating, Adam turned the wheel as he entered the drive, his rear wheels fishtailing as he made the curve. Just at that moment, a golden retriever ran across the car's path, and Adam clipped its hindquarters as he hit the brakes, sending the dog spinning and then tumbling across the drive. Julie screamed as the car came to a halt.

They got out of the car, and Julie and Barbara ran to the animal lying thirty yards further ahead. It was panting feverishly and mortally wounded. Adam walked up.

"You jackass! It's Sport, Mrs. Higgins's dog," said Barbara.

"He jumped right in front of me. It's not my fault. Anyway, it's just a dog."

"How can you be so insensitive?" said Julie, tears in her eyes. But Adam didn't hear her. He was already halfway to the front door.

Adam threw his keys on the table in the center of the foyer. Passing Benson, the Wilsons' longtime butler, he mentioned a mess that needed to be cleaned up in the drive. Then he proceeded to the sitting room immediately adjoining the foyer and fixed himself a drink at the bar.

Julie and Barbara came in, Julie still in tears. Barbara

was furious and said, "Adam, you can be a right bastard sometimes."

"Come on, sis, what's the big deal? I'll buy the house-maid another dog."

"It's like no one else exists but you. You should go tell Mrs. Higgins how sorry you are. But you won't because you're not sorry, and you don't apologize for anything. That would take an ounce of compassion, and you're two ounces short."

"Relax, sis. You've gotta calm down. Come on, Julie. I could use a shoulder massage. I think I strained something."

"Uh . . . oh, yes, Adam," Julie said meekly, wiping away her tears.

They rose together and walked out of the room, Adam in the lead and Julie close behind him. Barbara went to find Mrs. Higgins to break the news about her dog.

∽

Tobias Bach wasn't in his office to take J.L. Wilson's call. He waited for the elevator in the hallway on the fifteenth floor of City Financial, where he had served as president for the last twelve years.

Tobias and J.L. met in France during the war, where their friendship was forged as members of the same battalion in the 165th Infantry. Together, they participated in a rescue operation that succeeded in saving the lives of several soldiers, American and French. Both men were wounded in the action. Afterward, Wilson was offered the *Croix de Guerre* but turned it down when he learned that it had not been awarded to Bach because he was a Jew. They'd been friends ever since.

Tobias left the City Financial building and took a cab south from Midtown Manhattan to the Chelsea Pier on the Hudson. He'd arranged to meet his contact at the Cunard Line ticketing office. It was a busy place this time of day, so they wouldn't be noticed in the crowd. Not long after he arrived, he spotted his man just outside the entrance.

"Hello, Alfred. Have you been keeping well?"

"Very well, and you, Mr. Bach?"

"Oh, just the usual complaints for a man who sits behind a desk all day. It's nice to get out." Tobias looked around to be sure no one was paying attention, then leaned in and said softly, "But Alfred, tell me. What of the shipment? Has it arrived as planned?"

Alfred smiled. "Yes, it was offloaded and delivered without incident. Our people are very pleased."

After months of worrying that the operation might fail, Tobias was relieved. He had feared discovery by various authorities at every step, certain that funding the operation was illegal, even though he hadn't participated physically. He was thankful that his part of the mission was over.

"I'll contact you again in two weeks," said Alfred. "I should have word from them concerning what we can do next."

Bach was unsure. He was afraid of the risk and wasn't sure he could face all the fear and angst of possibly being caught again.

"Very good," said Tobias, looking at his watch. "Until then." He looked up and was about to say keep well, but Alfred Adler had already disappeared into the bustling crowd.

❧

Not long ago, dinner at the Wilson home had a casual and upbeat air, but that evening, J. Leland felt the tension that seemed to have become the new norm—Barbara wasn't talking, and Adam was talking too much. J.L. knew the signs well. It meant Adam had somehow offended Barbara, and his continual one-sided conversation was a vain attempt to get through the meal without it coming up.

"All right, what's up?" asked J.L.

Adam feigned innocence, which was quickly replaced by annoyance that his blathering had been interrupted.

Barbara said, "Adam murdered Mrs. Higgins's golden retriever this afternoon."

"Sport ran in front of the car. That's hardly murder," Adam said in his defense.

This started a back-and-forth series of accusations and denials that had become common whenever the two were in the same room. J.L. tried to keep order in the family, but nothing had been the same since the skiing accident four years ago.

Adam and his mother, Margaret, were skiing in California when they were caught in an avalanche and buried under a wall of snow and rubble. It took two hours to dig them out. Margaret was dead, her torso crushed by a boulder. Adam's leg and the right side of his face had been badly mangled, but he was alive.

Adam recovered from his injuries, save for a two-inch vertical scar under his right eye and the effects of an orbital fracture that caused enophthalmos. His right eye appeared sunken and smaller, not severely as can happen with such an injury, but noticeably so.

J.L. believed his behavior was primarily a result of anger stemming from his appearance.

After the accident, Adam's personality seemed to change. Where he was once a caring and thoughtful young man, he was now cold and distant. He felt his mother was the only family member who understood and supported him, and although his mother's death was an accident, he irrationally believed that she had abandoned him.

J.L. had hoped Adam would someday take a position with the company and rise to the top, but now he had doubts. He firmly believed that someone with the power to influence people's livelihoods should possess a sense of humanity, as well as humility and compassion. Adam's personality now seemed devoid of these qualities—either he disregarded people's feelings and emotions, or he was simply oblivious to their existence. J.L. wished it to be the latter, somehow thinking it would be less malicious.

He interrupted his children's bickering. "I don't want to hear anything more about it. Adam, I expect you'll offer Mrs. Higgins your sympathies tomorrow morning and apologize."

Adam didn't like being told what to do. Inwardly, there was a clash between his desire to control every aspect of his life and his inability to control his impulses.

He looked flat and emotionless as, almost whispering, he said, "Yes, Father."

◆

George Hansen was a senior member of the Union's board of directors. He had been with J.L. Wilson when they founded the company twenty years ago. He was also the second-largest stockholder after Wilson. Though they had successfully collaborated to grow the business, the two men couldn't be further apart in their worldviews.

While J.L. thought President Franklin Delano Roosevelt was the right man for the times, Hansen disregarded FDR, thinking him a dangerous socialist complicit in a Jewish agenda to dominate the American economy. Along with Charles Lindbergh and Henry Ford, he became an early member of the America First Committee, which opposed American intervention in the European war, which meant war with Germany to him. He also sympathized with the anti-Semitic leanings of some of its members.

Hansen knew Wilson was worried about their plant in Germany, which also gave him cause for worry, although for entirely different reasons. Over the past nine months, he had secretly communicated with Pierre Ter Meer, the head of operations in Blechhammer, through a German inter-mediary, a member of the German Abwehr, the German government's espionage and counterintelligence organiza-tion. Ter Meer had been a National Socialist Workers Party member since 1933. Both Hansen and Ter Meer saw the handwriting on the wall and knew that at some point, Union Chemical's assets would be pulled into the war effort, will-ingly or unwillingly. Hansen preferred willingly because, in that scenario, he could stand to realize a sizable profit.

Together, they secretly worked toward converting the plant to produce the raw material to support Hitler's armed forces. Hansen absconded with and passed on Union Chem-ical's proprietary technology to his contact, which would not only aid in the conversion of the plant but also provide a significantly more efficient process than current German science was capable of.

They'd managed to keep Wilson in the dark, mainly due to his trust in Ter Meer and his monthly financial reports, which showed consistent year-over-year growth and ever-increasing profit margins. Wilson didn't know that subsidies from the Reich bolstered these numbers. He suspected Wilson would move to shut down the plant at some point, but by then, it would be too late, and they'd keep producing. Not to mention providing a healthy and ongoing cash flow to Hansen's Swiss bank account.

It was nearly five o'clock, and Hansen had an appointment with his German intermediary at New York's well-known athletic club, where both were members.

Hansen's connection lived in New York under the assumed name of Bradley Compton. His real name was Rainer Heydrich, an Obersturmbannführer with the *Schutzstaffel* ("protection squadron," or SS), collaborating with the Abwehr. Compton had been sent to America to engage and manage Hansen and others colluding with the Third Reich. As such, he was Hansen's sole point of contact with Nazi Germany. He was the cousin of Reinhard Heydrich—"The Blond Beast" who served as Reich Security Main Office Director and head of the SS.

Compton (Heydrich) landed in Florida at the end of December 1941. With the help of operatives in place there, he made his way north to New York, where his new identity was waiting for him. On paper, he worked as a commodities broker on Wall Street—single, with a comfortable uptown apartment, a bank account, and, conveniently, a membership at the athletic club.

When Hansen arrived, Compton was already seated at a table in the club's second-floor dining room.

Hansen approached and took a seat. "Hello, Bradley."

"George! Good evening," said Compton, who had been trained to speak with a flawless Midwest American accent in preparation for his mission. "How about those Yankees, eh?"

"Baseball season doesn't start until April."

Compton smiled. "I know that. Just a little inside joke."

The waiter came to the table carrying a bottle of wine. "The '26 Latour, sir." He poured a sample into Compton's glass.

Bradley took the glass, examined the color and clarity of the wine, and inhaled the bouquet. He emptied the glass into his mouth and swirled it, appreciating the flavors and mouth feel, before finally giving the waiter an affirmative nod. The waiter filled both men's glasses and retreated.

"Good news, George. The conversion has been completed, and save for some final tests, they'll be in full production soon."

"And the company employees?"

"The few who outwardly opposed the conversion were disposed of. Some of the more senior engineers and their families who didn't support our objectives were, shall we say, persuaded to comply."

"The efficiency of the Germans never fails to impress me. I wish we could implement such methods here."

Dinner arrived. Compton tried his turtle soup. He signaled a look of pure pleasure, swallowed, and said, "I wish we could get soup like this in Potsdam."

Nervously, Hansen said, "Pierre's reports will only keep

Wilson at bay for another few months. What will we do when he finds out?"

"Nothing. He'll be powerless to do anything about it. Pierre will be exposed, of course, but he'll continue to act as chief of operations, and his reports will simply be routed to someone else. I'll move on to other matters that concern us in the United States."

Hansen didn't ask what those matters might be. Somehow, he managed to draw a mental line between his own treason and the greater conspiracy Bradley was involved in. Thanks to his rationalization, he slept comfortably at night.

They finished their meal. After exchanging goodbyes, Compton watched as Hansen walked from the table, thinking, *Enjoy the money, my friend. You've certainly earned it.*

❧

Upstairs in Adam's room, Julie was kneading Adam's shoulder muscles, fulfilling her duty as his occasional masseuse. He was edgy, and she could tell he was in a foul mood. Not that there was anything odd about that—he was, more often than not.

"Father told me that I didn't have respect for people and have no compassion. He said he couldn't picture me in a position of such responsibility with the company—the old bastard," Adam said, recalling their frank discussion where his father had told him he would support him in whatever other endeavor he undertook.

Julie felt Adam's shoulder muscles tense and saw the veins in his neck stand out. She knew the telltale signs of one of his fits. His hands clenched and unclenched, and she could see his cheeks turning red.

She knew the anger was welling up inside him, so she tried to calm him down. "Forget him. Let me make you feel better," she said, leaning over and kissing him in the crook of his neck. She let her hand travel lightly around and down his bare back to massage his left buttock.

Adam jumped up. "He's sorry? He has no right. I'm the heir, the oldest. I'm his son!" he roared, flushed with anger. He took a wild swing and swept everything sitting atop his dresser to the floor.

Julie sat back on her heels, still on the floor, trying to be invisible. Twice in the past six months, she'd witnessed these fits of anger, and both occasions culminated in violent outbursts. The first was with a waiter who had tripped and accidentally spilled the soup he was carrying—not on Adam but on Adam's jacket on the chair next to him. That incident ended with the waiter being sent to the hospital to get stitches for the torn lip where Adam struck him. J.L. had paid off the waiter, and in return, he agreed not to press charges. The second time, a little over a month ago, Julie had innocently called him crazy when he made a silly remark. He'd exploded and slapped her so hard she had fallen to the floor.

"I worked hard. I went to his alma mater, which I hated, with those lofty, better-than-thou teachers—so kind, so willing to help the failing student with tutors to help me crib for tests. Sure, but it wasn't out of kindness—it was for the money. Well, I'm not a boy anymore, and I'm better than all of them."

He stood naked in the middle of the bedroom floor, breathing hard. Slowly, his rage subsided, and bit by bit, his breathing relaxed. He was calmer now, under control.

Not wanting to provoke an angry response, Julie cautiously asked, "Feeling better now, sweetie?"

He looked at her, sitting on the floor by the edge of his bed. He walked over to her and whispered, "Almost, baby." She tilted her head back to look up at him, and he smirked and said suggestively, "You know how to make me feel better."

"Sure, sweetie."

∽

In time for his 11:00 appointment, Richard Todd was sitting outside J.L. Wilson's office, opposite his private secretary, in one of two leather upholstered chairs engineered for someone much smaller.

Sophie Campbell, a smartly dressed woman with horn-rimmed glasses and a dated hairstyle from ten years ago, sat up stiffly in the desk chair behind her desk. The intercom beside her buzzed, and she said, "Mr. Wilson will see you now." Todd stood, thanked her, and, hat in hand, went into Wilson's office.

Wilson walked around his desk and offered his hand. "Pleased to meet you, Mr. Todd."

"Please, sir, call me Richard."

"Well, in that case, you call me J.L. Tell me, how's old Wild Bill? I served with him in France during the first war, you know." He sighed. "The first war—I still can't get used to saying that."

"He's fine, sir, and sends his regards. He's heading up a new unit under the Joint Chiefs. That's part of the reason I came to see you today."

"He told me—the Office of Strategic Services, or OSS

for short. Bill's been working with the same network of people since the end of the war, doing the same sort of work—intelligence gathering, counterespionage, with a little sabotage mixed in. I expect the group will be expanding now that there's a war on."

"Beginning with me. I just transferred from Army Intelligence last month."

"You'll do fine. Bill's a great guy, and no one understands the intel game better than him. Now, what can I do for you?"

"Sir, it's not generally known, but in 1936, Germany launched a four-year plan to gain independence in the materials it needed for its territorial expansion. They fell short by a country mile. They're still reliant on the import of some critical materials, and now they're working to synthesize these resources in-country."

"Odd you mention it. I was speaking to my top executive about just that. We're afraid some of our plants may be redirected."

"I'm afraid they already have—or will be soon."

"What? I haven't gotten any word, and I'm regularly in touch with the operations chiefs."

"Our people in Heidelberg tell us that elements of the SS, the Einsatzgruppen, took over your Blechhammer facility in southeastern Germany. Key employees were taken into custody, and others who wouldn't go along were done away with."

"Murdered?"

"Yes. Your man in charge, Pierre Ter Meer, collaborated in the takeover."

"My God! Pierre's been with the company for five years.

Hardworking and seemed like a fine fellow. I had plans to expand his responsibility within Europe, grouping several plants with him in charge."

"And for all those years, he's been a member of the Nazi Party."

"A Nazi? Pierre?" J.L. returned to his chair, sat down, turned to the window, and stared out, seemingly at a loss for words.

"Mr. Wilson—J.L.—that's only part of why I'm here today. Two months ago, we intercepted an encrypted message intended for an agent bound for the United States, code-named Cassius. It didn't provide many details except that he was to take up residence in New York and contact other agents. One agent had the code name Geist—German for ghost—and another man wasn't named. The subject in the message header referenced Union Chemical."

✧

Tobias Bach was in his office early that morning. On his desk were several pink pieces of paper informing him who had called for him the day before. A message from J. Leland Wilson stood out.

After meeting with his contact at the pier the day before, he had decided to walk part of the way home and take the rest of the day off. He was tired of the cloak-and-dagger life he'd led for the past two years.

As he walked along the pier and saw the great Cunard White Star ocean liners, he imagined boarding one of the grand cruisers to steam home to his birthplace. He'd relax in its elegant salon for high tea in the afternoon, then nap on the promenade deck before dressing for dinner at the captain's table, followed by a concert in the grand ballroom. Then he would sleep a peaceful sleep and not wake until he was home.

Home? Home was here in New York. The dream he'd fostered all these years of returning to the house he'd known as a child had disappeared into war's cold fog of death and destruction.

He looked once more at the luxury liners. What a contrast to his arrival thirty-six years ago when he and his sister first came to the United States.

Their father was killed in the 1906 pogrom in Bialystok, Poland, which was then part of Russia. His father owned a textile mill and was a wealthy man. During the three days of anti-Semitic rioting, he was dragged from his home and killed. Their mother disappeared in the melee.

A neighbor who knew the family took them in hand and wrote to their Uncle Jakub, their father's estranged brother, in Warsaw. Jakub, who was active in a nascent Zionist group called Poale Zion, saw what was coming in Europe and wanted them to have a chance at a new life. So he sent them to New York to live with a Polish family connected to the group.

Tobias was twelve and his sister Miriam was seventeen when they embarked on the long journey to America. The first leg was by train, from Warsaw to Gdansk. There, they boarded a merchant steamer bound for New York. Their father's money was tied up in the Russian courts, so they had to travel third class. During the long eighteen days at sea, they were allowed only one hour each day on the aft deck to exercise and breathe fresh air.

He and Miriam were embraced by their host family, the

Bachs—Sara and Abraham. Abraham Bach was a wealthy man in the banking business, and he took to Tobias right away, having no son of his own. When Tobias was fifteen, Abraham adopted him, and he became Tobias Bach, later following his adopted father into the banking business. Miriam continued to use their birth name of Babinski until she married. Over time, their ties to the old world melted away.

All that changed for Bach in September 1939 when the Germans and Soviets invaded Poland. By October 6, the Polish armed resistance had been crushed. Then came the news that the Jews in German-held territory were being forcibly detained in crowded ghettos the Germans had established and made to wear a yellow star patch identifying them as Jews. This was followed by the opening of Auschwitz and other detention camps in early 1940.

So when Tobias was approached by people representing Poland's resistance groups, he felt compelled to help by providing money and whatever else he could through his business and political connections. He was relieved when Alfred Adler told him that the smuggled cache of weapons had made it into Poland.

The phone ringing brought him back into focus. Deidre, his secretary, an old Jewish woman, was like the bubbe he never knew and reminded him to take his heart medicine. She had seemed old when she first came to work for him fifteen years ago, and he had no idea how old she was now. Still, he was sure he wouldn't know what to do without her.

He reviewed the messages on his desk again. Finding the one from J.L. Wilson, he picked up the receiver and dialed the number.

"Mr. Wilson's office. How may I help you?"

"May I speak to J.L., please? This is Tobias Bach."

"Of course, Mr. Bach. I'll put you through."

"Tobias, I'm glad you got back to me. How are you?"

"Better than ever, Josh." Bach was among the few who referred to Wilson by his first name. He often jokingly told the devout Protestant that he was actually a crypto or secret Jew.

"I need your advice concerning a very sensitive matter, and I'm afraid we can't discuss it over the phone. Can you meet me for lunch tomorrow? Say, noon at 21?"

"Looking forward to it. See you there."

"Until then," J.L. said and hung up.

Tobias wondered what it was that he wanted to share. In any case, it would be good to see his old friend.

Barbara Wilson was finishing her undergraduate degree in political science and international relations at Columbia University. She'd hurried out of the morning lecture on American foreign policy at 11:00, as she had a lunch date with her father and was supposed to meet him at his office in Midtown at noon.

She thought she could make it by catching the subway just off campus at One Hundred Sixteenth Street, then leaving the train at Times Square, transferring to the Grand Central Station train, and then catching the northbound train to Fifty-first Street. From there, it was just a short walk to Park Avenue and the Union Chemical building half a block north. She had been lucky with the connections and might have a few minutes to spare.

It was eight minutes before noon, and she was on the final stretch of her journey, walking north on Park Avenue. That was where her luck ran out. A lanky man in a ragged dark coat and tattered plaid pants approached her from behind and grabbed her purse.

Barbara held on fast to the purse, shifted her weight, and, using both hands, swung the man around to her left as he passed, forcing him off the curb and onto the hood of a parked car. Upon impact, the would-be thief lost his grip on the purse and continued over the hood, landing in the street, while Barbara, suddenly free of the thief's counterweight, fell to the sidewalk. After returning to his feet, the thief gawked momentarily at the gathering crowd before taking off in a dead run.

Barbara was helped up by a tall, dark-haired man. "That was a very impressive maneuver you executed there," he said as he was helping her to her feet. "All the same, you took a nasty fall. Are you alright?"

"Thank you. Nothing broken." She laughed. "It may have looked impressive, but I think I managed to twist my ankle in the process."

Still holding her steady, Todd said, "Well then, I'd be careful putting weight on it." He walked her to a sidewalk bench a few steps away and helped her sit down.

"Thank you, Mr.—?"

"Todd. Richard Todd. And you are?"

"Clumsy." They both laughed, and then she said, "My name is Barbara."

Grinning, Todd said, "Barbara Wilson?

"Yes. How did you know?"

"I'd like to say I'm a master sleuth, but the truth is, I

just finished a meeting with your father, and your picture is on the credenza behind his desk. I work for a man in Washington named Bill Donovan. He arranged the meeting. I believe he's a good friend of your father's."

She cocked her head slightly and said, "Oh yes. My father's told me several stories about Wild Bill Donovan."

"There you go. We've something in common. Maybe we could catch dinner later this evening and chat some more."

"You work quickly, Mr. Todd. I think I'll wait to answer that. I'd like to hear my father's assessment first."

"Call me Richard."

TWO

Zemel was angry and frustrated. They had closed the chemical plant where he'd worked for three years, turning out adhesives and lubricants, and he'd been furloughed. He was told they'd open again soon after a plantwide retooling. That was six weeks ago. His anger stemmed from having to live off the largesse of his wealthy brother-in-law, who ran a successful farm outside Bytom, twenty kilometers away.

His wife, Pesha, didn't make it any easier, constantly nagging him to find other work while the plant was shut down. "A real man would have money to support his family. What do you do but sit around?"

He thought it would be for only a few weeks, but now he didn't know. He had heard that the plant was sold to German investors and no longer called *Unijna Rafinacja Chemiczna* (Union Chemical Refining) but now known as *Deutsches Staat Hydrierwerk* (German State Hydrogenation Plant). The rumor was that Himmler was a significant investor.

Zemel wasn't sure what the plant would produce, but it used coal as a raw material. He knew that because he'd seen rail cars full of it parked on the spur adjoining the site.

However, none of this mattered to him. He was still out of work. It didn't matter to him whether the Americans or the Germans operated the plant or refined the coal. He just wanted to draw his pay every month.

"What are you doing, Zemel, you lazy good-for-nothing? You'll never find work sitting in that chair. You shouldn't be in the house. Go out and make yourself useful. The gate in the backyard needs fixing. The hinge has separated from the post. Go on!"

Zemel rose slowly from his chair, cursing Pesha under his breath, and walked to the door. He'd seen that the hinge had come loose a couple of weeks ago but had neglected to tighten the fasteners holding it in place. "It's still working," he said to himself then—his lax interpretation of the adage, "If it isn't broke, don't fix it." But each time the gate was opened, it worked itself out a little further until it finally came off. Now was the time to fix it.

He went out to the barn, undid the latch that kept the doors closed, and pulled the right one open. As he walked inside to the bench that held his toolbox, he thought he caught some movement in the empty stall to his left. He glanced in that direction, but not seeing anything out of place, he opened the box and began rummaging through it for the tools he required. Then he heard a cough. Worried that a bandit might be hiding in his barn, perhaps waiting until nightfall to invade their house and rob them of their few worldly possessions, he picked up the hammer from the bench.

"Come out! I heard you. I know you're in there." There was silence, but then another cough, followed by several more.

"Wait. Please, we don't mean any harm." A few seconds later, an old man's head slowly emerged above the gate to the stall. "My name is Dovid Broder. My wife and I were just looking for a place to rest. My wife, Chasya, is sick, you see."

"Where are you coming from?" asked Zemel, still wary of his unwanted guest.

"Krakow. We're going to Prague. Chasya has relatives there."

Zemel knew almost immediately that these were Jews on the run. Just last month, the Germans had ordered all the Jews in Krakow moved into a single neighborhood of Krakow called Podgórze.

"I know who you are. Juden, trying to escape the ghetto."

The old man said nothing. He simply stared at Zemel with pleading eyes.

"You have money, Dovid Broder?"

Dovid knew what Zemel wanted. In the past year, the Nazis had moved beyond merely curtailing Jewish rights. Now they planned to herd the remaining 18,000 Jews in Krakow into a ghetto and leave them to starve. As Dovid and others tried to evade this fate, they faced a new threat—blackmail. Rather than immediately reporting the runaway Jews, some locals would demand payment for their silence, weighing what the families or individuals could pay against the bounty the Germans offered.

There was a name for people like Zemel—*szmalcownik*, a blackmailer who extorted money from Jews in exchange for not turning them over to the Nazis. There was nothing that Dovid could do. Finally, he replied, "I have some money, but we need it to eat."

"Let me see!" said Zemel, opening the stall gate. The woman, Chasya, was huddled in the corner of the stall. All their possessions, a few bags, were piled around her. Zemel stepped past Dovid and retrieved the bags. He took them out of the stall and over to the workbench, where he could inspect them in a better light.

He found what he was looking for in the second bag. A cloth satchel covered a small box. When he opened the box, one hundred gold coins sat in a neat row inside a hollow designed to hold them. *This is worth over twenty thousand zloty.* He turned to Dovid and said in a derisive tone, "You have a healthy appetite if this is all for food."

"Please. I will share if you keep your silence and allow us to stay a few days. Until Chasya is feeling better."

"What's to keep me from informing the police and keeping it all?"

Dovid expected this. When Zemel asked about money, he knew what kind of man he was dealing with. "I have more. I hid it away," he lied. There was no more money, but he knew Zemel's greed was his only chance. If he didn't bite, he would surely inform the police about them, keep the gold, and collect the bounty.

"More hidden, you say? I'm not a greedy man, and I sympathize with your plight. What say I keep this? You go get more, and I'm willing to settle half again as much—and then your secret is safe."

Dovid looked at Chasya. She had a cold sweat from the fever. He looked back at Zemel

and said, "I will do as you ask."

Pierre Ter Meer saw Christian Becker, his engineer, approaching him from across the factory floor. Becker reached the stairs that led to the metal gangway Ter Meer was standing on and started up.

"Are we just about ready, Christian?"

"All is well, Herr Direktor. We need to finish training

the supplemental laborers from the camp, and then we'll begin validating the process."

"Nothing complicated, I assume."

"No, material handling for the most. Silesian engineers and technicians will manage the controls and maintenance."

"Can the camp laborers be trusted?"

"I expect so. Hauptsturmführer Balsiger's security detail has thoroughly vetted them. They were screened in the camp. Jews mostly and a few Romani."

"How long will it take to complete the process validations?"

"About a week, granted all the equipment is sound, and the proper calibrations have been made."

"Excellent. Then we'll recall the rest of the men from furlough and be in production by the end of next week."

"That is my goal, Herr Direktor."

"You've done well, Christian! Please talk to personnel to announce the recall and inform Balsiger. He'll want to interview the furloughed men before they're allowed back."

Christian believed having the experienced men back now that they were ready for production would ensure there would be fewer problems. The regular employees could help keep an eye on the camp laborers until they gained experience. There would be some redundancy until they added extra shifts to boost output. *I'm sure our new masters will demand that,* he thought.

Ter Meer left Becker on the gangplank, exited the building to an external staircase, descended to the car park, and walked to his two-tone black and silver 1938 Horch 853 Voll & Ruhrbeck Sport Cabriolet. It was one of the perks he had allowed himself after starting work at Union Chemical.

He drove to his estate near the small village of Pławniowice, north of Gliwice, and eighteen kilometers from the plant—a small twelve-acre property, with a white four-thousand-square-foot Bauhaus-style home. Also on the property was a tennis court—his passion since he attended university in England as a young man.

He parked the car in the garage, then walked inside the house, through the kitchen, and into the main hall. Helga Blunt, an Abwehr agent posing as his private secretary, greeted him.

Helga performed all the duties of a private secretary and executed these tasks flawlessly. However, her responsibility also included keeping a watchful eye on Ter Meer. The Reich could look the other way concerning his sexual peccadillos, as they were primarily interested in his loyalty. All the same, she kept records of his trysts.

Early on, she had become aware that he was a homosexual, considering the company he kept and the overnight stays of many different men. They would take advantage of one of the guest rooms, and they always looked like they hadn't slept the next morning.

Helga had a liberal upbringing in Freiburg and thought, *Why should I tell them?* She decided not to inform her Abwehr controllers, seeing him guilty of nothing other than being human. She would later discover how thuggish and uncouth they were.

"Guten tag, Her Ter Meer. Everything is ready for your dinner guests this evening."

"That's fine, Frau Blunt. Have all the guests confirmed their attendance?"

"Ja, mein Herr. Herr Doktor Crowning, Herr Fusshuller, Hauptsturmführer

Balsiger, and Herr Becker have all confirmed."

"Good. I'm going to rest before dinner. Please ring my room at five o'clock."

"Ja, Herr Ter Meer."

Ter Meer went upstairs to his room and locked the door behind him. He walked across the room to his dresser and pushed a slide lock behind the lower right corner of the mirror, allowing it to slide up and reveal a compact shortwave radio receiver and transmitter. Then he walked to his nightstand and retrieved his dog-eared 1932 edition of *Mein Kampf* from the drawer, his key to the ciphers he had transmitted.

The coding method was both simple and ingenious. First, you chose the book that would act as the key to your ciphers. The only requirement for the receiver to decode them was to have the same edition of the book. The sender would find each word for his message in the book and code the coordinates for each word. For example, the number series 2,3,4 might represent the first word, meaning that the word could be found on page two, the third line, and the fourth word on that line. If anyone were to intercept your coded message, it would seem to be nothing more than a long series of numbers. Brilliant in its simplicity, such a cipher was nearly impossible to decode without having the correct book key.

Ter Meer constructed his message, tapped out each number string, sent the message, then calmly concealed the transmitter and returned the book to the night table.

That's done for now. I think a martini before dinner would be in order. He went to the fully stocked bar he kept in his bedroom so that he didn't have to walk downstairs when engaged with one or more of his lovers.

Pierre pondered his life, his sexuality, and the fact he'd been gay as long as he could remember. Through his younger years, he had hidden it because it was socially unacceptable, and he still did, since the physical danger had significantly escalated from being beaten up to being stood against a wall and shot by the Nazis.

In time, he learned that if he was somehow outed, he could still be relatively secure even in an atmosphere as homophobic as the Reich. Ter Meer found that if you provided a product or service—or both—that were crucial to the success of the Reich and couldn't easily be replaced, you were safe. After all, Friedrich Krupp, the armaments magnate, could spend the season in Capri cavorting with nubile Italian boys to his heart's content, and the Führer would look the other way as long as he continued to supply the canon and other armaments necessary for his war machine.

If I provide the fuel Hitler desperately needs for his tanks, trucks, and airplanes and remain indispensable, the Nazis will overlook my dalliances.

Of course, the corollary to this was that once this critical product or service ceased, he would no longer be indispensable, and his life might be forfeited.

He looked around and thought about all the worldly goods he had amassed during his career—the car, the house, the expensive furniture, and artwork—and sighed. *All this will soon be gone. I'll have to leave it all behind.* He would miss his art collection most of all.

It seemed so long ago when he worked for an engineering company in Northern Germany. A friend and former lover, Dieter, confessed to him that he had been approached by the English Secret Intelligence Service (SIS) to work for them. They wanted him to collect information about government-commissioned technologies currently under development in their company.

"Pierre, I know that you, too, feel no kinship with the National Socialist German Workers' Party and its leader, Adolf Hitler. Hitler's a madman, and if he continues, it may mean the destruction of the entire country."

"I agree with you, Dieter, but he now holds the reins of power—the Reichstag, the army—and has brutally shut down all forms of dissent in the press. I fear there's very little we can do about him."

"That, my dear friend, is why I've decided to work with the British. They can help us overthrow Hitler's regime and bring sanity back to the country."

They spoke through the night, and in the end, Pierre agreed with his friend. He allowed Dieter to put his name forward to the SIS as another German willing to work with them for the good of his country.

It wasn't long before a British undercover agent contacted Ter Meer. When the SIS agent was convinced that Pierre was genuine, he told him that he would be his controller (handler) from that point forward and that he should be his only contact.

His first instruction to Ter Meer was to join the Nazi Party, and since that time, his life had changed radically. He'd become an agent whose mission was to collect intelligence through his connections within the Nazi Party and convey it to the British. He found these connections in some less-celebrated corners of Nazi society.

After joining the party, he found that it wasn't difficult to identify and gain admittance to certain private Nazi cliques populated by gay men, which included a broad cross section of bureaucratic and military elites. Most importantly, not just a few of them were ready to impress a young, good-looking man like Ter Meer by recounting their meetings with other prominent officials and the weighty topics discussed. There were gatherings where drugs were used, and aided by this influence, a party official or Wehrmacht officer sometimes let slip information that would prove interesting to Ter Meer's handler.

It thrilled him. Here he was, an ordinary professional with a career and a degree in chemical engineering, playing the role of a covert spy, a secret agent, even if most of the intelligence he collected was low-level and inconsequential.

To advance his career, he took a job with Union Chemical in 1936, which sent him to Blechhammer in the easternmost reaches of German Silesia. He remained on the SIS's active list, but there wasn't as much opportunity to mingle with Nazi officials or higher echelons of the military in what would become a place where the Reich sent Jews and others to labor and die in concentration camps.

Then came the invasion in '39, and he found himself in the thick of things when, not long after he arrived in Blechhammer, he was propositioned by Generalfeldmarschall Göring's people.

Göring, a former World War I ace fighter pilot, had been the third and last commander of the first *Jagdgeschwader* (Air Wing), initially commanded by Baron Manfred von Richthofen. An early member of the Nazi Party, he was wounded in the Beer Hall Putsch, Hitler's failed coup d'état in Munich. After Hitler was named chancellor, he made Göring a minister without specific duties, and Göring rose to become Germany's second most powerful man. He oversaw the creation of the Gestapo, was made commander in chief of the Luftwaffe, and as minister of the Four-Year Plan, he was responsible for marshaling all sectors of the German economy for war, holding the rank of *Generalfeldmarschall* (general field marshal), the highest rank in the German military at that time.

The Office of the Four-Year Plan wanted to establish an *autarky*—an independent and self-sufficient national economy. Though it was a pipe dream, these men specifically aimed to boost the production of fuels and rubber not found in the homeland. With technical modifications, they believed fuel could be synthesized at the Union plant in Blechhammer.

Around this same time, the SIS had spawned a new wartime entity in Whitehall—Military Intelligence Section Six, or MI6. After reporting Göring's plan for autarky, Ter Meer was upgraded from a low-level controller he seldom heard from to a new and dedicated handler at MI6 headquarters.

Almost simultaneously, George Hansen approached him, offering cooperation along with previously unshared company proprietary technology that would significantly enhance the Blechhammer plant's production output. Ter Meer didn't believe in coincidences. Hansen was capitalizing on the inevitable—but how did Hansen know the Germans would commandeer the plant and convert it to synthetic fuel production? Ter Meer had his suspicions. When he reported this to his new man in London, he was told to play along with Hansen for the time being.

Ter Meer also knew that everything would change once more. Great Britain and the United States, which had only recently joined the fray, could not allow the plant to remain standing.

❧

Helga Blunt was thirty-eight years old and unmarried. Before the war, she served as the secretary to the general manager of a family-owned department store in Freiburg, southwestern Germany. She'd been engaged once, but her fiancé failed to attend the wedding, and she was left at the altar.

Frau Blunt was a genuinely caring, intelligent, and not unattractive woman. She was tall and blonde with a pleasant smile and a curvy figure—wide hips and large, well-proportioned breasts. She was every inch the perfect woman, all seventy-six of them.

Still, her height intimidated most men, and her substantial figure and long blonde hair in braids lent her the appearance of a Wagnerian Valkyrie. While some men might entertain the idea of having a Brünnhilde to carry them off to Valhalla, her almost crippling shyness and distrust of men kept her from reentering the dating world.

A friend had told her about an administrative position with the Freiburg *Polizeidirektion* (police headquarters). It sounded like a way to bring excitement into her life, so she applied and was given the job. It was all she expected—dealing with criminal records of thieves, murderers, and con men—and all very exciting.

Her efficiency and dedication to duty soon made her stand out. She constantly scanned the lists of positions that would take her far away from Freiburg, where she could play a more active role. She dreamed of being a field operative with the *Sicherdienst* (security service).

She landed a job with the Reichskommissariat Ostland, the Reich Commissariat for the East, and found herself in Bialystok, occupied Poland. The environment was utterly alien to her experience, and although she was excited to be somewhere far from Freiburg, the work consisted mostly of rote paper shuffling, compiling lists, and checking those lists against other lists.

Then, only a month after her arrival, an opportunity came along that promised all the excitement she hoped for. The Abwehr recruited her as an undercover intelligence agent assigned to Pierre Ter Meer, acting as his private secretary while informing them of Ter Meer's activities and associates. She soon discovered they were not interested in his sexual proclivities. They were more interested in his business and social acquaintances—their names and the nature of their relationship with him.

After a year working for Ter Meer, she had grown fond of him, and they had developed a close rapport. Unlike what seemed like the majority of fellow Germans, she was liberal-minded and saw past his sex life. He was a good man and treated everyone at the house with respect. He also did what he could to relieve the suffering of the laborers pressed into work from the concentration camp.

She had only one misgiving.

❧

Dressing for dinner, Pierre Ter Meer took one last look at his tie. *A fine knot. A perfect knot*, he mused to himself. Sighing, he knew it was time for him to go downstairs and meet his guests. He wasn't looking forward to it. Except for Christian Becker, he loathed them all.

As he descended the stairs, he saw Herr Crowning in the entry hall. Crowning was his backup at the plant. He didn't know if he was there because his German masters distrusted him or were planning to let him go at some point, but Crowning showed up one day, and Ter Meer was informed that they would run the operation together.

"Guten abend, Herr Doktor Crowning. Tell me, what do you think of our progress with the conversion?"

Crowning, good Prussian that he was, quickly bowed, clicking his heels together as he did so. "I believe it's going along splendidly. I expect we will finish ahead of schedule." He turned and saw Franz Fusshuller walking toward them from the living room.

Smiling and extending his hand, Fusshuller greeted both men. "Mein Herren, what a lovely evening. Thank you, Herr Ter Meer, for having us." He shook hands with both men in turn.

Fusshuller was the head of the technical department and a capable engineer. At the same time, he was a zealous Nazi whose sole mode of conversation was spewing party propaganda and espousing the brilliance of the supreme leader.

The door chime sounded, and the maid moved quickly to answer it.

Two men, arriving at the same time but not together, walked through the doorway into the entry hall.

The first was Hauptsturmführer Balsiger, who oversaw security for all prisoner work assignments. This was an enormous responsibility because, aside from the Union Chemical plant, several nearby plants constructed by IG Farben were utilizing over 13,000 men and women from the Auschwitz camp as forced labor. Balsiger, a sadistic butcher, used his uniform to legitimize what he would ordinarily be hanged for in a civilized society. He held a mid-level rank in the SS and was suspicious of everybody.

The other man was the plant engineer, Christian Becker, who strived to be apolitical, was a brilliant engineer, and was the only hope for decent conversation this evening.

After another round of greetings, Ter Meer said, "Well, it seems our party is complete. Please help yourselves to drinks in the living room while I go and check on dinner."

Entering the living room on his return, he saw that Fusshuller had cornered Christian by the bar, no doubt telling him about the latest accomplishments of their glorious leader. Balsiger stood studying an abstract painting on the wall, painted by a little-known Polish artist, no doubt judging it by its degree of degeneracy.

Crowning approached Ter Meer and said, "Pierre, what a wonderful home you have. So clean and functional. A German architect, no doubt."

"Thank you, Herr Doktor. He was a Pole, but after the Bauhaus style. No worries—I had him investigated. Not a trace of Jewish blood."

Crowning gave him a knowing smile. "That's good. I would guess our friend the Hauptsturmführer would have already sniffed it out if there had been."

Balsiger joined them, and Ter Meer greeted him. "Hauptsturmführer. I'm glad you could make it this evening. Thank you for finding the time in what I'm sure is a busy schedule."

Balsiger nodded and turned to Ter Meer. "Herr Ter Meer, thank you for inviting me. I suppose we have cause to celebrate this evening. The plant conversion is nearly completed, and we will be in production soon."

"Well, we still have to finish the process validations, but I am confident we'll have full production by next week."

"Very good. Have we prepared the logistics?"

"There'll be outbound railcar shipments every other day direct to Munich and Frankfurt and redistributed from there to supply depots and air bases throughout the Reich."

Crowning interrupted Balsiger and Ter Meer's conversation, saying, "Gentlemen, we talk about these matters all day. Let's consider our host and spare him the business chat."

Ter Meer laughed, while Balsiger's expression remained thin-lipped and emotionless.

"I suppose you are correct, Herr Doktor. It's a dinner party, and I've instructed the chef to prepare a meal that reminds us all of home—*kartoffelsuppe* (potato soup), steamed asparagus, and *schweinshaxe* (braised pork knuckle with sauerkraut). And no wine tonight. I've had twenty liters of fresh Münchener Pils trucked in for the occasion."

"How thoughtful, Pierre. We all could use a good German meal after months of this local fare," said Crowning.

"Then I suggest we all make our way to the dining room. I believe dinner is served." Ter Meer led the way.

Midway through the soup course, Fusshuller remarked, "By this time next year, we'll be sitting in London having dinner."

"I don't know, Franz," said Becker. "The Americans are in the war now, and they've expanded their materials supply with this new program they started in March."

"Nonsense! Our U-boats sink thousands of tons of shipping every week. Those supplies will never reach England."

"Herr Becker, do you lack confidence in the ability of

the German armed forces?" said Balsiger, a noticeable hint of accusation in his voice.

"No. I just thought it might take a little more time since the Americans have gotten involved. That's all."

"I'm sure that's what you meant," Fusshuller said. "Hauptsturmführer, what is it we're feeding the laborers from the camp? They're useless after midday."

"Herr Fusshuller, you must understand. The Romanis are lazy, and the Jews are devious—when you turn your back, they start slacking. In either case, what's required is the proper type of motivation. I will bring it to the attention of their overseer, Oberfeldwebel Krieger, and he will advise his men to apply whatever corrective measure seems appropriate."

That idiot Fusshuller, Ter Meer thought. *Thanks to him, an extra ration of pain will be dished out to the camp laborers tomorrow.* He needs to learn not to say the first thing that comes to mind when speaking with Balsiger.

Despite his true feelings, Ter Meer said, "You are correct, Hauptsturmführer. The Jews are devious. After all, they did secretly work to prevent us from winning the last war through rampant war profiteering, secretly aiding and abetting the enemy, and avoiding military conscription. The Führer is correct when he says they stabbed us in the back!"

"The international Jewish conspiracy is both vile and insidious," added Fusshuller. "Look at how they wormed their way into the American economy and politics. They control the banks and the media—and now there's a Jew lover in the White House."

"It's true," said Balsiger. "They are subhuman filth, and we are doing our best to free the world of the Zionist disease."

"However, I fear that continuing along this line of conversation will ruin our appetite," Ter Meer said, and then jokingly added, "We cannot allow the Jews even that small satisfaction." He raised his glass of Pils and toasted. "Prost!"

✺

Dovid followed the instructions the resistance in Krakow had given—find shelter for himself and Chasya near the village of Ujazd and leave a small pile of seven stones at the base of the *kapliczki* (road shrine) to the Virgin Mary on the western road into the village. On the following day, he was to wait by the abandoned mill just south of that on the Klodica River. He would be contacted by a man carrying a walking stick with a green sash tied to it. He was told the contact would help them obtain the documents they needed to travel to Budapest. With luck, they could then secure letters of transit for the journey to Turkey.

Dovid had found shelter. Unfortunately, he had chosen Zemel Kowalski's barn, and he had to leave Chasya in the barn that morning as he went to find the road shrine. When he came back, after leaving the stones piled next to the shrine, Zemel found them and coerced them to hand over their life savings. Dovid had told him two lies. First, there was more money—there wasn't. The second was that they were traveling to Prague, and Chasya had family there— they weren't, and she didn't.

But there was something else he didn't share with Zemel, and it was on his mind now as he crouched low against the brick foundation of the mill in the chilly morning air. He had made his way there in the earliest light of the day, fearing that if he got there too late, he would miss his contact.

What had he not told Zemel? The truth—that instead of fetching more money to pay him off, he was meeting a member of Zegota, also known as *Tymczasowy Komitet Pomocy Żydom* (Provisional Committee to Aid the Jews). They assisted the Jews by providing forged documents, German identification cards, birth certificates, baptismal records, and marriage certificates.

Dovid huddled in the cold for over an hour before he saw the man. At first, he was walking in tall grass, and the walking stick wasn't visible. But when he reached the outer grounds of the mill site, he could see the staff clearly, and it had a narrow green ribbon of cloth wrapped around it.

He remembered the words he was supposed to use. "Have you seen a sheepdog? Mine seems to have gone astray."

"The only dog I've seen today was a greyhound."

"All right. Well then, my name is Dovid Broder."

"You can call me Alexi. Pleased to meet you, Mr. Broder."

Dovid, relieved, smiled and said, "And you, Alexi." Still relieved, but the smile gone from his face, Dovid continued, "My wife, Chasya, is sick, and I had to leave her in the barn where we found shelter."

"I'm sorry," said Alexi. "Is it serious?"

"I hope not. However, neither of us is particularly young anymore, and it took us a week to get here from Krakow, walking at night and sleeping under bridges or behind bushes during the day."

"I can get medicine for your wife. Do you need food?"

"We'd greatly appreciate both."

"Did you bring the pictures?"

"Yes. A friend in Krakow took them for us. He developed

them to conform to the measurements we were given. Four sets. That's one extra."

"Very good. It will take three days to get your identification papers, birth certificates, and marriage license."

"There's just one problem, Alexi."

"Problem?"

Dovid swallowed hard and told him the whole story, explaining that he had lied to Zemel about having more money to avoid what would have been the man's immediate betrayal of the couple's whereabouts.

"The provisional government has made it clear what should be done with blackmailers like your Mr. Zemel. Death. But it would be better to postpone that for now and put this filthy *szmalcownik* to good use."

⁂

Chasya was feeling better. She slept through the morning, but her fever hadn't completely broken. Dovid announced himself as he entered the barn to avoid startling her or having her think that Zemel had returned.

"You're back. Thank goodness."

"You look better, Chasya. Are you feeling better?"

"I slept for a long time and had the strangest dream. I dreamed Jan was with us, and he was rich."

"Your brother is rich, you say?"

"Yes. In my dream, he had fine clothes and was driving an expensive car. I know it's silly. It's just so long since I've seen him. I wish he could have come to Krakow."

"He was safer staying north—he would have been swept up like the rest of us. He still managed to send us the instructions that got us this far."

Dovid paused for a moment while they reflected on that. Then he took Chasya's hand and said, "I have good news. I contacted his comrade and gave him the pictures. He said we should have the papers in three days. Then we will go to Katowice and take the train to Budapest. It's safer to take the eastern route."

"But how will we pay for it? That man has taken all our money."

"The man I met, Alexi, says he can get our money back, and we can stay here safely until our papers arrive."

"Oh, I hope so, Dovid. So much depends on it."

The *Armia Krajowa*, the Polish Home Army, was inconsistent in assisting the Jews. While they did much to help, and courageously so, some units openly thwarted the Jews. Antisemitism still existed even under the boot of a common oppressor.

Perhaps owing to this inconsistency, the idea for Zegota was proposed by a Catholic colonel in the Home Army who had a Jewish wife. Empowered by the Polish government in exile, Zegota worked to aid the Jews who were being persecuted and targeted for extermination throughout the country.

Of course, Alexi was not the real name of Dovid's contact. He had been working for over a year in Krakow and west through Silesia, trying to help however he could. First, by smuggling food and medical supplies to those denied such things by the Germans. Then, with the underground network of people that comprised Zegota running a more and more sophisticated operation, they supplied Jews with forged documents so they could hide or, as many wished, escape to freedom.

He worked with a group of twelve volunteers. Some were members of Zegota, while others were sympathetic and willing to help. All had held everyday occupations before the German invasion—a doctor, a seamstress, a butcher, an office worker, a town official, a housewife, and himself, a lawyer. Ordinary people with a sense of humanity in a world gone mad.

He received word from Zegota's Warsaw headquarters of the arrival of the Broders from Krakow. Jan Berman, a member of Poale Zion, would be traveling from Warsaw to oversee the Broder case, but Alexi didn't know why. Over the past year, they'd provided these services to dozens of other individuals and couples. He wondered what made this one special to Berman.

He gathered two men and two women from the group. Together, they walked to Zemel Kowalski's farm to speak with him about the Broders.

∽

Sitting comfortably with his beer, Zemel Kowalski was pleased with his newfound wealth. *When the old man comes back with more,* he thought, *I'll take it all and throw them out. Maybe give them a little head start before I go into town and tell the SS Corporal that I discovered two Jews hiding in my barn. Then I'll collect the bounty on their heads.*

He knew the bounty wasn't as substantial as what he'd collected from the old Jewish couple. But in his mind, more was more and more was good.

There was a knock at the door. Pesha yelled at him to get

off his lazy ass and see who it was. Perturbed at his drinking being interrupted, Zemel rose from his chair and went to the front door. He opened the door to find a group of five villagers. "If you're collecting for charity, we don't have any money."

Alexi stopped the door with his foot when he started to swing it shut. "We're not collecting charity but have come to provide some." He pushed his way in, and the others followed.

"Who are you people? And what do you mean by letting yourselves into my home?" It was Pesha, and she was indignant.

"We've come to bestow an act of mercy on Zemel here. May I ask who you are, kind lady?"

"I'm his wife."

Zemel stood there, confused, trying to understand what was happening.

"Madam, my name is Alexi. Your husband has committed a crime against the Polish State, and I'm afraid the punishment is death."

"What?" cried Pesha. "Zemel, what have you done?"

"I've done nothing, and what do you mean by the Polish State? This is Germany."

Alexi strode over to Zemel and took him by the collar of his shirt. "If you weren't aware, Poland is at war with Germany. You have blackmailed two old Polish Jews who made the mistake of hiding in your barn, threatening to inform the Germans and extorting money from them. The criminal punishment for *szmalcowniks* is death."

Zemel couldn't get his words out after that. He just kept repeating, "I-I-I . . ."

"Zemel, is this true?" asked Pesha.

Her husband's eyes went to hers, and he stammered a weak, "I didn't mean to."

Pesha stared angrily at Zemel, then turned to Alexi, her eyes pleading. "Sir, he's a worthless, lazy, good-for-nothing, but he's all I've got."

"Madam, when we entered, I said we were here to provide charity. We will suspend sentence provided Zemel is prepared to agree to certain conditions."

"What must he do?"

"He will return their money in full, personally guarantee their safety while staying here, and provide them with food and any other needs they may have. Once they're gone, he must never divulge that he knows about them nor discuss them with anyone but you and me." Alexi pulled Zemel closer and, looking into his eyes, said, "Do you understand?"

Meekly, Zemel said, "Yes, yes. I understand."

"One more thing. The woman is sick. You will relocate the Broders out of the barn and into the house this afternoon once we've left. I will have you and the house watched the entire time the Broders are here. If you fail to meet these conditions or try to trick us in any way, you will be killed."

His head lowered, Zemel nodded.

Pesha moved in front of him and, with a calm voice, called his name. "Zemel." He raised his head just in time to meet her right hand as it completed its wide, violent arc. "You have brought shame to this house!"

THREE

Adam Wilson made his announcement midway through dinner in time for the fish course. Both Barbara and Julie were in attendance.

J. Leland spoke in an elevated and incredulous tone. "You did what?"

"I joined the Marines. I report to Parris Island in four days."

"You didn't say anything to me about this. Why didn't you tell me, sweetie?" asked Julie.

"I didn't think you needed to know."

"What am I supposed to do?"

"I don't know. Leave, maybe."

Julie burst into tears. Sobbing, she got up and ran out of the room.

Barbara wanted to go after her, but she thought the sooner she was away from Adam, the better for her.

She stared coldly at Adam and said, "Jesus, Adam. You're a regular turd."

J.L. said, "I'd tell you to apologize to her, but I know you wouldn't do it. Maybe this is just what you need. Although I don't know if you'll get much guidance about respecting other people's feelings from the Marines."

"Just the kind of encouragement I expected, Father."

"Son, I wish you the best of luck and Godspeed."

"What's your hurry? Don't you want to get all sappy and tell me how much you love me and how much you'll miss me while I'm gone?"

"Adam," said his father.

But before J.L. could continue, Adam stood up and threw his napkin onto his plate. "I think I'll go and pack now. Why not get an early start?" With that, he turned and walked away from the table.

I got a good one in on old Pops. Showed him I know he doesn't give a damn about me. The sooner I'm out of here, the sooner I can put him and Sis in the rearview mirror.

He climbed the stairs and opened the first door to the right. Julie was still in his room, sobbing as she packed the few things she had brought for an overnight stay.

"What, you're still here?"

"Bastard."

He walked over to her and stood toe-to-toe. "Ah, get over it. You got yours, and I got mine."

"Is that what this was all about? Sex?"

"What do you think?"

"I think you overrate yourself. I saw your dad changing by the pool. His is a lot bigger than yours. Man-sized."

Adam turned red. He slapped Julie hard enough that she fell back onto the bed. He bent down and grabbed her by the blouse, swung, and hit her a second time. This time, his hand was closed into a fist, and he cut her lip. Then he hit a third time and a fourth time.

He brought her to her feet, slapped her again, turned her around, and pushed her back onto the bed. He pulled down her skirt and underwear, fell on top of her, and said, "Tell me if this doesn't feel man-sized."

❧

Richard Todd and his OSS mission team were ready to go. Their operation's objective was to destroy the synthetic fuel plant in Blechhammer, rendering it useless to the Germans.

He went to J.L. Wilson's office to tell him the plan. J.L. was meeting with Tobias Bach, but when he heard that Todd was there, he told Sophie to wave him through.

"Hello, Richard," said J.L. "Welcome. I'd like you to meet Tobias Bach."

Tobias stood as Todd walked forward and extended his hand. "Hello, sir. A pleasure to meet you."

"Don't worry, Richard," said J.L. "We can discuss anything in front of Tobias. I can vouch for him. So can Bill. The three of us were in the same squad in France during the Great War."

"Well, I did come on a matter of some sensitivity. We've decided the mission is a go for May. I've come to tell you the objective is to destroy the Union Chemical plant in Blechhammer."

"I suppose it had to happen. The finance boys will determine how to write it off and claim it as a loss. I've briefed Tobias. He's originally from northern Poland."

"Mr. Todd," said Bach, "I understand the Nazis are using slave labor from the concentration camps to build and work in their factories."

"You're very well informed. Not many people in the West had heard about this until recently, including myself. We're only just now getting reports."

"I have my connections. You see, I'm Jewish, and I'm very much concerned with the way the Nazis are treating the Jews. I've heard worse rumors about hundreds of thousands of Jews being rounded up and confined to parts of the city as small as half a square mile. They lack sufficient food, water, and medicine. These ghettos, as they're called, are just a slow means of execution."

"May I ask where you got this information, Mr. Bach?"

"Oh, word of mouth. You know us Jews. We're thick as thieves."

"Come on now, Tobias," J.L. interjected. "Richard is a friend."

Todd said, "Sir, I, too, am worried about the plight of your people or any people treated in such appalling ways."

"I'm sorry. I didn't mean to offend you. You should know I've been working with a group of Polish nationals. Members of an underground resistance group."

"I'll caution you not to tell me anything more, Mr. Bach. As a US citizen, working with foreign nationals can get you into trouble."

"I understand," said Bach. "Well, gentlemen, I must be on my way. J.L., I'll see you Friday night for dinner. Mr. Todd, it was a pleasure to meet you."

Todd nodded and said, "A pleasure, sir. Pleased to make your acquaintance."

When Bach left the office, Todd turned to Wilson. "J.L., I need to know what Mr. Bach's resistance connections are and whom they're affiliated with. Could you help me with that?"

"He's never confided in me on this matter—that was the first time I've heard mention of it—but I'm sure I could ask him. I suppose he was trying to be transparent since we were on the topic of covert operations. You know, get all his cards out on the table."

"I'd like to think so. I'd like to know all the details, but would prefer to hear it from you. It would protect him if I ever had to testify against him. That way, anything I knew would have to come from you secondhand, which would render it hearsay and likely be judged inadmissible. Oh, I almost forgot. I have some good news for you."

J.L., looking tired, exhaled and said, "I could use some."

"Mr. Donovan has always been on good terms with the SIS in Great Britain. Stewart Menzies, the head of MI6, is his good friend. Bill knew him from the war. Relations with the SIS have expanded since the Germans invaded Poland. We've learned from the Brits that your man Pierre Ter Meer has been working for them as an undercover mole since 1933. That's why he joined the National Socialist Party. He's given them invaluable information about your Blechhammer plant's capacity and physical layout."

"Ter Meer, that son of a bitch. I guess, in a way, he had us all duped. But it's a relief to hear he's not a traitor. I like the man."

"The British haven't decided whether they'll extract him when we blow up the plant."

"That raises a question," said J.L. "Why send a team in and blow it up? Why not just bomb it?"

"For the simple reason that we don't have any heavy bombers with the range to hit that far into the continent. I wish we did. It's going to be tricky getting in there and back."

"You mean you're going on the mission?"

Todd smiled. "That's what they hired me for. Anyway,

I have to have something to show for the fifty bucks Uncle Sam pays me every month."

"You'll tell me if there's anything the company or I can do to assist you or your team?"

"Well, there's the matter of Tobias Bach and whom he's working with. We should know to ensure there's no way it could affect the mission."

J.L. paused momentarily, then said, "Bach's a good man. Listen, I thought of something. Why not have Bill Donovan call him or visit him? Bill knows him, although I'm sure it's been a while since they were in touch."

"Thanks. I'll do that."

Todd left J.L.'s office, and as he descended in the elevator to the lobby, he couldn't help but wonder, *Who is it that Bach's dealing with?*

Todd met Donovan at the offices Allen Dulles kept for the New York headquarters of the OSS on the thirty-seventh floor of the RCA building at 30 Rockefeller Plaza.

Bill Donovan waved his hand toward the leather side chair next to the desk. "Have a seat, Richard."

"Thank you for taking the time, sir. I wanted to ask you a favor regarding Operation Bermuda."

"Ask away. But first, how is Josh Wilson? I heard about the troubles with his son."

"As good as can be expected. I didn't speak with him about it, but from what I heard from his daughter, Barbara, there was no arrest. They made a formidable settlement to this girl, Julie—the poor kid suffered a broken nose and severe facial bruising. At least they managed to avoid formal charges. Mr. Wilson tossed the boy, Adam, out of the house. I understand he's started his first week of boot camp with the Marines. I'm not sure I like that."

"I agree. A boy with anger issues and Marine training seems like a recipe for disaster. So what's this favor?"

"I was in Mr. Wilson's office to apprise him of the mission. He already had a guest. A friend of his by the name of Tobias Bach."

"Tobias Bach. It's been a while since I've seen him. I used to know him well. We served together in France. Damn good soldier. I hear he's done quite well for himself in the banking business. He's well respected in the community."

"As we spoke, he mentioned he was working with a Polish underground resistance group. I warned him that, however good the cause may be, doing so without government approval may be illegal. I asked Wilson if he would convince Bach to be open with him, and he suggested you call him."

"I think I know what's going on here. You'll want to speak with his sister, Miriam, not Tobias. He and his sister lost their parents in the old country, and an uncle sent them to America to live. The family wasn't related, but they and the uncle were tied to a right-wing faction of Poale Zion (Workers of Zion), now an underground Jewish nationalist group, minus the original group's Marxist ideology. It was her new mother, Sara Bach, who was the activist. Sara is now semi-retired, and Miriam heads the group. It was Miriam who probably had someone from the group contact Tobias."

"Does he know that?"

"I doubt he knows about her connection to the group."

"Are they a threat to the operation, sir?"

"I believe not, but we should try to connect with them. They have valuable regional resources, even in German Silesia, and their cooperation could be useful. You don't want to be stumbling over each other."

"Then I should get in touch with Miriam?"

"Yes, and you can get more details from the British intelligence, their MI6 branch. They keep closer tabs on Poale Zion's activities and are actively in contact with them." Donovan chuckled and said, "You won't have to go far."

"Sir?"

"It's one floor down right here at 30 Rockefeller Plaza. It's run by a man named Stephenson, William Stephenson. He reports to 'C' in London—that's Menzies codename. He's the head of MI6, which is another name for the SIS. They came up with it at the beginning of the war. He reports directly to the Foreign Secretary."

"May I ask, sir, why British intelligence is present in the States?"

"Just started. It was Churchill's idea. Menzies was against it. Ostensibly, they're here to seek out enemy saboteurs and spies. They're also here to spy on us. I don't blame Churchill. That's the reality of the intelligence business. We all do it."

Todd grabbed his hat, left Donovan's office, and headed for the elevator.

⋙

He had driven twenty-five miles into the city from where he lived upstate. It was already seven P.M. when he parked near Fifth Avenue and Seventy-third Street. His instructions were to walk into Central Park and meet him on East Drive by the footpath to the Loeb Boathouse.

The last rays of sunlight filtered through the trees as he entered the park. After a few minutes' walk, he was at the rendezvous point. A man in a black suit and hat walked toward him along the boathouse path. He stood facing the other man, silent at first, and then, with a peculiar shake of his leg that Lindbergh couldn't help noticing, the man said, "Do you like to sail?"

"Yes, but I haven't got a boat." He paused, then said somewhat hesitantly, "Cassius?"

"That's correct. I have to say, it's an honor to meet you."

Lindbergh took the oft-repeated compliment in stride. He observed the person standing before him, taking measure of the man—blond hair, symmetric facial features, a square jaw, perhaps six foot two. Not one for chit-chat, he said, "I came because you mentioned something very few people would know in your communication. It concerns the phrase *Meine Ehre heißt Treue*—my honor is loyalty."

"Please, call me Bradley," the man said. "And concerning those words, they are written along the blade of the SS Ehrendolch, the Gestapo 'honor' dagger Field Marshall Göring presented you when you saw him last."

Lindbergh was sure no one else was aware of the event. It was at a private dinner—no press, not even his wife. There was a much-publicized photo of Göring holding up a sword to him, and the press described it as a gift from Göring to him. In reality, Göring was only showing him the sword from his wedding ceremony.

"Very well," said Lindbergh, "I trust you represent those whom you say you represent. What can I do for you?"

"I believe it's what we can do for each other. You worked diligently to keep America out of the war. I imagine the foundations of your reasoning support a much greater, nobler struggle—the struggle to keep the Northern European race pure."

"I'm listening."

"The die is cast. America has joined the war, and that is done. But the work must go on. Many people in the world oppose that struggle. People who have accepted the mongrelization of our race."

"Yes. There is a struggle, and I do what I can."

"You could do so much more."

"In what way?"

"Strike a decisive blow to their leadership. To the one man who has done precisely the opposite of what our glorious Führer has done for the future of the race and our children—Franklin Delano Roosevelt, an active Jew collaborator who will be responsible for the decline and fall of white American civilization."

"What do you want me to do? Kill him?"

"Quite simply, yes."

Surprised, Lindbergh said, "It's been an interesting conversation. Good evening, sir."

"No, wait. What if I told you that you could do it and never be caught or even suspected?"

Lindbergh looked at him and thought, *At least listen to the man's proposition, Charles.* "Supposing I were to say yes? How would I go about it?"

At that moment, Bradley knew Lindbergh was hooked. And once he explained how easy it would be, he'd be all in. He told himself he'd have an extra cocktail tonight at the

Carlyle before going home to compose the coded message to Berlin, informing them that Lindbergh, now Geist, was active.

❧

The apartment on Central Park West was Barbara's sanctuary. For the past two years, while attending Columbia, she had discovered her own identity and become independent of the extended Wilson family. Fascinated by new ideas and challenges to the status quo, she'd cultivated that independence and developed a circle of friends outside the ones she'd been given at birth. And like her free-thinking friends, she had taken the occasional lover, which made her feel empowered, free to choose what she wanted, and unshackled from the staid mores she'd acquired in her youth.

Preparing a cocktail at the bar in the living room, Barbara thought how funny it was how things had worked out over the past couple of months. How just a chance meeting with a man purporting to know her father had progressed first to a date, and then a second. By their third date, she realized how exceptional this man was—serious but witty, sensitive, and kind—and that he genuinely cared about what was happening in the world.

Over time, Barbara knew she was in love with Richard Todd, and not long after, he confessed his love for her. They truly enjoyed being together, and she wondered where their relationship would end up. Marriage? Perhaps. She decided she was happy and resigned herself to that happiness, choosing not to worry about the future.

She and Richard had caught a movie earlier in the evening. The latest Hitchcock thriller, *Saboteur*, was a suspenseful story about a man on the run after being accused of committing an act of domestic sabotage at the aircraft plant where he was employed. Following some clues, he managed to track down the people responsible—Nazis sabotaging America's war industry. He duped them by posing to be an accomplice and accompanied them to New York, where they planned to blow up a battleship during its christening. Ultimately, he managed to thwart their plan in an exhilarating final sequence.

She called to Richard in the next room. "Do you want a drink, Richard?"

"Sure. One part vodka, one part gin, and a small dose of Lilith Blanc. I got it from one of the MI6 boys. Try one."

"I'll stick to Sazeracs. Does your cocktail have a name?"

"This Stephenson fellow said he got it from someone in the London office. Fleming was his name, I think. Call it a Fleming."

Barbara took her mixology seriously as she prepared the cocktails. "Damn, I'm out of Peychaud's. Angostura isn't the same. Oh well." She stirred each concoction with ice before straining into two stemmed cocktail glasses.

Naked except for Richard's white button-down shirt, she strolled back into the bedroom. Richard lay in the bed under a single linen sheet, propped up on one elbow. She discerned the outline of his tight buttocks and, reaching out with his cocktail in her hand, admired his broad shoulders.

Todd accepted the drink. "Thanks. I better catch up. You're one ahead of me."

Barbara assumed a pouty look. "You shouldn't have made that phone call and abandoned me."

"I had to call to confirm the flight. We take off for Portugal at nine o'clock."

"How long will you be gone?"

"The plan says one week. But you know what they say about plans. The main objective shouldn't take too long. However, separate from the mission, Donovan wants me to contact an underground armed Zionist faction trying to help Jews emigrate to Palestine. The man I need to see is in the same area."

"One week, two weeks. You just better make sure you get back here, mister!"

Todd pulled her down on the bed and kissed her passionately. Her body relaxed, allowing him to advance unchecked. His right hand found her left breast as his left hand planted itself in the small of her back and pulled her closer to him.

They lost themselves in each other's bodies as their unfinished cocktails sat untouched on the night table.

❧

Todd went to meet with Tobias Bach's sister, Miriam. Her British intelligence contact had called and arranged for the visit. She lived in an unassuming three-story walk-up near Murray Hill. When he arrived, she was alone in the apartment.

Miriam Abramowicz was tall and slim with piercing gray eyes. Todd couldn't help but notice how smartly dressed she was when she answered the front door. "Mrs. Abramowicz, I'm Richard Todd. I believe William Stephenson called to tell you I would be visiting?"

"Good afternoon, Mr. Todd. Yes, he did. Won't you please come in?"

Todd thanked her and crossed the threshold to the entrance hall. The stairway leading to the second floor was in front of him on the right, and on the left was a set of double doors. One of the doors was open, and Todd followed Miriam through it.

Most of the neighborhood's families would have reserved this room as a parlor. However, the room was more like an office, with a moderately sized desk, three file cabinets, a bookcase filled with additional files, and several bound notebooks. Still, the room seemed warm and comfortable, with a couch, a fireplace with a couple of wingback chairs placed in front of it, and a truly extraordinary collection of paintings.

They stood there for a while, and Todd said, "May I compliment you on your paintings, Mrs. Abramowicz? If I'm not incorrect, this one is by Marc Chagall, and here is a Picasso, and this one is from Sonia Delaunay."

"My, my, you know your artists, Mr. Todd. But please stop calling me Mrs. Abramowicz. It sounds like I'll be passing out homework assignments next. My name is Miriam."

Todd thought for a moment. "Miriam, sister of Moses?"

She moved to the couch and sat down. "Yes, and the name is ancient. It's a form of Mary, and in Hebrew, it means 'beloved.' If we go further back, it could be Egyptian for 'beloved of Amun.'"

Todd sat in one of the wingbacks and smiled. "But the sister of Moses seems more fitting. Leading your people to the Promised Land."

"Perhaps. Please, what can I help you with, Richard?" said Miriam, assuming the familiar.

"I'm sorry. Excuse me. I didn't mean to be forward with my comment."

"Your comment was perfectly appropriate. It's just that I have another appointment in thirty minutes."

"Your brother commented in a meeting the other day that he was working with an underground resistance group in Poland."

"That is true." She paused and then continued, "But you see, Tobias is blissfully unaware of the role I've played in those activities since shortly after arriving in America."

"He doesn't know?"

"No, and I would ask you to keep that between us. He was only twelve when we first arrived, and I was seventeen. I was captivated by the stories my adopted mother told me about our struggle and history, of settling in our ancestral homeland and establishing a nation of our own where we could be safe. Tobias was very close to Mr. Bach, and Abraham looked at him as his son, and the son grew up to be the father. In that time, I learned more and more from Sara, and when she retired, I took her place. Tobias has his own life, and I didn't want to complicate it with mine."

"And the money Tobias gave them funded arms for Poland?"

"He felt at least he was doing something good—and he was, even if all he did was to come up with the money and have three or four clandestine rendezvous with our man. Those weapons went mostly to the Home Army. You see, Poland is a funny country, Richard. There are many groups trying to do something good, but their efforts are not always well-coordinated. Poale Zion is a political orga-nization forced underground by the German invasion. It has its own objectives, but we will fight alongside the Home Army when it's called for.

"Although my stepfather Abraham knew my mother led and guided the American wing of Poale Zion, he never actively participated other than fundraising and the like. All the operational and political details were her burden. She wanted him to be free of that.

"I felt something like that about Tobias. You see, during a brutal anti-Semitic pogrom, my father was killed, and my mother disappeared. Tobias was deeply affected by this, and to support him, I had to take on the role of both parents. After all that has happened to us, I just want Tobias to live a long and happy life. Free from war. So, following Sara's example, I try to keep Tobias at arm's length with regard to these matters."

Todd believed he understood. They had both suffered so much. "Miriam," he asked, "you told William Stephen-son one of your men was going to be close to an area we're visiting."

"Yes, to meet up with yet another group that provides Jews in Upper Silesia with forged documents to escape the country. His name is Jan Berman, and his sister is one of the refugees they're helping. Jan is Poale Zion, but he also works with another group, Zegota. As I said, so many groups, so many people."

"We hope to form a relationship with these under-ground groups. The larger our network, the more effective we'll be."

"I don't feel comfortable revealing the whereabouts of our people."

"It's your decision, but we could use their cooperation and intelligence in special tactics and ground operations."

"This isn't something I can decide on my own. I'll take it to the governing council, but I understand what you mean. We could certainly use your help to overthrow the Hun. That's how we refer to the Germans in our country."

Rising from the chair, Richard said, "Thank you for your consideration, Miriam. That's all I can ask."

She rose to see Todd out, grasping his left elbow as they walked to the door. "If this does happen, and someone from the Allies connects with Jan Berman, try to help him and his sister. They're special, Richard."

He sensed a hint of desperation in her voice. When they stopped at the door, he turned to her and said, "Yes, ma'am. We'll do all we can."

Miriam didn't smile or say goodbye, but the look in her eyes communicated a mixture of thankfulness and, he thought, concern.

FOUR

A BRISK WIND met Jan Berman as he descended the steps from his train onto the station platform. He stood there for a moment, trying to stretch away all the knots his body had accumulated after so many hours of sitting in a third-class railcar. Before the German occupation, one could travel from Warsaw to Krakow by train in six hours. However, with all the German control points, unscheduled stops, and delays, the trip had lasted nearly eighteen hours.

He looked around the platform. It was filled with German soldiers, both traveling and on duty. He saw the sign that read *Wyjście* (exit) and proceeded along the platform to the staircase that led to the connecting tunnel, which, in one direction, took him to the Lubicz Street exit and in the other, the main terminal. He wanted the terminal.

Since it was breakfast time, a waft of warm air carrying the scents of the different foods the kiosks offered blew out of the tunnel connecting the main station and the platform—fried potato pancakes with sides of cabbage, sausages cooking on the griddle, pierogis filled with sautéed onion and mashed potato, and slow-cooked cabbage rolls in tomato sauce. Berman's stomach screamed to be fed, and he briefly considered buying something to eat, but then thought better. People like him didn't linger in train stations overrun by suspicious SS stormtroopers itching for a kill.

It was enough of a gamble just making the journey, but his forged documents were impeccable, and though he had yet to get used to making the trip, he had done it many times before.

He'd agreed to meet his contact on the footpath between Castle Wawel and the Vistula River, specifically by the entrance to the dragon's cave. Berman enjoyed the myth of *Smok Wawelski*, a fire-breathing dragon that plagued Krakow in the twelfth century during the reign of King Krakus and dwelled in the cave in a rocky outcrop overlooking the Vistula River. It was barely a mile from the train station, and he could do with the walk. He passed through the large oak French doors at the front of the station and strolled across the plaza that took him to the street that led through the old town to the castle and the appointed spot above the Vistula.

He entered the castle and walked through the Renaissance courtyard to the other side. As he passed the castle walls, he had a commanding view of the Vistula and could see the footpath below him.

Berman had never met Alexi, but he was well known for his work with Zegota. They had both been shown pictures of each other, so the secret sign wouldn't be necessary. When he spotted Alexi on the footpath near the cave entrance, he was surprised to see a captain with the Waffen SS speaking to him. Keeping low, Berman made his way down the path and continued cautiously until he was around the bend, perhaps fifteen meters away. He could hear the captain speaking—his voice was raised in anger.

"These papers have expired, and you have no other form of identification."

"My work permit is at home. Perhaps if we go there, I could show you."

"All the same, your state papers are out of order. I will have to arrest you."

"No, please, I—"

But Alexi stopped mid-sentence when he saw the captain draw his pistol.

The captain said nothing for a moment. Then, a crooked smile came across his face, and he said, "It's a long way to the post. Perhaps I should shoot you here. That would save me time."

The German took two steps backward to allow for a clean shot. Suddenly, he felt a sharp pain in the lower left of his back. At the same time, Jan's hand came from behind, grabbed his right arm, and pulled it down and around the captain's back, causing the gun to fall out of his hand.

With a knife driven deep into his lower back, the captain struggled to speak and tried to move, but Jan's left hand held the blade firmly in place. The officer did not have time to think long about what to do because Alexi buried his own knife between the man's third and fourth ribs just left of the sternum. He fell straight to the ground.

Jan and Alexi looked at each other, instinctively knowing what to do. Alexi took his legs and Jan his arms, and they carried him into the bushes beneath the castle. They stripped him of his papers and money and kept his pistol.

He'd be found eventually, and that would prompt reprisals from the Germans. Regrettably, it couldn't be helped.

"Thank you, Mr. Berman. I thought I'd had it. Your appearance was fortuitous."

"It's Jan, and you're Alexi?"

"Yes, more than pleased to meet you."

"Do you have a last name, Alexi?"

"I could give you one, but it would be a similar fabrication as Alexi."

"Very well. My people told me you are Zegota and will assist the Broder couple with papers."

"Yes, but may I ask, why send a man from Warsaw? Surely, Poale Zion has people here in Krakow?"

"And the Krakow people did help them. They provided them with an escape route, and it was them who got Dovid and Chasya in contact with your lot. I'm here because Chasya Broder is my sister. I plan to accompany them to Budapest and help them secure transit papers for Turkey. Once they're on the train, I'll return. Connections in Turkey will see them safely to Palestine."

"I'm happy to take you to them, but tell me, why not go with them to Palestine?"

"There are too many Jews in Poland who need to emigrate. I don't care if they want to go to Palestine or any other place as long as they're out of the reach of the Nazis. I'll stay to help them."

Alexi found new courage in this man's words. It was so easy to give in to what seemed like an impossible task to free these people. He had seen people in Krakow beaten, shot, and starved to death. For some, death was the only escape from the horror. Anger fueled his sense of resolve, but Jan's words gave him new hope.

"We help them with forged documents. You help them escape to a new land. We share that common objective and one other."

"And what's that?"

"To kill every last fucking Nazi in Poland."

�

"What's so urgent that you needed to see me with such short notice?"

George Hansen sat in a far corner of the athletic club's bar. All the booths around him were empty. "I thought you'd be interested in something that came to my attention, Bradley."

"And what would that be?" said Compton, signaling for the waiter.

"Judging by the value of what I'm about to tell you, I'd like to think that you would consider a quid pro quo."

"I'll pay for the drinks if that's what you mean." The waiter approached the table, and Compton ordered a vodka gimlet.

"I think you'll find the information is much more valuable than that."

But Compton already had something else in mind that he wanted from Hansen. He thanked his stars. *How could I be so lucky? George needs a favor, and it's important to him. How will I play this?* He leaned back in his seat and said, "Precisely what do you want in return?"

"I want you to dispose of two people and make their deaths look like accidents."

Compton's eyebrows rose. He knew Hansen to be unethical but thought him incapable of murder. Now, he was intrigued. It didn't matter to him if two people would have to die. He wanted to know what this information was that Hansen thought was worth murder.

"Very well, George. If what you tell me is worthwhile and useful to the Reich, I'll consider it."

"The Allied forces are planning to blow up the Blechhammer facility."

Compton tried not to react to Hansen's startling proclamation.

"And how did you come by this particular news item?"

"I came into possession of a secret report commissioned by J. Leland Wilson. It detailed the possibility of converting the Blechhammer plant to synthetic fuel production. After that, it was a simple matter of hiring a private detective to do some snooping for me. I gave him access to J.L.'s office, and one evening after hours, he checked J.L.'s appointment calendar—Sophie, his secretary, leaves it in plain sight. My man copied down the names written in next to each appointment, and after making some inquiries, I found that one appointment was with Richard Todd, who works for the government. Specifically, the OSS. It was easy enough to put two and two together."

Although the evidence was circumstantial, Compton knew from a leak in Whitehall that MI6 was aware the Reich had commandeered the plant. It was highly plausible that the American OSS was working with the British to sabotage it. *Now it's time to bargain.*

"That wouldn't be good for either of us now, would it? But murder could jeopardize my position and risk exposing me to the authorities."

"But it threatens your main objective."

Compton laughed. "Dear George, don't flatter yourself that this is my sole purpose for being in the United States. It is only one of many objectives, and not the main one. As

I said, we both have something to lose. We couldn't provide you with production royalties without production."

"Those trade secrets I passed you are worth more than my royalty."

"Enough to commit murder? I'm not sure. But perhaps you could give me something else to—how do you Americans put it?—even the kitty."

Hansen looked at Compton. *Okay, here it comes.* Then, aloud, he said, "Like what?"

"We've come to understand Union's research and development unit has been working on a new solid rocket propellant for the government. It's entirely new and based on ammonium perchlorate as an oxidizer. If we receive the latest research documents, I could, perhaps, persuade my masters to help you with your assassinations."

"That's treason, Bradley."

"I might point out that it's just *another* treason. What's the difference between one and two secrets? As my British friends say, 'In for a penny, in for a pound.'"

Hansen weighed his options. He'd given up the news about the sabotage and received nothing in return, but to achieve his long-term goal of becoming Chairman of the Board of Union Chemical, he needed to get these two people out of the way. Having Compton's people do it guaranteed it could never get back to him.

"Damnit! All right, Bradley, I'll see what I can do. But it won't be easy. They don't leave information like that just lying around."

"Wonderful. Speaking of lying around, how did you get your hands on that report Wilson commissioned?"

"It came in the mail. My guess is somebody wanted it leaked."

"Yes, having that information before it became known publicly could allow someone to sell their stock while it was still high."

"Or sell the stock short."

"Just one other thing I need to know, George. Who are these two people you want eliminated?"

"Adam Wilson and Anthony Scrivner."

⁌

It took Ter Meer over thirty minutes to decipher the unusually lengthy coded message.

After securing the transmitter and sliding the mirror back into place, he paused and studied his reflection. He was getting older. He'd turned forty-five last summer, and he could see faint lines forming under his eyes. It was a fate everyone endured, but he couldn't help thinking he was no longer that young gay bon vivant, the center of attention at parties, attracting equally young and vibrant men. *I'll be an old queer in a few more years. Young partners will only come by way of favors and what I can do for them.* Ter Meer had yet to find the one person he could spend the rest of his life with.

He shook off the momentary self-regret and refocused on the matter at hand. The Allies had coined the mission Operation Bermuda, and a team would arrive in three days. The message didn't give Ter Meer the details, but he already understood what would happen.

Four men—two MI-6 and two American OSS operatives—would parachute in from a stripped-down B-24 Liberator, modified to give it the range needed to make it from a secret airfield north of Istanbul, near the Bulgarian border. Turkey, being a neutral country, was, officially, unaware of the airstrip's existence. They would use twenty-five kilos of RDX explosives to blow up the reactor and hydrogen storage tanks. That would take out the entire building and anything within six hundred feet of the blast. Starting from scratch, it would take the Germans nearly eighteen months to rebuild it, and it was doubtful they had the capability.

The question on Ter Meer's mind was whether he should maintain his cover and stay on or escape with the team. If he stayed, there would be little left for him to do—his only contribution would be to keep the Allies apprised of the reconstruction. However, the Germans would be fanatical in tracking down all those they believed responsible, and he'd be living in constant fear of being discovered and shot. Escape was beginning to sound more and more agreeable to him.

He went downstairs and sought out Frau Blunt, finding her in her office, where she was busy filing memoranda. "Helga, I'll be traveling to Krakow the day after tomorrow. I'll be gone for three days."

Frau Blunt liked it when he used her first name. After all, he was a handsome man. "Will you need me to arrange for accommodations?"

"No, thank you. The people I am meeting have made the arrangements. You can cancel any appointments for those days. Nothing critical, if memory serves. There's an angel." He bent over and pecked her on the cheek.

She blushed profusely and looked down, trying to make it look like she was examining some paperwork. "Don't forget you have the security briefing with Hauptsturmfüh-rer Balsiger at the camp tomorrow. It starts promptly at ten."

He smiled and said with mock sincerity, "I won't forget. I wouldn't miss it for the world."

Helga wondered what he would be up to during the three days in Krakow, if he was going there at all. She'd found the radio transmitter during a routine search of the home and his items after she first arrived. The Abwehr had instructed her to search for anything incriminating or compromising. Not because they suspected him. They just wanted to have leverage should they ever need to black-mail him into performing a task that, due to his morals, he would not be willing to do, such as spying or informing on a friend or relative.

During her search, she started to suspect that something odd was going on when she found a dog-eared copy of *Mein Kampf* on his night table. *Seriously, what educated man reads that insufferable pap?* Then, when she tried to look behind the dresser mirror, she found that it didn't move. She told herself that there was nothing strange about it, but when she knocked on the mirror, it returned a hollow sound as though there was nothing behind it. She felt around the edges until she found the catch in a corner that freed the mirror, allowing it to move upward to reveal a cubby that housed a transmitter with a telegraph key that could be pulled out onto the dresser.

This proved to be a turning point for Frau Blunt. Until now, Ter Meer had been guilty only of inviting men into his bed. Now he was a spy, a traitor to the Reich.

She searched her soul. Since moving here, she had seen

men working in the refinery who were barely capable of pushing a coal cart because their half-starved bodies didn't have the energy. Then, there was the day she had, at Hauptsturmführer Balsiger's request, accompanied him to the Auschwitz detention camp to perform some clerical work. She wasn't prepared for the horror of what she saw—starving people moving about like specters, faces with enormous sunken eyes peering out of skulls with skin stretched over them, and the stench of death pervading the camp. A little girl who had not obeyed an order or acted fast enough for one guard was kicked and stomped until her head was completely crushed.

She decided not to inform the Abwehr about Pierre Ter Meer's clandestine activities. She would do nothing further to support the Reich and its brutality. No, Herr Ter Meer's secret was safe with her. But she still wondered what he was doing and how it might affect her.

Jan and Alexi arrived at the Kowalski farm. Alexi stayed downstairs with Zemel while Jan ascended the stairs to the bedroom where the Broders had been moved.

Chasya saw Jan enter the room, and her heart leaped into her throat. "Jan! Can that be you? How did you get here?"

Jan Berman looked down at his older sister in the bed, dismayed by how frail she looked. He sat on the side of the bed and took her hand. "How are you, dear sister? I came after I heard you and Dovid were seeking help from Zegota and planning to leave the country."

She looked lovingly at her younger brother, remembering

how she dressed him as a baby. "They took everything—our home, our belongings." Her eyes filled with tears. "When they threw us out of the house, we were allowed to take only what could fit in two suitcases. Dovid wasn't allowed to teach at the gymnasium anymore, so we had no means of support." She started to weep.

Dovid, standing at the end of the bed, continued for her. "They were gathering all the Jews and crowding them into three square blocks in the southern part of the city. We knew we had to go. A Zegota woman told us to come here and how to make contact again, so we crept out in the middle of the night. We were nearly caught several times, but we made it safely here thanks to God's benevolence."

Jan took Dovid aside. "Dovid, tell me, what's her condition?"

"At first, it was malnutrition. We ate very little for several days. But the trip here was too much for her. She had a cough and was weak. Yesterday, she started having difficulty breathing. I fear she may have pneumonia. She needs penicillin."

"I'll see what I can do. How are you holding up?"

"I am well enough except for Chasya. She is my world."

"I know. I'll talk to Alexi about the antibiotics, but with the war, there's a great demand right now." Jan moved back to the bed. It hurt him to see his sister in such pain. "Chasya, everything will be better soon. I'll get you some medicine to make you feel well."

"You're a good brother. I can't tell you how good it is to see you again. Now it is you who's taking care of me."

Jan remembered his sister taking him everywhere—the park, the library, festivals, and, later, the theater. He'd enjoyed the theater the most because he could live in a different world for a brief while. Afterward, in his imagination, he would become one of those characters and return to that world—a world where he was never hungry or cold, and people were good to each other.

He didn't realize until much later that the nine-year age difference between them cast her more as a parent than a sister. Without her, he may never have survived. Their mother had run away from her first husband, a cruel man who beat her. She had met the son of a baker in the city of Bialystok, where she grew up. They moved to Krakow, where he and their mother died in an influenza epidemic shortly after he was born. They were orphaned, and as a result, he and his sister were placed in the same state-run home. When she was eighteen, Chasya found a job and a small apartment and took Jan out of the home. He had never been happier in his life.

Jan stood and said, "Dovid, Chasya, I'm going with you to Budapest, where I'll help you secure letters of transit that will allow you to travel to Turkey unmolested. My organization has contacts there who can help."

Hungary had become a temporary haven for Jews. Although still subject to anti-Jewish laws, they weren't, at the time, being deported to the camps.

"We must get your identity papers, passports with the Hungarian visas issued by the consulate, and train tickets. We have plenty of time, so we won't go until you're well enough. Dovid, do you need anything else?"

"Other than the penicillin, we have everything we need. Alexi said he could bring the papers by tomorrow. We'll see how Chasya feels. I know Zemel will be glad to be rid of us.

I still don't trust that man. He has so much anger for the world bottled up inside him."

"Alexi told me about him. He says he's got him under control."

"I hope so, Jan."

&

Hauptsturmführer Balsiger was drinking his tea, a cold cup of East Frisian, when the adjutant entered his office. The man stopped abruptly in front of his desk, raised his right arm from the shoulder, hand straight, and offered his Hitlergruss, the familiar Nazi salute, "Heil Hitler!"

Balsiger looked at him and wearily told him, "At ease, lieutenant."

The adjutant handed him a message that had just been received, decoded, and transcribed.

Balsiger reached into his breast pocket, retrieved his pince-nez glasses, and started to read the dispatch. He stood up, still looking at the page, rereading the message from *Schutzstaffel Hauptamt*, SS Headquarters in Berlin, marked secret.

It read, "Attention: Obersturmbannführer Hoss; Hauptsturmführer Balsiger. Reichsführer Heinrich Himmler will be arriving to inspect the Blechhammer facility and all facilities related to and including the Auschwitz camps and the Blechhammer hydrierwerks on Friday at 0930, 15 May 1942."

Astonished, and speaking under his breath, he said, "Good God! That's not much time to prepare." No longer interested in his tea, he raised his voice and shouted, "Lieutenant, get me Commandant Hoss on the phone and convene a meeting of all my staff officers here in twenty minutes."

Typical to give such short notice, he thought as the lieutenant left. *Everything—the camp, the soldiers, the barracks, and the factories—must be in perfect order before he arrives. I'd better notify Herr Doktor Crowning and Ter Meer that they must wrap up the validations and have the refinery in full production by the time he sees it. Scheisse!*

His adjutant came back to the door of his office and announced, "Commandant Hoss on the phone, sir."

FIVE

Adam Wilson won a unique commendation during his first week at boot camp—he was voted recruit most likely to have the shit kicked out of him. He made no friends, and it amazed everybody that he lasted even two weeks before being invited to leave and receiving his discharge. A week later, he was in a Savannah flop house with one pair of shoes and a half-full bottle of cheap rye.

He'd spent what little money he had and was facing his second day without food when someone knocked on his door. He was paid up through the end of the week, so he couldn't think who it could be.

Probably holy rollers, he thought as he swung his legs off the bed. He ambled toward the door, shouting, "Go away! We don't want whatever you're selling."

He stumbled on the rug and went headlong into a small table before falling to the floor.

"I think you might want to speak with me, Mr. Wilson," came a voice from the other side of the door.

Adam raised his head, confused. "Who is it?"

"I'm a friend, Adam, and I think you'll want to hear what I have to say. Would you kindly open the door?"

Slowly, Adam picked himself up off the floor. He grabbed his T-shirt off the bed and put it on, then walked back to the door and opened it. Standing there was a well-dressed man, perhaps in his mid-thirties, holding a bottle of scotch.

"I told you I was a friend. I even brought my own booze, but I'm willing to share. May I come in?"

Adam turned, sat in a small chair next to the table, and said, "Sure, why not? The more, the merrier."

The stranger retrieved Adam's glass by the side of the bed and poured Adam a double. "What? Aren't you going to drink? There's a clean glass over there on the dresser."

Bradley Compton said, "My name is Fredrick Pole, and I know you, Mr. Wilson."

"Know me, how?"

"I run a detective agency. I have a complete dossier on you."

"What the fuck for? I'm nobody special."

"Oh, on the contrary. You're the son of a very important man who runs Union Chemical, a company that employs thousands of people and contributes significantly to the country's defense."

"Get out! Like I said, whatever it is, I don't want any."

"Come, come, Mr. Wilson. I think you have great potential. I want to make you a proposal to do some work for me, and if adequately performed, it could mean a substantial cash payout for you."

"What kind of work?"

"Mr. Wilson, or Adam, if I may call you Adam?"

"Why not?"

"Adam, from what we gather, you possess a certain—how shall I call it?—character. You have the ability to see above it all, and you aren't distracted by the same petty human concerns as everyday people. You act as you feel—forthrightly. I'm asking you, as that man who set aside senseless and outdated ethics, to, well, kill somebody."

Adam stared at him. Half drunk, he was trying to process what he had just heard. "Did you say kill someone?"

"Indeed, I did, and the pay is quite generous. Fifty-thousand dollars."

Adam thought for a moment. *The guy is right—I couldn't care less if someone was alive one moment and then dead the next. And if I had a part in it, it would be no skin off my nose.*

"Who do I have to kill?"

"First, are you open to such an endeavor?"

Christ, this guy talks like Edward Everett Horton. Aloud, he said, "Yeah, I'm open to it. Who's the stiff to be?"

"I think you know him—Anthony Scrivner."

New York's spring got a cold start. So far, the temperature hadn't gone above sixty degrees. It was much too cold for lunch on the Tavern on the Green patio, so George Hansen was seated inside the restaurant. Looking out the window, he found the view of the park quite pleasing, despite the weather. Fledgling green leaves on the trees outlined in morning dew glistened, capturing the sunlight and reflecting it outward.

Hansen had come here to escape from the office, J.L., and all the troubles crowding his mind. He needed some quiet time to reflect on where he was and what he wanted to accomplish in life.

With the money I have now, I might be assured comfort for the rest of my life, but that isn't enough. I've nearly reached the pinnacle of man's hierarchy of needs—but not the apex of power. To reach that summit, I'll need much more than what I already possess.

Hansen thought he had been cheated out of the CEO position and should have been named Chairman of the Board, his ultimate goal. He knew others thought he wasn't sharp or savvy enough and lacked the people skills he needed to succeed. He listed these points in his mind, but there was still something else. Something that they all thought and perhaps mentioned in hushed tones, but he refused to recognize—he lacked the principles a man must have for the top job.

He used this rejection and his resentment to rationalize his decidedly unprincipled actions, such as colluding with a dictator and an enemy of America purely for personal gain. That and stealing proprietary technical property for that same purpose—all things that could lead to his arrest, trial, and conviction as a traitor.

And now it was beginning to escalate. In his plan to gain the power he craved, he'd asked a Nazi spy to murder the two people who could potentially stand in his way of achieving the CEO spot. Equally as bad, he'd just agreed to give away vital military secrets in compensation—a hanging offense.

Still, he hadn't thought of how to eliminate J.L. or force him to step down. *Am I putting the cart before the horse? I thought it would all happen so quickly, so easily.*

༄

Compton returned home from Savannah at nine in the evening. It was a long, boring train ride, but he was happy with how things had gone with Adam Wilson. He'd given him enough money to get to New York, find a decent hotel, and get some food. He enjoyed manipulating people to do what he wanted them to do.

Hansen would never have suspected that Adam Wilson would murder Scrivner and that the bullet that killed Adam was from the gun they'd find in a dead Scrivner's hand. The police would conclude—and the papers would report—that they shot each other in an exchange of gunfire.

Yes, it was perfect, but he wouldn't put anything in motion until he saw the specifics of the new solid fuel research. Hansen seemed uncertain whether he could lay his hands on it, but Compton trusted that he would find a way. Compton had chosen not to share the knowledge he had about the Wilson family fallout, Adam's near arrest for the assault and battery of Julie Warren, and his brief military career. Hansen may as well continue to believe he still had two competitors.

He made himself a drink, thinking he should try to calm down. The exhilaration he felt after recruiting Lindbergh lasted for two days. Himmler had chosen the code name *Oststurm* (Eastern Storm) for the assassination. The only thing he knew for sure was that Roosevelt would die, and Lindbergh would never be suspected.

The German Secret Service provided him with an SE88/5 radio receiver-transmitter with a signal capable of reaching one of the German U-boats stationed in the Caribbean. At scheduled times, twice a day, the U-boat would send and receive coded messages to and from Berlin and clandestine operatives in North America. The U-boat could remain submerged at a shallow depth and receive coded messages, but it couldn't transmit. For that, it had to surface. Hence, it would receive in the morning and surface to transmit at night to avoid being sighted by the Allies.

Compton knew he could, in an emergency, transmit at any time of day as the U-boat constantly monitored incoming signals. But this was reserved for movement orders, and he should transmit only during his allotted time. He thought he should probably switch the transmitter-receiver on and ensure the receiver was set to twenty-eight point five megahertz on the *Kurzwelle* (shortwave bandwidth), which reminded him that he would receive details of the operation at ten thirty, a little more than an hour from now.

Compton set about his task, humming a song to himself, and when he reached the end of the song, he sang the lyrics out loud, "Wie einst Lili Marleen. Wie einst Lili Marleen."

Barbara had looked forward to this weekend, and she and J.L. went to the duck blind on the estate shortly after daybreak. They had a good morning. Barbara brought down three mallards and J.L. two. On the way back, they talked about various ways to prepare them for dinner, although it would be Benson and Mrs. Higgins who would pluck, clean, and prepare the fowl.

Barbara enjoyed these outings with her father. He had taught her to shoot when she was twelve. The Wilson estate comprised a country house on a large swath of land in western upstate New Jersey. Barbara and her father often went there on weekends to hunt and shoot skeet.

By fourteen, she had advanced to the point that she wasn't far behind J.L.'s shooting ability. That was when

J.L. had a blind constructed by the lake on the estate. They would go out early on Saturdays, bringing sandwiches and a thermos of hot cocoa, and sit with Sassy, their chocolate Labrador retriever, passing the time, talking and discussing all sorts of things, waiting for the ducks. Both she and her father cherished these moments together.

After they got home, they sat in the kitchen in the curved breakfast nook under the window. The morning sun was bright now, and they could see signs of the garden outside the window beginning to come to life, particularly the bougainvillea that surrounded the entire length of the arbor.

"Dad, it's lovely being here with you on the weekends, and not just because Mrs. Higgins makes the best pancakes in the world."

J.L. sipped his coffee, wisps of steam still rising from the cup. Barbara wondered how he could drink hot black coffee straight from the pot.

"Hon, it's wonderful to have you here. I confess that when I come here from the city on the weekends, it gets a bit lonely. Especially since your mother passed, and now with Adam . . ." He stopped talking, not wanting to dwell on the situation with his son.

Barbara saw the change in his expression. She reached across the table, placing her hand on his, and said, "Dad, you're not to blame for Adam's shortcomings. Don't put that on yourself." Then, changing the subject and assuming a bright smile, she said, "Richard told me he'd be back in three weeks. I hope it's true."

"You've been seeing a lot of him over the past month. Is it serious? I mean, your relationship with him."

"Maybe. I like him a lot and enjoy being with him. We seem to have much in common."

"You mean he's got a brilliant and handsome father too?"

"Yes, but not half as brilliant and handsome as he thinks he is."

"Barbara, I asked you up here for a reason, not just because I'm lonely."

"Okay, so what is it?"

"I know you have your sights set on the State Department, and I confess it's a pretty dynamic prospect right now considering the war, but I want you to consider something seriously." He paused and drew in a breath. "Barbara, I'd like you to consider taking a position with the firm. I think you could take my spot in a couple of years."

Her face crinkled. "I've never thought of it. I always thought . . ." She stopped before she said that it was Adam, the oldest, who had always been pegged for that opportunity. "I've had my eyes on a career in the diplomatic service for years. I'd be a fish out of water with Union."

"The education you have in politics and diplomacy is just what you need to be the head of a multinational corporation. You may need some help with the finances and operations, but you'll pick it up in time. Anthony can help you. He's a good man."

"I don't know, Dad. What about you? You're still a relatively young man." She jokingly emphasized *relatively*.

"I'm not getting younger, and besides, there might be other things I'd like to pursue. I built this company for you and Adam. It's a legacy and responsibility that will allow you to pursue your dreams and, in turn, provide for your family."

"It's like jumping into the deep end, don't you think, Dad?"

"Think it over. It's hard work but satisfying. It will give you the means to effect substantial good in this world. God knows we need it."

"Dad, I have to ask. Have you heard from Adam?"

"Not since he left that night, leaving that poor girl unconscious in his room."

"Nothing about the Marines?"

"Well, to be truthful, I hired private detectives to check up on him. They lost track of him in Savannah. After he was kicked out of the Marines."

Barbara was sad but not surprised at this latest failure, and she knew it was hitting her father hard. She reached over the table, took his hand again, and said, "Are you okay, Dad?"

Wilson was silent for a while before smiling at his daughter. "I have to keep reminding myself we aren't meant to understand life. And if you try? Well, that's a pretty deep rabbit hole."

"Want some more pancakes, Dad?"

"I sure do, Pumpkin."

SIX

THEY'D BEEN FLYING for five hours at fifteen thousand feet and were north of the outer Carpathian Mountains, coming into the rolling hills of Silesia. They were flying a British B-24 Liberator, supplied to Britain as part of the Lend-Lease Program the United States extended before joining the war. Congress and isolationists in the general population didn't want to get involved in what they saw as Europe's war. To some extent, the program mollified the isolationists' concerns by providing that materials could be sent only to countries deemed necessary to the defense of the United States.

The B-24 Liberator flew out of a secret airfield near the small town of Begendik, Turkey, north of Istanbul near the Black Sea coast, then northwest through Bulgaria, Romania, Hungary, and Slovakia to the designated drop area one click—or .62 miles—northwest of Gliwice, in Southeast Germany.

The plane, initially built by Consolidated Aircraft of San Diego, California, was equipped with four Pratt & Whitney twelve-hundred-horsepower engines and was modified for the purpose it served this evening. Flame dampeners had been fitted to the engine exhausts. The plane was painted matte black and had blackout glass on the waist windows. The pilot's window was extended for better visibility. The belly ball turret had been removed, and the hole was fitted with a lift gate known as a Joe hole—a reference to OSS agents who were often code-named "Joe." The bombs in the bomb bay were replaced with a British H-type cargo container. Both the container and commandos were fitted with parachutes, allowing them to drop through the Joe hole at the appropriate time.

Now that they were out of the mountains, they would descend to no more than two hundred feet above ground level and cut their airspeed to just ten miles an hour faster than the stall speed of ninety-five. Flying at night made it particularly dangerous, as the B-24 was difficult to maneuver at low speeds owing to the 110-foot wingspan that gave it superior range.

There were four men aboard besides the pilot, copilot, and navigator. Two of them, including Richard Todd, were OSS agents, and two were MI6. All were dressed as typical Silesian farmers and armed with High Standard HDD semiautomatic .22 caliber pistols with integral suppressors.

They would drop the H-type container that held British-made Sten guns with silencers, 9mm and .22 caliber ammunition, hand grenades, twenty-five kilos of RDX explosive, PETN detonators, medical supplies, rations, and an SSTR-1 shortwave radio. All, except the Sten guns, were neatly separated into four backpacks.

"Strap in, gentlemen," announced the pilot. "We're about to go low and slow. It's seventy miles to the drop point, so we have another forty minutes before we get there."

One of the MI6 men, still active in the British navy, was Commander Michael (Mick) Stafford, who asked, "How low will we be when we jump?"

"I'll lift her a little from where we are now, but it's still low for a jump. That's why you'll be attached to a static line, so your chute opens automatically. It'd be a shame if you lost count."

Stafford flashed a nervous smile, moved aft, and hooked his safety strap. He turned to Todd across from him, both sitting in the part of the plane where the two waist guns would typically have been mounted. "Captain Todd, I suppose now's not the time to mention I've never jumped out of a plane at any height."

"That's a remarkable coincidence. Neither have I. I'm sure the training was adequate to see us through. Right, Joe?"

Lieutenant Joe Hendricks, a former US Marine, was their explosives expert. Stocky and built like the first six feet of an oak tree, he was a good-hearted fellow and saw how nervous the English commander was. "I'm used to getting someplace on a boat or using my two legs to walk in. I kind of like the idea of jumping. I guess this will be the third time I've done it, and believe me, once you go through the Joe hole, all your worries disappear. From that point on, it's a matter of pure terror."

Commander Stafford laughed along with Todd and Lieutenant Commander Reg Newley, a short, thin man with round glasses, a narrow face, and an overly large Roman nose that seemed disproportionate on his lean frame. Newley and Hendricks were the two most important members of the team. Both men were trained in the use of high explosives, but Reg brought additional experience—before enlisting in the Army, he had studied in medical school. When not blowing things up, he served as a field medic. They all hoped his medical skills wouldn't prove necessary.

The copilot left the cockpit and walked past them to prepare the H-container, which would go out first, for the drop. He looked up from what he was doing and said, "Almost there, chaps. Eight minutes to go. Get in position, please."

He unlocked the belly hatch, lifted it upward, and slid it aside to reveal a round five-foot opening. The space between the compartment in which they stood and the outer hull had a smooth metal finish so that nothing would snag on it. They felt the cold air rushing past as the plane plowed through it.

"Not very sophisticated technology. Now I know why they call it a hole," said Todd as the four men stood around it, looking down at the blackness they were about to drop into.

At the specified time, the copilot attached the static line to the container's chute, slid it toward the edge, and tipped it up. They watched as it descended into the cold abyss.

The order for the jump was predetermined. Each man checked the anchored static line attached to their chute. As Todd disappeared through the Joe hole, they saw the static line go taut for a second, then limp again. That signaled Stafford to jump, followed by Hendricks and Newley.

At first, Todd was disoriented, not knowing which way was up, but as the chute deployed, he was jerked violently upward, making it clear. It was dark, and there was no moon, but he could still see the ground coming up fast. In their briefing, they were told they should land in fields, but it was slightly hilly below him, with bushes, a few small trees, and, luckily, a few patches of what he thought to be grass. Todd noted that he had only about a hundred feet left where he could use the risers on the chute to adjust the angle of his descent. He pulled on the two left risers to shift in a direction that should land him in one of the clearings. He bent his knees as he landed and rolled right. He got to his feet, released the chute, and began to reel it in.

The others came down in roughly the same place, and based on the direction they had flown in, he judged that the supplies would be a little further to the south. Once they had all found each other, they buried their chutes and headed for the supplies.

Commander Stafford walked beside Todd. "It's just midnight," he said. "We've got two hours before Ramrod's due to transmit." Ramrod was the code name for Pierre Ter Meer, the German national working for MI6.

They came to a clearing and saw two men inspecting their supply container, struggling to release the clamps that held it together. Todd and Stafford ducked down. The Sten guns were in the container, but they had their HDM-silenced pistols.

"What do you think?" whispered Todd. "Shoot them or find out who they are first?"

"They're not wearing uniforms, so they could just be farmers."

"Out here after midnight? Highly unlikely."

"Well, we can't just murder them in cold blood, old man. I say we confront them and find out who they are."

"And swear them to secrecy if they're innocents? That's a big risk."

"What else can we do? After all, as you Yanks say, we're the good guys."

Todd turned to Hendricks and Newley and said, "Joe, you and Reg work your way around the other side of them and cover us while we move in." They nodded and moved off to the left. Todd and Stafford gave them time to get into position, then stood and walked into the clearing, their pistols leveled at the two men.

Over the centuries, several other languages had influenced the Upper Silesian dialect, including Polish, German, Czech, and Slovak. Knowing that, Stafford spoke in Polish, the only language he knew other than English. "Can we help with that? You're going about it in the wrong way."

Quickly, the two men rolled off to either side of the container, retrieved rifles lying on the ground, and aimed them at Todd and Stafford. Alexi peered at the two men, wondering why they were here and carrying weapons. He responded with a query. "Who are you? Boche?"

"No," said Stafford, "we're not the Germans, but first, who are you, and why are you out here in the middle of the night?"

Alexi looked at Jan and said under his breath, "They're not dressed like the Boche."

"And I don't think I've met a German yet that can speak Polski," Jan said before speaking to Todd and Stafford. "We were on our way back to our village. We were out hunting today and stayed late at the Gasthaus afterward."

"Stand up and drop your weapons."

"Maybe you drop yours first," said Alexi.

At Todd's signal, Joe and Reg stepped out of the bushes, their pistols aimed directly at the two men. Seeing this,

Alexi and Jan laid down their rifles and slowly stood. Todd and Stafford moved forward while Joe and Reg kept their weapons trained on the two looters.

Stafford said, "These gentlemen and I are visitors to your country, and I'm afraid you will have to remain with us as our guests until we leave." Then, in English, he said, "Reg, bind these two gentlemen."

"No, wait!" It was Jan speaking in English. He looked questioningly at Alexi. Alexi gave a slight nod, and Jan continued. "My name is Jan, and he is Alexi. We're both members of the underground. We, too, are on a mission. We were headed to a town a little further east when we saw this canister drop from the sky. We didn't know what it was."

"If you're underground," asked Todd, "what group are you attached to?"

"Alexi is with Zegota, an organization created by the Polish government to assist the Jews with forged documents. I'm with another organization independent of the government known as Poale Zion. We help the Jewish people to immigrate to Palestine. Sorry, but neither of us carries papers to prove it. Alexi can give you the name of someone with the government in exile who can vouch for us. He's in London at the invitation of the British goverment."

"We'll do that once we get the radio squared away," said Stafford. "We don't have enough signal to reach England, but we can have someone relay the message. For the time being, you will surrender your weapons."

Jan looked at Alexi. "What choice do we have? In any case, I believe them. The tall one has a definite British accent, and the other sounds like the American Don

Ameche I've seen in the movies. Why would Germans affect such a disguise?"

"We'll return the weapons once we've confirmed your identity." Nodding toward their rifles, Stafford said, "Reg, be a good lad and pick those up and secure them."

"Right, commander!" said Newley, stepping forward and retrieving their guns.

"Let's get these supplies sorted and the radio powered up."

The four men undid the clamps that held the sections of the container together. As they did so, Alexi and Jan stared in muted appreciation, not only of the efficient packing but also for the cornucopia of weapons and equipment stowed inside.

Lieutenant Hendricks got the radio working. They still had half an hour before Ramrod would transmit. Todd asked him to send a coded message back to the base with a request to relay it to OSS HQ in London.

"Message as follows. 'Have encountered two friendlies. Please confirm names and any relation to an organization known as Zegota.'" Then he added their names and requested they also contact the man whose name Jan had given them.

They hid the container sections and asked Alex and Jan to sit and wait patiently, as they'd all be on the move in a few more minutes. The men sat silently, waiting. Then, at the prescribed time, the message from Ramrod came. Hendricks signaled to Todd and Stafford that he had an incoming message.

Listening through headphones, Lieutenant Hendricks heard the Morse for the five-letter code authenticating the sender. He tapped out the coded response and wrote the coded message using a pencil and paper, followed by the code for "End of Message." Once finished with the decoding, Hendricks read the message to the others out of earshot of Alexi and Jan.

"Bermuda in go stage. Meet at the shrine one-quarter kilometer south of Ujazd by the bridge that crosses the Klodnica River at 0600 hours. Ramrod."

"That's it," said Todd. "We're a go. Lieutenant, how far do you make this Ujazd from here?"

Hendricks consulted his map and compass and said, "Assuming our location to be a little over one click west of Gliwice, it's about seven to eight kilometers in that direction." He pointed northwest.

"We can cover that in two hours," said Todd. "Maybe we can get two hours' shuteye before meeting Ramrod." He walked over to Alexi and Jan and said, "I'm sorry, but at best, we won't have confirmation of what you say until the next scheduled transmission at 0800 hours, and we must be moving. We'll have to bind your hands until then."

"Look, Captain, there are two people we're helping to escape—a man and his wife. She's very ill," Jan said, distraught. "We were coming from the farm where they were hiding, heading into Gliwice, when we saw the canister fall from the sky. She needs penicillin, and we can get that in town. Can't you trust us? Her life hangs in the balance."

"Again, I'm sorry. We can't risk the mission. How far is this farm?"

"It's six kilometers from here, on the south side of the Klodnica River."

Todd pulled Stafford aside and said, "That man claims

they were on their way into Gliwice to secure some penicil-lin for a sick woman. It sounds as though she's not too far away from the rendezvous point. We've got penicillin in our medical kit. You think we can go there after we meet Ramrod and see what we can do?"

Stafford looked miffed and seemed bothered by Todd's request. "I'm sorry to say, old man, it's a no-can-do. We haven't the time, and God only knows what our next step might be after we meet Ramrod."

Todd was torn. His instinct was to trust the man and save a life, but he had to agree with Stafford—the mission came first. If helping them meant they had to go out of their way, it would be impossible. He also knew that if he bluntly told the two men no, they would try to escape every step of the way. He went back to the two, thinking about what to tell them. If London confirmed their identities, he could give them the penicillin when they released them. However, London might not be able to verify their stories right away or might say they were still working on it. Todd decided to stretch the truth.

"Jan—that's your name, right?"

"Yes, sir."

"I'll give it to you straight. We have penicillin in our medical supplies, and we'll stop by this farm if it doesn't interfere with our mission. I'm afraid that's the best we can do."

Alexi and Jan looked at each other. Alexi said, "It might be faster than if we were to go to Gliwice and back, and there may be more they can do for Chasya."

"Very well, sir," said Jan. "We will accompany you and not cause any trouble. God willing, you'll be able to help."

Hendricks took the point as they started. The moonless night meant they'd be making their way in the dark, but he was thankful that the stars were bright, standing out so much that he felt he could reach out and touch them. Getting his bearings, he said, "This way, gents."

Alexi and Jan, their hands bound behind their backs, walked along with the others in single file.

⁓

Ter Meer stowed the radio set and decided he'd better get a few hours' sleep while he had the chance. It'd been a long day at the plant, and they'd had problems maintaining the correct temperature in the hydrogen-fueled reactor. If the temperature went too low, the process would produce a metric ton of useless sludge. Too high, and it would bypass the liquefaction point, resulting in an equally useless amount of oxidized product. He, Christian Becker, and the production team had worked late into the night and finally found the problem—a valve on the hydrogen intake to the reactor wasn't appropriately calibrated. He'd had to rush to get home in time to make his radio transmission.

He walked downstairs to the kitchen to get a glass of warm milk, his trick for falling asleep immediately. He noticed on the way that a note was sitting propped up on the table in the foyer. The handwriting on the envelope was Frau Blunt's, and it was marked "Urgent." He supposed he'd missed it on the way in because he was in a rush. He opened it and was astonished at what he saw. It was from Hauptsturmführer Balsiger.

"I wish to inform you that Reichsführer Himmler

will inspect the Blechhammer plant at 9:00 A.M. on 16 May. Please attend a meeting tomorrow at 10:00 A.M. in my offices to discuss preparations."

"Fuck! Why now? I just told Bermuda I would meet them in Ujazd at six. I've got no way to contact them. I don't even know where they are." Then he looked down and read the second half of the message.

"I have extended your kind invitation for Reichsführer Himmler to enjoy the comfort of your home during his stay. Please make the necessary arrangements. Heil Hitler! Balsiger."

Christ! That tears it. Should we abort the mission or at least postpone it? Ter Meer thought it over. *If I meet them at six, I should have time to drive to the meeting in Auschwitz since the camp is just under a hundred kilometers from the rendezvous at Ujazd. But how do I manage Balsiger's invitation to Himmler to stay in my home?*

He knew Helga must have rung the plant dozens of times, but they had been on the plant floor, and there hadn't been anyone to answer the phone in the office.

He looked at the clock—no sense in trying to get any sleep. He decided to get his things together and head for the rendezvous, hoping they'd already be there. Not an exceptionally safe thing to do, arriving early to a clandestine assignation—one could get shot—but he had to risk it.

Suddenly, he got a tingling sensation in his neck and felt like someone was watching. He turned quickly to see

Frau Blunt in her nightgown. She was holding a glass of warm milk.

❧

Sara Bach lived in the same West Village brownstone on Perry Street she and her husband had purchased before Tobias and his sister arrived in the United States. Her husband, Abraham, passed away in '31. Now, she lived alone, having insisted on remaining in the five-thousand-square-foot home after his death.

It was customary for Tobias to stop by every other week to see how she was and if she needed anything. He was walking up the street toward the house when he noticed a man talking to Sara on the front stoop. Ducking into the basement stairwell of another house, he continued observing the conversation.

The man smiling and chatting with Sara Bach was Alfred Adler, his contact with the Polish underground. *What is he doing visiting my mother?* Sara, laughing, placed her hand on his shoulder and kissed him on the cheek. Alfred then descended the steps and headed down the street in the opposite direction from Tobias, with Sara waving as he went.

She walked back into the house, and Tobias stood thinking for a minute. What connection could the man possibly have with his mother? He decided he would have to ask her, so he climbed the steps to the front door and rang the bell.

Sara came to the door almost immediately. She opened it, her eyes beaming as she smiled broadly. "Toby! Come in, come in."

"Hello, Mother. How are you?"

"I'm well. Come into the kitchen. I was preparing something for tonight's dinner. You'll have to stay."

"I'd love to, but maybe some other time. Tell me, what are you cooking?" They continued chatting as they walked through the first-floor hall to the back of the house and the kitchen.

"I'm cooking a recipe I got from a friend during my travels in Palestine. Dumplings stuffed with lamb and pine nuts, cooked in goat's milk yogurt. It's delicious. You sure you won't stay?"

"I can't, but I'm sure you'll have plenty of dinner guests. I don't know many people with as broad a network of friends as you." He thought about the word as quickly as he had said it—*network*.

Tobias loved his mother, but growing up, he spent most of his time in the company of his father, Abraham. Sara was never lonely. People circulated through the house on a regular basis. As he remembered, their discussions were always political, but he paid little attention.

All at once, he realized why Alfred Adler was visiting his mother. Her political leanings, her network of acquaintances, Palestine, and Alfred Adler—a man not only fighting for the lives of the Jewish people but also for their ancient homeland and their return to Zion. How else would Adler know about him? Could the connection be Sara?

He glanced at his mother, humming to herself as she prepared the dough on the large kitchen table in the middle of the room. He wondered why she wouldn't just ask him for help. Why be so secretive?

"Mother?"

"Yes, Toby."

"Why didn't you tell me about Alfred Adler?"

She stopped what she was doing and looked up at him. "What about Alfred?"

"I saw him talking to you in front of the house. Why did you tell him to ask me for money to help with the struggle in Poland instead of just asking me yourself?"

A perplexed look came over her face. "Toby, I didn't ask Alfred to speak with you. You saw him in front of the house because we're old friends."

"But Mother . . ."

"Tobias, sit down. I need to explain something to you. I don't know why I didn't do it long ago."

He took a chair at the kitchen table. She sat and reached over to him and took his hand in both of hers. "Tobias, I never told you about the work I once did with a political organization in Poland and later here in New York. Here, we would lobby politicians and collect money to support the organization. Some of us were involved with the work being done in Palestine. And now, Alfred and others—the Polska in particular—are working to eject those beastly Germans from our country. That's probably what Alfred wanted money for."

"Probably?"

"As I said, I had nothing to do with him approaching you, but it seems logical."

"If not you, then who?"

Sara looked at him. She didn't have to say anything because Tobias knew.

He said flatly, "Miriam?"

"If I had to guess."

"Is she involved with this organization?"

"Yes. She took over when I stopped being active. She has a real gift for this sort of work. She's raised a substantial amount of money for the cause."

"Poland?"

"Yes. Much more for the past couple of years since the Boche invaded."

"Where does the rest go?"

"To the cause of creating a Jewish homeland in Palestine."

"Zionists?"

"Yes. Poale Zion was the name of the movement. Alfred and I started the New York branch in 1903. We were budding young communists in those days, but Trotsky and the Comintern would have nothing to do with Zionists. So the group split in 1920, and a less Marxist and more nationalistic branch was formed. Alfred and I agreed that this was where our priorities should lie. As the years passed, Abraham focused more on his business here in New York and became less involved, while I continued with Poale Zion."

"Why didn't Miriam just ask me? Why the subterfuge?"

"You would have to ask Miriam. Speaking for myself, your father and I rarely discussed Poale Zion. He had done so much and so well in business, and he was helping people in the community in many ways. We wanted to avoid arguments, and I didn't want to weigh him down with politics."

"I wish you had told me. Did you ever think I might be interested and want to be part of this?"

"You were so young, and Abraham loved you so much that he capitalized on your time—and I allowed it. You were happy, and that was all that mattered to me."

"May I use your phone?"

"Of course, dear."

"I'm going to move some appointments around, and if the offer's still open, I'll stay for dinner."

Sara smiled at him, happy to see him stay, but in her mind, she also wondered why Miriam had not been forthright.

⌘

Miriam Abramowicz was worried. The last communication from Jan Berman was over a week ago when he was still in Warsaw. She thought he may still be in Krakow or perhaps had moved on with the people from Zegota to where Dovid and Chasya Broder were hiding. Jan was a capable agent, and she was sure that he could see the couple safely to a neutral country and, hopefully, from there to one of our settlements in Palestine. She said a quick prayer for their safety.

Mother had called and given her an account of her visit with Tobias yesterday, revealing that he had seen Alfred Adler speaking with her. Miriam expected Tobias would be visiting her next, and as expected, she received a call from him earlier in the morning asking if she would be in today. She would see him for lunch.

He mentioned that Mother had sent him home last night with a chafing dish and several lamb dumplings and that it was one of the most delicious meals he had ever had. He'd bring it for their midday meal. He had asked if she had any yogurt, and if not, he'd stop and pick some up.

She was a little nervous, anticipating that Tobias would confront her and ask why she had withheld the truth from him for so long. As she thought about what to say, the door-bell rang. She walked down the hallway to the front door and saw Tobias through the sheers that covered the glass panels on the front door. He was holding the chafing dish she recognized as one mother had used to serve hundreds of meals over the years.

She opened the door, and they looked at each other a moment before saying hello—he with a hurt look of "why?" and her face emoting sorrow and regret.

"Good morning, Toby."

He walked in and said, "Good morning, Miriam." He handed her the chafing dish and shed his hat and coat, hanging both on the wall-mounted coat rack by the door. Together, they walked to the kitchen.

Miriam got plates and settings for the table while Tobias took a seat in a chair next to it. They'd eat in the kitchen the way they used to do.

"Miriam, are you going to tell me why?"

As she collected flatware from the cabinet drawer, her back to Tobias, she said, "About what, Toby?"

"I'm sure you've already spoken with Mother about my seeing Adler in front of her house yesterday."

"And how would you know that, Tobias?" He noticed she dropped the diminutive. A sure sign she was vexed.

"Because I've known Mother for thirty-six years and you for forty-eight. I know because the two of you have always been as thick as thieves, and when one of you knows something, it isn't long before the other knows it as well."

"All right, yes, she telephoned and told me."

"So why did you send Alfred rather than ask me when you or your group needed money? And why keep your involvement with this organization a secret from me?"

"I suppose because it was something special I had with

Mother, and you were Father's pride and joy. Later, as an adult, I found I had a talent as a leader. Things progressed, and I was as passionate about the cause as Mother was. It didn't occur to me that you might be interested."

"I can understand that, but it doesn't explain Alfred."

Miriam put the dumplings in the oven and then sat next to Tobias. She looked at him and said, "I'll tell you why I sent Alfred instead of approaching you myself. It was because I always wanted you to be happy, and I wanted to safeguard you from all the ugly things in life. You'd seen too much horror and sadness for a twelve-year-old boy. You'd worked to be successful in America. You fought for America in the First World War. I just wanted you to be free from the pain and live a fulfilling life.

"I sent Alfred because the situation is desperate in Poland, and I knew you could raise the money we needed. You would help, of course, but I didn't want you to take on the entire burden of the struggle. That's your nature, Tobias—when you get involved, you give it your all. And I knew that's what you would do if you learned of my involvement with Poale Zion and aiding the Home Army and the resistance."

Miriam took a deep breath before continuing. "There's something else I've never shared—something about the family when we lived back in the old country. As the years went by, I told myself you didn't need to know, and I wanted to forget. I should have told you, but every year that went by where I didn't, the worse I thought your reaction would be. I was afraid you would hate me for not revealing the truth."

"Something painful?"

"You were so young, and I thought the truth would hurt you more than you already had been."

"Just tell me. I won't be mad, and I certainly won't hate you."

"You were too young to notice, but father was a horrible man, a contemptible *paskudnyak*. He beat Mother and kept her locked up in the house while he was at the mill."

God, how awful. Tobias never had a close relationship with his birth father, but he looked up to him all the same and worshipped him as a hero. He was never treated poorly and had no memory of any abuse.

Miriam held his hand. "Tobias, I should have told you long ago once you had grown. When Mother disappeared during the riots and never reappeared, you believed that she must be dead, that she was killed during the pogrom. But the truth is, she ran away."

Instantly, Tobias's mind filled with a thousand questions. *Why didn't she take us with her? Why didn't she come back? Why didn't she at least contact us?* And the most important one—*Is she still alive?*

Tears welled in Miriam's eyes. "She ran away because she was carrying the baker's son's baby. Together, they fled Bialystok and later moved to Krakow. A married woman with another man's baby would have been a pariah in the community, so she stayed away. Uncle Jakub told me about it the day before we left for America. The first letter I received from her wasn't until almost ten years later. She wrote me to say she was remarried to the baker's son, and they had two children. A nine-year-old girl and a baby boy—Chasya and Jan."

"Did she write often?"

"No, I received only the one letter. I never heard from her again. Then, miraculously, a few years ago, just before the invasion, I received a letter from Jan. He was a lawyer in Warsaw and worked with Poale Zion. He met Uncle Jakub, and when Jakub heard his story, he realized who he was and told him that you and I were in America. In his letter, he said that Chasya is married to a teacher in Krakow."

Miriam wiped a tear from her eye and sighed. "He also told me that mother and her husband had died in 1915 during the flu epidemic. He was still an infant and had never really known them."

So we have another brother and sister. Tobias was silent a moment and then said, "I remember the old baker. He had a shop not too far from our home. Yes, Mr. Berman. He'd give us sweet babka whenever we went there."

Miriam smiled. "So many years ago."

Then, the realization came to Tobias like a bolt of lightning. "But Miriam, they're in danger. We must get them out!"

Miriam sighed resignedly. "That's right, Tobias. Welcome to Poale Zion."

Barbara Wilson walked across Central Park to Fifth Avenue, then down to Fifty-sixth Street toward her destination between Fifth and Sixth Streets. Bonwit Teller was her favorite department store, and she did most of her shopping there. Today, she planned to buy a new evening dress, something she could wear when she took Richard out to celebrate his return.

She had the whole evening planned in her mind.

Because she knew he'd first want a rare steak, prime cut, accompanied by a Manhattan, she would take him to the Homestead, a restaurant in the Meatpacking District. Then she'd whisk him back uptown for drinks and dancing at the Rainbow Room, ending the night back at her apartment.

"Yes," she said to herself, "the perfect evening. But first, the dress." Something sensual and inviting. Something not too complicated so he could quickly undress her with just a few easy motions. Men could be so clumsy when it came to women's clothing.

She had just passed East Fifty-eighth when she heard a loud crash and the sound of glass breaking, followed by car horns blaring. Everyone on the sidewalks stopped and turned toward the sound. A large black Plymouth had crashed into a beige Studebaker Champion.

All the car horns fell silent except for one. She moved to the sidewalk to get a better view and saw the driver of the Plymouth slumped over the steering wheel. Through the broken windshield, she could see his weight pressing against the horn. Barbara stared, embarrassed but fixated, like all the other onlookers. She came to her senses and was about to turn and continue her journey when she saw that one of the men standing next to the curb on the opposite side of the street was Anthony Scrivner. She started to walk to the next corner to cross over when she was surprised to see her brother, Adam, standing in the crowd further behind him. As she approached the crosswalk, she saw Anthony turn away and start walking in the opposite direction, back toward Central Park.

Odd, she thought, that when Anthony started to move, Adam did the same. Then she noticed that Adam seemed to be looking directly at Anthony as the two moved together toward the park, Adam keeping pace with him but not attempting to catch up.

Deciding that Bonwit Teller could wait, she turned her back on the street, moved to a storefront display, and pretended to be window shopping. Once they'd passed her, moving north, she began to walk. Keeping to her side of the street, she stayed parallel to Adam but a few steps behind.

This was the first time she had seen Adam since the night he assaulted poor Julie. Now, at least, she knew he was back in town, but why on earth would he be following Anthony?

They turned left on Fifty-ninth. She ran across the street, narrowly missing being hit by a cab, the cabbie shouting something rude as he passed her. Rounding the corner on Fifty-ninth, she caught sight of them again and moved closer, afraid she might lose them. Then Adam suddenly stopped. She ducked into a doorway and peered out.

Anthony had stopped as well and was speaking to a woman.

Barbara had met his wife at company functions, and this was not her. She wore a form-fitting blue dress, beige nylons, black high heels, and a fur wrap. She looked to be in her mid-twenties, smiling and speaking animatedly. After their brief conversation, Anthony took her by the arm, walked a bit further, and then both turned into the lobby of the Plaza Hotel.

Adam stood in place for almost a full minute, then abruptly turned and started walking toward her. She stood her ground, and he saw her after walking only a few paces.

He paused briefly before continuing toward her, breaking out in a broad grin.

"Hi ho, Sis, how're tricks?"

"Hello, Adam. Why didn't you tell us you were in town?"

"I'm persona non grata these days, you know. Dad would rather I not bother him any longer."

"That's not true. He's been worried sick about you ever since we lost track of you in South Carolina."

"You mean since I got booted out of the Marines, don't you?"

"Not at all! How are you doing?"

Adam had been wondering what he'd say this whole time, but if he was good at anything, it was lying. "I'm working for a private detective agency. A friend recommended me. A hundred a week. Not bad, 'ay?"

"Is that why you're following Anthony Scrivner?"

So she saw that. The next lie came as easily as the first. "Yeah, that's right. I'm not sure, but I think his wife hired the agency," he said, implying that the man was cheating on his wife and meeting that woman wasn't entirely coincidental. He was, of course, really following Scrivner to understand his movements, planning to plug him in some quiet, out-of-the-way spot.

"Oh, Adam, I'm happy for you. I wish you'd come out to the house for dinner some night. I'll let Dad know you're in town. Can I get your phone number?"

"Uh, just moved in. I haven't gotten hooked up yet."

Barbara hid her disappointment. By the look on his face, she knew Adam hadn't told the truth about that. Now she doubted everything else he had told her, but she decided not to push it.

"Well, you've got my number, right?"

"Sure."

She reached into her purse, took out her notebook and pen, and said, "Just in case you've lost it, take this." She scribbled her number down and pulled the sheet from the book.

"Thanks, Sis. I'll call real soon."

"Do that, Big Brother," she said, knowing that he probably wouldn't.

She leaned forward and pecked him on the cheek. They smiled at each other, and then he slipped past her and continued down the street and around the corner.

✍

Ter Meer was shocked but not surprised. After all, Frau Blunt's room was on the house's first floor. For a moment, he believed the glass of milk was for him, then thought better of it.

Frau Blunt stared at Ter Meer briefly and then said, "Guten abend, Herr Ter Meer."

"Yes. Good evening to you, Frau Blunt. A glass of milk?"

"I find it helps me sleep. You are just now reading the message I left from Hauptsturmführer Balsiger."

"Yes. I wish I'd seen it when I first came in, but it was late, and I . . ." He was about to say he was in a hurry but caught himself. "I wanted to get to bed."

"Are you worried about Reichsführer Himmler staying in the house?"

"Why no, not at all. Though there are so many things I must do before he arrives."

"Pardon me, Herr Ter Meer, but I would start by finding another place to put that radio transmitter."

Ter Meer froze. What had she said? He looked at her, eyes wide, and fumbled for something to say. "I'm sorry. I don't know what you mean. Did you say radio transmitter?"

"Ja, Herr Ter Meer. That is precisely what I said. I'm sure the Reichsführer's people would find it during the compulsory security sweep of the house."

Knowing he was exposed, he replied, "Yes, I suppose they might."

"I did in the first thirty seconds going over your room. I apologize, but you know this is part of my duties."

"Not specifically, but I assumed you were Abwehr when they told me I would have an assistant, and you arrived the next morning." He paused momentarily, then said, "I suppose it's also a part of your duty to report me."

"Yes, that is my duty, but I don't think I will."

For a second time, Ter Meer was stunned by the words coming out of her mouth. "You won't?"

"I had already seen things but rationalized them by telling myself we're in a war." Frau Blunt stood silent for a few seconds as if trying to summon the words. "When I first arrived in your home, Hauptsturmführer Balsiger took me to the camp to help him with some labor records." Her voice started to crack. "I saw what they were doing to those people. Starving them. Their faces were skin-covered skulls, gaunt with sunken eyes. Then I saw this one guard . . ." She started to cry. "A little girl, not more than five years old, was standing in a part of the yard where she didn't belong. He grabbed the girl and threw her to the ground and began stomping on her with his boot." Blunt broke down, sobbing. "He killed that little girl."

She sat down and used the sleeve of her nightgown to wipe the tears from her eyes.

"It isn't a detention camp—it's a death camp. They're murdering these people—the Romani, the Jews. And I know there are hundreds of camps here in Poland and back in Germany. I feel so stupid."

Too late, he thought of his handkerchief, but he took it from his pocket anyway and handed it to her.

"I realized then that I was part of a hideous crime and wanted nothing more to do with it. So, no, I'm not going to report you."

He took her hand, realizing that despite her imposing physical presence, she was fragile—like all of us, he thought.

"Thank you, Helga. May I call you Helga?" It was typical in Germany to refer to people by their surnames or titles. Calling someone by their first name didn't happen until you had known that person for an extended period of time, and then only with their permission.

"Ja, you may. But I will call you Herr Ter Meer. I am your assistant."

"Okay, Helga. That would be fine. Now, where do we go from here?"

"First, we move that radio and replace it with some nude pictures. Maybe of your girlfriend to justify having so obvious a hiding place."

She made him feel like he was an amateur, and why wouldn't he be? When he had started, he was passing along bits and pieces of conversations he overheard at parties. Now, he was sending coded radio transmissions and setting up furtive rendezvous with commando teams. He wasn't afraid to say he was overwhelmed at times. Now, thankfully, he had somebody he could share the burden with. But he asked himself how much he should share.

"That's fine, but I don't own nude pictures of a girlfriend."

"Herr Ter Meer, why does that not surprise me?" She gave him a half smile. "I found some in the gardener's shed. They'll have to do, although the Boche will think you have low standards."

Now he wondered just how much she knew about him. His overnight friends always had their separate rooms to maintain a semblance of propriety. Truthfully, he'd been lax about maintaining proper appearances with his guests, despite having a live-in Abwehr agent in his home.

"I have to leave again in a couple of hours, but not for three days in Krakow, as I told you. It's an appointment that I have to keep."

"So early in the morning? You have the meeting at 10:00 with Balsiger and his staff."

"I know. This message has—how should I put it?—complicated my schedule." He was struggling with what he should tell her. Her story about Balsiger and visiting the camp could be a fabrication to draw him out. But she seemed to have known about the radio for some time, so why had he not already been arrested? He remembered his new handler's words, and they were screaming at him in his head—*Don't trust anyone!* "We've got a day to prepare. I'll tell you more after I get back." Then he foolishly asked, "Can I trust you?" He felt like an idiot as soon as the words left his mouth.

"Yes, of course. I can only say that I like you and respect your actions. You are very brave."

Damn. I must decide. Do I trust Helga or not? Do I share this with the Bermuda team? I can hear their answer already. No, they certainly wouldn't trust me beyond that point. It would compromise the success of the operation or even scuttle it. Best I keep this to myself.

"Good night, Helga."

"Good night, and be careful, Herr Ter Meer."

Bradley Compton thought it best that he and Geist—Lindbergh—meet outside the city. He chose the boardwalk at Rockaway Beach because it was easy to get to yet still remote from places they usually frequented. The plan was to meet at a hot dog stand at the corner of the Playland facade at eight. It would be closed, and they'd be there before the beachgoers arrived. The radio transmission he had received from the U-boat off Nassau in the Caribbean included the time and place for Operation Eastern Storm. He would brief Geist on that, but he wanted to hear a firm commitment to the mission first.

Compton arrived at a quarter to eight. He was dressed informally, wearing casual slacks, a tan short-sleeved shirt, slip-ons, and a straw porkpie hat. He carried a light jacket but hadn't found it necessary.

He eyed the menu hanging inside the window of the restaurant. Seeing a picture of a hot dog, he thought about how the Americans owed a debt of gratitude to the Germans for providing them with frankfurters. Admittedly, the Americans did innovate by nesting it in a split bread roll and placing the mustard and sauerkraut on the inside, rather than serving them separately. *I'll have to try that someday. It does look rather delicious.*

From the corner of his eye, he saw Lindbergh walking up to him on his left. He turned to greet him and, with the same queer little shake of the leg, said, "Good morning, Charles. Are you well?"

"Well enough, but we could have met someplace a little more convenient." Lindbergh, in an effort to appear incognito, wore a baseball cap, cheaters, denim trousers, and a light blue jacket.

"I endeavored to pick a place where you would not normally be found."

"I'd say you got that right."

As the two men started to stroll down the boardwalk toward the park, Compton said, "I have the operation details, but first I must ask, are you committed to seeing this operation through? A substantial amount of effort has gone into the planning and preparation, and there will be much more over the next weeks."

Lindbergh stopped and turned to face him. "Sir, I've given quite a bit of thought to this task, and I have set my mind to complete it. You have my word."

Inwardly, Compton was ecstatic. He had worried that Lindbergh might have second thoughts, but now he was sure he would go through with it.

"In that case, Charles, let's find a seat somewhere, and I'll brief you." They sat on one of the beaches facing the Atlantic. Compton tried to be as concise as possible without leaving out any important details.

"On Saturday, May 30, America will be observing the

fifth Decoration Day since its inauguration in 1938, a day for the nation to decorate the graves of her war dead with flowers. The president will be laying a wreath at the Tomb of the Unknown Soldier in Arlington Cemetery across the Potomac River.

"After the wreath laying, he traditionally says a few words to the nation in the cemetery's amphitheater. You'll be among the host of military, political, and society elite in attendance, along with dozens of newspaper and radio reporters representing the national press.

"The president will enter through the Fort Myer Gate, then on to the Old Post Chapel Gate, into the cemetery, and from there to the west side of the amphitheater. He will exit his limousine and be escorted along the north path to the sarcophagus. The dignitaries and press will be assembled on either side.

"It would be best if you stood by the northwest corner of the plaza, close to the path where Roosevelt will enter and exit. Stand adjacent to the path, but not on the path itself."

Compton handed Lindbergh a small black leather case with a latch that opened like a clamshell. Inside was a formed insert designed to secure seven items in place. The largest was a black copy of a Montblanc Meisterstuck 4810. Alongside it were six small metal capsules.

"Charles, let me explain what you are holding in your hands. It is the centerpiece of our plan."

Compton reached over and took the pen out of its niche. Holding it between his fingers, he said, "This pen is actually a small but very powerful pellet gun. It has an effective range of thirty feet and can only achieve its purpose within that distance. That is to say, it will penetrate a coat, jacket, and shirt or trousers and deliver its content only if fired within thirty feet."

Lindbergh took the pen and hefted it. "It's very solid. How much does this weigh?"

"Two hundred and twenty-four grams. Almost half a pound."

"And these?" Lindbergh said, motioning to the capsules.

"Ah! Those are a wonder of German ingenuity. Each capsule contains both the pellet and the propellant." Compton showed him how the pen opened to accept the capsule. "Once you have a pellet loaded, you pull the bottom cover off the pen as you would if you're about to write something, point it at your target, turn the back end of the pen clockwise ninety degrees, and press to fire." Again, Compton demonstrated. "The firing mechanism is disabled when the cover is in place."

"Ingenious! So I have six cartridges, as it were?"

"No. Those are for you to practice firing. The real ammunition will arrive toward the middle of the month, and there will be only two capsules."

"I don't understand. Why only two?"

"Because the pellets are very special and are being prepared as we speak. The pellets themselves are nearly microscopic, but they're encased in soft gelatin to give mass during their flight. When they hit their target, the gelatin disperses, and the pellet continues its progress, piercing the skin. This is possible because even though they are microscopic, the material they are made from makes them quite heavy."

"What are they made of?"

"A highly radioactive material. Polonium 210."

"I don't know what that means."

"Not many people outside of academia do. It was discovered in the last century by Madame Curie. She managed with great difficulty to refine a very small amount by processing an ore called pitchblende containing radium—the same stuff that creates the glowing numbers on watch faces."

"I'm still not following."

"Put simply, it's five thousand times more radioactive than radium. Each pellet is made from one microgram of polonium. Allowed to enter the body, it will result in ever-progressive organ failure and death within two to three days. Our scientists have perfected a method of producing it in a lab environment. Still, the yields can only be measured in micrograms."

"Is it safe to handle?"

"Yes, if it's contained within the capsule. Even then, you would have to swallow it to cause any severe harm. One thing to note is that it has a half-life of only a hundred and thirty-eight days. After that, its radioactivity diminishes by half. That's why we won't have the pellets until mid-month. They will be sent directly to you in the post. Having them delivered by mail was determined to be the surest way to get them into the country without raising suspicion. Agents can be caught or searched at the border, but the postal system's efficiency with millions of pieces of mail delivered each day was the best way to get them to you undetected. Nonetheless, another two capsules will be mailed to me as a precaution, should yours not arrive."

"You meant it when you said much planning and preparation. What do we do next?"

"Nothing for the time being, but I would suggest that

you travel to Virginia in the interim and familiarize yourself with the location."

Compton spent the next few minutes instructing Lindbergh on how the ceremony would proceed and where best to position himself for a clear shot at the president.

After that, they noticed the first groups of people coming onto the boardwalk and the shops beginning to open. It seemed time for them to be on their way. Lindbergh returned the pen to its niche in the box, closed it, and pocketed it. Together, they stood and began to walk.

"I'll wait for your call, Bradley. Are you going to stay and experience one of New York's amusement parks?"

"No, but I think I may get a hot dog on the way out."

❧

As Pierre Ter Meer barreled down the narrow one-lane roads toward Ujazd, he thought of what he would say to the Bermuda team. They had to delay the action, that was sure, but until when? Himmler would no doubt monopolize his time. If not him, then Balsiger, with his incessant need to micromanage everyone's schedules to ensure everything was perfectly coordinated during the Reichsführer's visit.

He slowed the car as he approached the bridge that spanned the Klodica River and led into Ujazd. It was nearing six o'clock, and he saw the shrine off the road on the right side. He drove past it, and before he got to the bridge, he pulled off on a dirt road that paralleled the river. He stopped where he was sure the car couldn't be seen from the main road.

He got out of the car and started walking back to the

shrine. It was cold, and there was dense morning fog. He hadn't gone far before he heard a soft voice.

"Ramrod?"

He stopped and looked in the direction of the voice.

"Bermuda?" Ter Meer asked, peering through the haze. He saw the outline of two men emerging from the fog and moving toward him.

"You're punctual. I'll give you that." Stafford chose to speak German.

"I am always punctual," Ter Meer replied in English. "Have you been here long?"

"Not long—only about forty minutes. You said we're a go for Bermuda?"

"Not by the current schedule. There's been a complication."

"What complication?" said Todd, speaking up.

"It seems we have a dignitary coming to visit. He'll be inspecting both the camp and the hydrierwerks. Moreover, the head of security, Hauptsturmführer Balsiger, has offered him my home for his lodgings."

"Surely we can work around one visitor's agenda," said Stafford.

"I'm afraid that's not that easy when the visitor is Heinrich Himmler."

Stafford and Todd were dumbfounded. The number two man in Hitler's Reich was coming.

The men were mute, and Ter Meer guessed they were thinking things through. He said, "There will be extra security men on and off at both locations, not to mention his personal guard. We'll have to postpone the operation until he's left."

"That will be tricky," Stafford said. "The plan and timetable for our exit will have to be reconsidered. I suppose we could bivouac somewhere out of the way."

"I don't think HQ will be very pleased with the development. Changing the timetable isn't as simple as canceling and reissuing a train ticket," said Todd.

Ter Meer sensed their disappointment, but there was little he could do. Then, a crazy, outrageous idea came into his head, but he dared not share it. He told himself he was fantasizing, but the more he went over it in his mind, the more plausible it seemed. He said out loud, "I just thought of an alternative. It may sound a bit fantastic at first, but I think it might just work."

Todd and Stafford listened attentively to Ter Meer's scheme. Like him, they initially thought it was too wild an idea, but the more they thought it through, the more its potential for success became apparent.

"For this to work," Stafford said, "we would have to overcome his personal guard and find a way to ensure his cooperation at the critical moments."

Ter Meer planned to capture Himmler, and once they completed their mission, they would smuggle him out of the country. It would be a coup for the Allies.

Ter Meer added, "I'll know more after I attend this morning's briefing about the visit with the camp security officer, Balsiger."

As they talked, Hendricks, Newley, and the two captives, Alexi and Jan, approached. Stafford introduced the two Allied officers and referred to Alexi and Jan as temporary detainees.

"You wouldn't happen to know these two gentlemen?" asked Todd.

"No, Captain, I'm afraid not," replied Ter Meer.

"They claim to be members of two Polish underground organizations assisting Jewish refugees. Have you heard of either Zegota or Poale Zion?"

"Apologies, Captain. Though I've lived in this part of Germany for six years now, I was born in Mainz and raised Catholic. I am keenly aware of and familiar with the plight of the Jews, but I've had only incidental exposure to Polish politics. Though I work for MI6, I have no connections with the Polish underground."

"We've asked London if representatives from the Polish government in exile can confirm their identities," said Todd. "With the change in plan, they may be useful. What do you think, Commander?"

"Yes, they could, but only upon hearing confirmation that they are who they say they are."

"Will we have time to deliver the penicillin now?" Jan asked.

"Things being what they are now, yes, I suppose we will," Stafford said.

"Thank you. The farmhouse is only three kilometers away on this side of the river."

Ter Meer, mindful of the time it would take him to drive to Auschwitz, the opposite direction from the plant—told them he had to leave to get to the SS briefing in Balsiger's office at the camp on time. "I'll see if they've already posted additional security at the plant when I get there this afternoon and what plans they may have for my home. We can meet at the house tomorrow if they're not sending anyone there until Friday. I'll radio from home at 01800 this evening to tell you if it's safe."

"We'll be ready," said Hendricks.

"Well then, I'll be on my way. Keep safe." Ter Meer walked back to his car and drove off.

Todd turned to Jan and Alexi and said, "What's the best way to go, staying off the roads?"

∽

Anthony Scrivner sat in his office, staring out at the Manhattan skyline. He was furious. J.L. had told him earlier that he had spoken to his daughter, Barbara, about joining the company and asked if Anthony would act as her mentor. "Wonderful idea," Scrivner had told him. "Yes, of course. It would be my privilege."

He swore out loud. "Damn!" He thought his ascendancy to the CEO position was assured since young Adam Wilson had imploded. "The idiot hung on to that dream well past the time it was obvious the boy was unstable."

Funny, he thought. The other day, as he was leaving the Plaza after his rendezvous with his amoureux, Eileen Simpson, from the typing pool, he had seen Adam standing on the corner. *Fool, he didn't even notice me.*

Wilson had told him he had presented the proposition to her at breakfast the other day, and she had said she would think about it. *Now I have to deal with the daughter, but how?* He turned from the window. *Get a grip, Anthony. She may not even want the job.* But he still needed to do something. It had become clear that J.L. never intended to nominate him for CEO after he left.

Hansen came to mind as a potential ally in his dilemma.

Sure, Scrivner had anonymously had a copy of the Blech-hammer report sent to him, but that was only to get some leverage on the board to oppose any decision to close the plant. Closure and loss of business would cost the company over one hundred and twenty million dollars in revenue annually.

I'll be damned if I'm going to lose my annual bonus because some joker suddenly developed scruples. Each year, top executives would receive a bonus or shares of preferred stock based on the company's profitability.

Scrivner didn't want J.L. ousted. At least not yet. If he were to ascend to the top spot, he would need more support on the board. At the moment, he was in a dead heat with Hansen, with the geriatrics on the board supporting Hansen. He had counted on J.L. being the tie-breaking vote until he came to him with this nonsense about his daughter.

No, there had to be some other way. *I could murder Hansen. No, too big a risk. Not that I wouldn't enjoy it.*

He knew only one option was open to him, short of murder. He had to convince Barbara or J.L. that she wasn't fit for the job. He supposed he didn't have to hurry—it would be years after she joined the company before J.L. relinquished the reins.

That's it, Anthony, old boy. Just bide your time for now and think of a way to discredit her with the board or persuade her to believe it's not a woman's place. It isn't, after all. A woman only has two places in a man's world—in front of a stove or in bed.

This thought made him think of Eileen Simpson. She was excellent in bed. And all he had to do was promise he'd use his influence with her supervisor to promote her from typist two to three.

"An extra ten dollars a week," he said aloud and laughed. *Hell, it's not my money. Why not?* The intercom on his desk buzzed. "Yes, Sophie, what is it?"

"Barbara Wilson to see you."

Speak of the devil, Scrivner thought and pressed the switch on the intercom. "Please send her in."

Barbara Wilson entered the office and walked to Scrivner's desk. "Good morning, Anthony."

"Good morning, Barbara. Are you sure you're related to J.L.? He barely gives me the time of day when I enter his office. Just goes straight to business."

"Well, I didn't get these dimples from my mother. How are you?"

"I'm fine. Please sit down," he said, waving to a chair.

"I was here seeing Dad and thought I'd pop over and say hello." She paused for a moment before continuing. "Not just hello. I wanted to get your take on this idea of Father's."

"About coming on board? I think it's a marvelous idea. He's struggled quite a bit since . . . well, since Adam got in trouble."

"You're not opposed to it? I still really haven't made up my mind to do it. I wanted to talk to you about it and get your thoughts."

"Well, it's a great deal of responsibility and long hours that no one thanks you for."

"That's not what I mean. I mean, how do you feel about it? Did you have expectations of becoming CEO one day?"

"I might have fantasized about it once or twice, but I'm delighted with my current position. It has its rewards." He did his best to smile and seem lighthearted, not entirely pulling it off.

Barbara noticed and decided to take a different tack. "Where do you want to go in your career?"

He sensed she knew he was being disingenuous. "I'd be happy to retire as president. Perhaps take a seat on the board to stay connected and pursue public initiatives like children's education or medical assistance to the poor." Scrivner had a hard time holding a straight face, but he managed. He couldn't care less about children or the poor.

"I would need your help and guidance. And I'd have to be with the company years before I could even consider what Father suggests."

"I'm your man. I'd consider it an honor to act as your mentor. Be warned, however—I'm a rigid taskmaster." He smiled genuinely this time.

She doubted his sincerity but returned his smile. "That's wonderful. I can't thank you enough. Dad and I are going to lunch. Would you like to join us?"

"Sounds great."

"Okay, we'll stop by and pick you up." Barbara got up and shook Anthony's hand. Halfway to the door, she stopped and turned. "By the way, you haven't seen my brother Adam by chance, have you?"

He wondered if she knew that he had seen him, but he lied and said, "No, not in some time. Why?"

"Oh, no particular reason. I bumped into him the other day. He's back in town. He says he's working for some detective agency."

Detective agency? Could it be he was following me? Did he see me with Ms. Simpson?" Aloud, he said, "Oh, I see. Well, good to hear he's situated."

Barbara smiled and left. Scrivner, ever suspicious, decided right then that he'd have to keep a close eye on her.

§

For once, Zemel thought his argument with Pesha had weight.

"Look, underground activists and foreign soldiers are gathering at our farm. We must inform the Germans, Pesha, or it will put our necks in the noose as well as theirs."

"And whose fault is that, Zemel Kowalski? If you hadn't robbed the old Jew, we wouldn't be in this predicament. Besides, they came with drugs to treat that poor woman."

"I don't care what you think. I don't want the Germans to shoot me like a dog."

"If you turn them in, you can stay away. I won't live with an informer."

Zemel was a weak man, faced with more than he could handle. On the one hand, Alexi had bullied him into silence and forced him to return the money he had extorted from Dovid. He may or may not have killed him as he had threatened. On the other hand, he had no doubt that if the Boche discovered the Broders at the farm, he would be lined up with the rest of them and shot. He was more frightened of the Germans than Alexi's threats.

Maybe the Germans are searching for them now. They could arrive at any minute. The thought elevated Zemel's fear. He was sweating, terrified that there would be a knock at the door. *What if they torture us to find out what the soldiers are here for?*

His need to flee the situation was overwhelming. *No one*

is paying me any attention. I'll just slip out the back without anyone noticing.

In the bedroom, Dovid, Todd, Stafford, and Zemel's wife, Pesha, stood around Chasya's bed, while lieutenants Newley and Hendricks stood watch outside. Todd administered a shot of penicillin.

"I'm not a doctor," said Todd, "but considering her high fever and labored breathing, it could be pneumonia."

"Will the penicillin help?" asked Dovid.

"It should, but she needs rest and plenty of fluids." He was about to say she should be in a hospital, but why suggest the impossible?

Pesha, ashamed of her husband's actions, said, "I'll be sure the lady stays warm and gets plenty to drink. Mr. Broder, you and your wife are welcome to stay here as long as you like."

No one noticed as Zemel left the house through the kitchen door and headed across the vegetable garden toward the barn. Halfway across the garden, he broke into a run, anxious to put as much distance as possible between himself and the others.

Behind the barn was a path that led into the woods. His heart stopped as he rounded the corner of the barn—Alexi was there, standing in silence, his emotionless eyes focused on Zemel.

"In a hurry to get somewhere, szmalcownik ?"

"I was just going for a walk."

"But you were running, Zemel. Why? Are you afraid of something?"

Frantic with fear, Zemel stammered, "No . . . I . . ."

"You should be afraid. You know why?"

"No. Please." Zemel started to shake.

"You know what happens to all God-cursed szmalcowniks."

Alexi raised his revolver and, without blinking, pumped two bullets into Zemel's heart. He was dead before he hit the ground. Alexi dragged the body over to the compost heap, grabbed a shovel from the barn, and covered it with two feet of manure. Then he washed his hands in a bucket of water from the horse trough and returned to the house.

They were all downstairs now. Jan was speaking with Dovid, and the Bermuda team was setting up their short-wave, readying for the next scheduled broadcast.

Pesha saw Alexi come in through the kitchen. She caught him staring at her, and his cold, passionless gaze told her Zemel was dead. "Why?" she asked.

"He was going to inform," said Alexi.

Alexi felt sorry for her, not because her husband was dead but because she had married such a worthless shit. Before they left, he would tell her where the body was.

She turned around, went to the kitchen, picked up some beets, then returned to the people assembled in her living room. Raising her voice above the din, she said, "I hope everyone likes borscht."

SEVEN

Bradley Compton had placed Adam Wilson in a modest but comfortable hotel near Penn Station on Thirty-fourth Street, with a private bathroom and maid service. Adam was lying on the bed, wearing trousers and a T-shirt, his head propped on two pillows against the headboard. He stared up at the ceiling fan, watching it turn as he contemplated his life to this point.

When he was growing up, he adored his younger sister, Barbara, and often played with her. In many ways, she had always been the more mature and sensible of the two. But he had always been a bit jealous of her—she seemed to play catch with Dad more often than he ever did. Still, he didn't resent her for it. He resented his father.

He and his mother were very close. He had friends, but his mother was his best friend. She took him everywhere and helped him with all sorts of things—like pointing out which of his friends were trustworthy or which were "bad influences." She rarely approved of any of the girls he brought home. Sometimes, she would say, "Careful, Adam, I can tell that one's a dirty girl. You don't want a dirty girl."

Tears formed in his eyes as he remembered their skiing vacation—and the accident. He relived the shock and horror of the moment when a mountain of snow and rock swallowed his mother, and then him. When he awoke after the rescue, everything had changed.

She was gone, and he had survived. The loss was unbearable. He no longer had the strength to deal with life's setbacks, big or small. His mother had always helped him with that. Without her to guide him, to make things better, he became angry—lashing out at those around him, even the ones he thought he loved. It wasn't something he could control.

Probably better for everyone that I left. I miss Barb, even though she was pissed off at me half the time. And Dad? Well, he never understood. He was always trying to change me into somebody I'm not.

Adam got up off the bed, undressed, and went into the bathroom, where he showered, shaved, and put on a clean white shirt and a pair of slacks. Standing in front of the mirror, combing his hair, he stared at the faint outlines of the scars from where they had fitted his face back together after the accident. They were barely visible now, but he could always find them.

I know Dad blamed me for the accident. To him, my disfigurement was just a reminder of my guilt, an annoyance. So he waved his magic wand to hide the ugly truth that I was responsible for my mother's death—nothing but the best surgeons and hospitals for Adam Wilson. A near-perfect repair job for everyone else's peace of mind. But I was the one who endured eight surgeries over twenty-seven months.

Still looking in the mirror, he said aloud, "Perfect job. But who are you? Not me. That's not the face I woke up with the morning before the accident."

He put on his shoes and socks and grabbed his coat.

Why am I doing this? Am I really going to murder a man? And what happens after? God, I wish Mother were here.

Pushing his thoughts aside, he opened the door and stepped into the hallway. He was supposed to meet Compton to give him the lowdown on how—and where—he would kill Anthony Scrivner. He went downstairs, walked out to the street, and hailed a cab.

He was about to give the cabbie the address where he was supposed to meet Compton, but instead, said, "115 Central Park West." As the cab pulled away from the curb, Adam settled into the seat.

Hauptsturmführer Balsiger stood stiff and straight as Obersturmbannführer Rudolf Hoss, the man responsible for all operations in the Auschwitz complex, entered the room. The entire complex encompassed three camps—Auschwitz one, which was the main concentration camp, Auschwitz-Birkenau, a concentration and extermination camp, and Auschwitz Monowitz, the industrial complex built and staffed by the prisoners.

Hoss was Balsiger's superior, two ranks above him, and Balsiger reported directly to him. Balsiger had security responsibility for the three camps in Auschwitz and the hydrierwerks located in Blechhammer. As head of security, he would be overseeing both Himmler's stay and the inspections.

Balsiger raised his arm in a sharp salute. "Sieg Heil!"

Nonchalantly, Hoss took a chair. "At ease, Hauptsturmführer. There'll be enough formality over the next few days. Please, Otto, have a seat. Remind me. You received the communication from headquarters. At precisely what time does Reichsführer Himmler arrive?"

Balsiger pulled out his desk chair and sat, remaining stiff and straight. "Friday at 0930, Obersturmbannführer."

"And his schedule during his stay?"

"Upon arrival, he will meet with the two of us in your office for a general briefing on the camp's operational statistics—prisoner volumes by number series, work detail assignments, and the number of executions over the last six months, categorized by gassing, shooting, hanging, and starvation, again by number series.

"Following the briefing, he will tour the main camp and the industrial complex.

"Reichsführer Himmler will then retire to his assigned billet—Herr Ter Meer's residence outside Gliwice—for a two-night stay. On the second day, he will tour the hydrierwerks at Blechhammer, with Herr Ter Meer and Herr Doktor Crowning leading the visit.

"On Sunday, he will inspect the execution facilities and procedures at Birkenau, including the gas chambers and crematorium. He will depart for Krakow that afternoon."

"Excellent, Otto. I will accompany you and the Reichsführer on both camp inspections, but I don't think I need to be present for the hydrierwerks plant as it's mostly technical, and I'd be out of my depth. We will, of course, allow the Reichsführer to rest on his first night here. We'll schedule a dinner for Friday as a formal welcome. What do you think?"

"I agree, sir. We can have dinner at Ter Meer's residence. It's large, modern, and well-appointed, and that's why I chose it for the Reichsführer's stay. I've been there for dinner, and I must say Ter Meer is an excellent host."

"I received instructions outlining Reichsführer Himmler's diet. Did you know he cannot—or perhaps will not—touch cheese of any kind? He says it's rotting milk." Balsiger chuckled. "He must have been frightened by a cow when he was young."

His attempt at humor fell flat with Hoss, who raised an eyebrow in response.

"Well," said Hoss. "I think that's about all, except for one thing."

"Yes, Obersturmbannführer?"

"Be sure that there's been no recent usage when we inspect the gas chambers—the smell is horrible. And please keep the *Sonderkammandos* (prisoners forced to help clean the chambers and remove the bodies to the crematorium) away from the Reichsführer."

"I'll see to it, sir."

"Very well." Hoss stood, gave a halfhearted Hitler salute, mumbled "Heil Hitler!" and left Balsiger alone in his office.

Balsiger didn't lower his arm until Hoss closed the office door behind him.

Very well, indeed. If all goes smoothly, I think there'll be a letter of commendation for me.

He removed the notebook from the side pocket of his tunic and jotted down a reminder about the Sonderkommandos.

✧

Ter Meer left Balsiger's ten o'clock briefing dreading the idea of Himmler under his roof, knowing he could do little about it. What irritated him even more was that Balsiger had asked him to cater and host a dinner in Himmler's honor.

"Just make sure you don't serve cheese," Balsiger had said.

Ter Meer had replied, "But some people enjoy a cheese plate after dinner."

Balsiger had stood and shouted, "Scheisse, Pierre, Ich sagte kein Kase!"

Being spoken to like that by the Hauptsturmführer only deepened Ter Meer's resentment. He considered the man sycophantic, toady, officious—and not especially bright.

Most important, however, was that Ter Meer now had Himmler's schedule through Sunday. He decided to make a quick run to the plant to see Christian. He would tell him to expedite the delivery of the tanker cars of liquid hydrogen and have them parked on the rail spur beside the plant. His excuse for this would be to avoid any potential downtime due to short supply—even though two cars held enough to support three months of production.

If we detonate them, all that would be left of the plant would be a scorched hole in the ground, and there wouldn't be a tree left standing within a half-kilometer radius.

Afterward, he could still make it home in time to radio Bermuda with the message that it would be safe to meet at the house this evening. They'd need as much time as possible to devise a workable plan.

But what about Frau Blunt? Should I let her into my confidence? And if not, then what? I have to make a decision.

It suddenly struck him that if he couldn't trust her, he might have to eliminate her. He hadn't signed up for that when the British SIS recruited him. He'd never killed anybody. He was just a likable gay man who got along well at parties. But he had to face facts—if she couldn't be trusted, she'd have to go. But was he capable of murder? He supposed he wouldn't know until the time came. Either way, he had to know where Helga's loyalties lay.

He finished at the plant quickly. Christian would do as instructed, and the tanker cars of liquid hydrogen would be in place by Friday.

It was half past five in the evening when he turned off the main road onto the private drive to his home. He drove around the side to the carport and parked. As he was getting out of his car, he saw Frau Blunt wrestling a large suitcase into her '35 Adler cabriolet.

"Where are you going, Helga?"

"Back to Freiburg. I can't stay here."

"May I ask why?"

"Because I know the dilemma I pose to you. Nothing I can do will convince you I meant what I said last night—and there are any number of tricks the Abwehr could employ to make me seem loyal. If I were in your position, I would have to consider liquidating me, just to be safe. I'm not leaving just to save myself. I'm leaving to solve your problem—and to let you get on with the business at hand."

Ter Meer looked at the giant of a woman before him and decided he had to trust her. The thought crossed his mind that even this could be a trick, but he decided enough was enough—murder was beyond his capability, at least in this case. He had worked with Helga for some time now, and though she acted with an unemotional efficiency most of the time, he saw hints of a warm and caring human being.

"You are correct to think I was debating what to do, but

I've come to the realization that I trust you. And to be frank, I don't think I could ever kill you."

Helga yanked her bulky suitcase out of the car. "Thank you, Herr Ter Meer. Now, if you don't mind, I will put away my things and see you at dinner in precisely one hour and forty-five minutes." She hefted the bag, turned, and strode into the house.

Under his breath, Ter Meer whispered, "Jawohl, Frau Blunt."

The following day, Alexi, who had spent the evening in Gliwice, returned to the farmhouse. Jan Berman met him at the door.

"Good morning, Jan. Did you sleep well?"

"Yes. I think it's the first full night's sleep since leaving Warsaw. I woke up to the sound of Pesha humming to herself in the kitchen as she made breakfast. I think she's starting to understand she's better off now that Zemel is gone."

After getting the all-clear in Ter Meer's coded radio message the night before, the Bermuda team had left before dawn that morning for his home.

The team had also received confirmation from London that Jan Berman's identity was legitimate and that he was a member of Poale Zion. They also confirmed that Szymon Janko was Alexi's true identity and that he was a member of Zegota. Stafford, however, was none too pleased when he realized that Alexi must have had another weapon he used to shoot Zemel. Nonetheless, the evening before, they allowed him to leave to retrieve the forged papers.

Alexi sat with Jan. "I've brought the Broders' papers. They were sent to our people in Gliwice as I requested."

He handed the small bundle of documents—German identification cards (*Kennkarten*), a marriage certificate, and a work permit (*Arbeitskarte*) for Dovid—to Jan. They were now identified as Antoni and Freyda Wojcik. The identification cards were gray, signifying that they were ethnic Poles—unlike the yellow cards they had originally been issued as Jews. On Dovid's work permit, he was still listed as a teacher. There were also two German passports (*Reisepäss*) that would allow them to travel to Budapest.

Jan had seen these kinds of counterfeit documents many times before, but he was always impressed with the quality of the forgeries.

"You'll need their fingerprints on their identification cards," Alexi said.

"I'll take care of that. Unfortunately, I don't think Chasya will be able to travel anytime soon."

"She's not getting better?"

"No. I gave her the second shot of penicillin this morning, but I'm afraid she's getting worse. Dovid won't leave her bedside, and it's taking its toll on him as well."

"The longer you stay here, the greater the risk of being discovered."

"I know, but what am I to do? She's my sister, and Dovid won't leave without her."

"If she doesn't get better soon, we may need to move to another location. I can get us a car to help with that, but if we're stopped, we'll have to tell where we're going, and they might follow us to be sure we're telling the truth. They've been known to do that."

At that moment, they saw Pesha descending the stairs. "The dear lady is not at all well," she said, "and her husband kneels at the side of the bed, holding her hand. He is so devoted." She paused, and Alexi wondered if she was thinking about how Zemel had never treated her in such a kind way. "The husband is much older than the lady."

"Yes, seventeen years older," said Jan.

He remembered when Chasya had introduced him. She was in her late thirties, recently abandoned by her first husband for another woman, and Dovid was fifty-six at the time. He had proven himself a good man and truly loved and doted on Chasya.

"She is blessed to have a husband so kind." She looked at Alexi, frightened of him yet strangely grateful for what he had done. "Mister . . ." She paused. "I'm afraid I do not know your last name."

Alexi smiled briefly. "I don't have a last name, madam. Just call me Alexi."

"Mister Alexi, would you care for some breakfast? It's just some warmed *kluski slaskie* (potato dumplings) with eggs and sausage."

"That sounds delicious, Mrs. Kowalski, but I've already eaten."

"Pesha, please. You may call me by my first name."

Alexi smiled, bowed slightly, and said, "Thank you, Pesha."

Blushing, Pesha hurried back to the kitchen.

"I can't thank you enough, Alexi, for helping my sister and her husband," said Jan.

"Not at all. We all help each other. You saved my life in Krakow not too long ago."

"I think we can catch the train in Gliwice—there's less security there. Then we'll travel to Katowice and transfer to a train bound for Budapest. That route will take us across the frontier to Ostrava, Czechia, then down through Slovakia with a stop in Bratislava before continuing on to Budapest. I know a safe house there where we can stay. My contact at the Swiss consulate will issue papers for travel to Turkey, and once they're on their way, I'll return to Krakow."

"That should work well. I wish you and your family all the best." With that, Alexi stood and placed a hand on Jan's shoulder. "It's time I left. God help us—there are so many other people."

"Aye. Shalom, my friend."

Alexi knew Jan had only come to see his sister safely out of the country. *Please, God, let the sister be well.*

Barbara Wilson had been expecting a courier to drop off papers her father wanted her to read. She heard the bell and, upon opening the door, was surprised to find her brother Adam standing there, an ear-to-ear grin on his face.

"Hi, Sis. How're tricks?"

She grabbed his hand, pulled him inside the apartment, and hugged him. "This is a surprise. I wasn't expecting you." She showed him to the sofa. "I know it's a bit early, but would you like a drink? Vodka on the rocks with a twist of lemon, right?"

"That would be fine. Join me?"

"Sure, my afternoon's open. But just one." She poured herself a scotch and soda and sat on the sofa next to him. "What brings you around?"

"Do I have to have a reason? Couldn't it be I just wanted to see my adoring sister?"

"That would be a first. Not that you aren't welcome, but I know you, Adam, and I know that look on your face. Something's eating you."

Adam downed half his drink and set the glass on the coffee table. "You do know me, and you know I'm not the touchy-feely type."

Not since Mom died. But she didn't voice her thought, deciding it was best to just let him talk.

"I've been thinking about things since we bumped into each other. I mean, you and me, where I'm going, and how it used to be."

Barbara hadn't heard this level of personal discussion from her brother for a long time. "You mean when we used to be best friends?"

Adam shrugged. "Yeah, when we used to have fun just hanging out together."

"Adam, I'm still your friend, your sister. If something's bothering you, I'll listen, and I promise I won't judge."

She could tell he was on the verge of crying and reached for his hand, but he quickly stood, took his drink, walked to the radio, and leaned on the console.

"I guess I've made a mess of things. You know, with Dad and . . ." He hesitated, then started to talk again, but was having trouble getting the words out. "And Julie." He fell quiet and stared down his nose at his glass, swirling the ice cubes with his finger.

"You think you need help?"

"No, it's just that Julie was a swell kid—and I know what I did. What's bothering me is that . . . and what my life is turning into. I have a huge chip on my shoulder, and I go around looking for someone to try and knock it off so I can deck them."

"You're carrying around a lot of anger. That's not good."

"Yeah, I guess so. Anyway, I met this guy with the detective agency I told you about. He wants me to do something, and I'm afraid that if I do it, there's no going back. That's what I meant about where my life's going."

"What does he want you to do?"

Adam stiffened, anxiety swelling inside him. Abruptly, he set his glass back down on the table and grabbed his hat. "Never mind, Sis. I should never have come." He walked to the door.

"Wait, Adam. Whatever it is, we can work it out." She got up and moved quickly to his side, placing her hand on his arm in an attempt to stop him from going.

"Thanks for the drink."

"Please don't go."

"I'll be all right. I'll call you." He opened the door, bent down and gave her a peck on the cheek, and left.

Barbara watched the door close.

I wish Richard were here. I could use a shoulder to lean on, someone to talk to. But maybe it's too soon in our relationship to burden him with this. There's Dad—but no. Uncle Tobias! Perfect. He's always been there for me.

Thanks to Balsiger's briefing, Ter Meer had not only Himmler's schedule by the hour but details of who would accompany him during each of his stops, including the number of officers, support staff, and security personnel.

For his Friday and Saturday night stays at Ter Meer's home, Himmler would be joined by his adjutant, Oberleutnant Ambros Kilmer. Oberleutnant Dieter Stamn, head of Himmler's protection squad—six hand-picked SS men—would remain outside, positioned close to the house. Balsiger's men would patrol the estate grounds, securing a perimeter one kilometer from the building. Radio voice checks between Balsiger's men and Stamn's would take place at the top of every hour.

The plan was simple. Ter Meer would give his cook and maid the day off and hire a competent catering service for the evening, warning them that any cheese on the menu would be met with severe consequences.

Todd and Hendricks would secret themselves in the house while Himmler and his entourage were touring the Auschwitz main camp.

At the same time, Stafford and Newley would go into Pławniowice and pick up a truck that Ter Meer had arranged to be transferred from the hydrierwerks to the village. He had told a shift supervisor he needed it to move some furniture, and the supervisor was only too happy to help the boss as a personal favor. It was perfect for their purposes—large and unmarked with a covered rear bed that could accommodate passengers.

Stafford, who spoke fluent German, and the other team members carried forged German identification papers. He, Newley, and Hendricks would pretend to be with the caterers, coming to pick up the cleanup crew, the actual catering staff having left earlier. Ter Meer would leave the space next to the side door in the car park open for the truck.

Before Stafford and Newley arrived, Todd and Hendricks

would come out of hiding and overpower Himmler and his adjutant, Oberleutnant Kilmer. They'd warn Himmler to remain silent—or forfeit his life. Todd trusted that, fanatic though he was, Himmler wouldn't carry it to the grave and would grudgingly comply. They would disguise him as one of the waitstaff, dressing him in one of the white smocks Ter Meer would steal from the test lab at the plant, shaving his mustache and removing his glasses.

The Oberleutnant would be bound and left in one of the bedrooms. Then, with everyone disguised as members of the catering staff, Todd and Hendricks would sneak Ter Meer and Himmler out to the truck. Ter Meer had made up his mind—he would leave Silesia with the Bermuda team.

Together, they would go to the plant, set the explosives, and hopefully make it to the rendezvous point to meet the B-34 Liberator scheduled to land at 0300 hours on Saturday before anyone discovered Himmler was missing. All this had to happen within six hours of leaving the house.

That was the plan, and it would all start tomorrow, Friday, when Ter Meer would meet Himmler for the first time when he arrived at the Auschwitz main camp.

Ter Meer was not looking forward to it. Balsiger had proudly told him that the Reichsführer was the chief architect of what they were calling the "Final Solution." They schemed to liquidate the entire Jewish population of Europe—scapegoated by Hitler to justify his rise to power and his wars of aggression. According to their twisted beliefs, the Jews had killed Christ, denied the word of God, betrayed Germany in the First World War, murdered children for religious rituals, and conspired to dominate the world through banks and corrupt politicians.

One item, however, was left unresolved. Although Ter Meer had elected to put his trust in Helga Blunt, he had not yet told her of their plan to kidnap Heinrich Himmler.

Hendricks sat in front of the shortwave at Ter Meer's kitchen table, sending the mission status message, which was just a few words in code indicating that the mission was proceeding according to the original timetable. The only change was moving the rendezvous out to 0300, done in a previous transmission and acknowledged.

Todd and Mick Stafford stood on either side of him, and Newley sat across from him at the table, cleaning his pistol—a custom HDM series manufactured by High Standard Firearms in Hamden, Connecticut. The "M" designated it as a military model, built specifically for the OSS.

"I hope Pierre is right about the radio checks being confined to the perimeter guards and Himmler's security on the grounds near the house," said Todd.

"I believe he's correct," Stafford replied, "but he wasn't briefed on the procedures Himmler's people follow. Who knows if they check in with Himmler or his adjutant inside the house on a regular basis?"

"We'll have to risk it, Mick. With luck, that's not the case, and they won't realize we're gone until the plant goes up. I assume someone will then come calling for Pierre to inform him, but we should be in the air shortly after that."

"Speaking of risks," said Stafford, "we have to clear out of this place early tomorrow morning. The woods by the farmhouse will be a good spot for us to hide. Then you and I will return while Himmler and the rest tour the camps."

"I agree. It's a good place to lay low." Todd laughed. "I think you might just want to stop in for another bowl of borscht—and I wouldn't blame you. That Pesha woman knows her way around a kitchen."

"Tempting, old boy, but we said our goodbyes and should leave those people to themselves." Stafford thought for a moment and then asked, "Aren't you a bit concerned about Pierre's assistant? What's her name? Blunt?"

"Pierre says she's safe. I would hope he'd know—he said she's been working for him for some years. But I suspect there's something about her that he's not sharing."

As they talked, Pierre sat in one of the two Barcelona chairs in his living room, and Frau Blunt perched on the edge of one of the two La Corbusier loveseats. The furnishings reflected Pierre's penchant for Bauhaus design.

Wondering why Ter Meer had called her aside, Helga asked, "So there is something you wish to tell me, Herr Ter Meer?"

"Yes, Helga. I'm leaving on Saturday evening, and I do not intend to return."

This caught her off guard. She hadn't expected such a declaration, and it prompted numerous questions. "Going? May I ask where?"

"I think England, to begin with. Maybe America. But I want to pose a question. Would you consider joining me?" Seeing that she was at a loss for words, he said, "It would be dangerous for you to stay."

"I assume you and your colleagues are going to do something . . ." She paused, looking for the right word, and then said, "Extreme?"

"Yes, quite extreme, and being my assistant, you would probably be held suspect."

"It appears I have no choice. I have no illusions about what they'd do to me if I stayed."

"You could plausibly deny any foreknowledge of our actions, but . . ." Now, Ter Meer paused. He leaned forward and looked at her. "Well, you know how the Gestapo operates. Your interrogation would likely leave you seriously injured or dead."

Helga swallowed. "Most likely the latter." She then sat up straight. "I will go with you, Herr Ter Meer, because I no longer wish to have anything to do with Herr Hitler or his Reich."

"Good. That settles that. You don't need to know our objective, only that we have expanded it. That part you need to know."

"I suppose it might be related to Reichsführer Himmler's visit?"

"Yes."

"Are you going to assassinate the Reichsführer?"

"That would be much easier, but no. We're going to kidnap him."

❧

Tobias Bach sat with J. Leland Wilson in Wilson's office, drinking coffee. After meeting for lunch, they had come back to the office so Tobias could witness changes to Wilson's will.

"That's an incredible story, Tobias—finding out you had another brother and sister all these years, that he's a member of the underground group you funded, and that his sister is on the run from the Nazis with her husband. And who'd have thought your sweet stepmother was behind the Poale Zion movement? And Miriam? Good God."

"I wish I could do more to help them, but I'm not even sure I know where they are. Somewhere in German Upper Silesia. Your plant's there, isn't it?"

"Yes, but not for much longer if things go as planned. You know that Richard Todd is part of the team that went there to deal with it. Barbara hides it, but she's worried sick about him. I hope for her sake he makes it back."

"People worldwide are worried about their brothers, sisters, and relatives because of this dreadful war. I thought we'd made the world safe for democracy in the last one."

"I thought so too. That reminds me—Bill Donovan just called. He told me to tell you he was going down to Washington for Decoration Day, and he asked us to come along. He's inviting the old squad members to dinner. You should come. We'll have dinner with the boys, and then on Saturday, we can see the president lay the wreath at the Tomb of the Unknown."

"I'd like that. I haven't seen some of them in years, and it'd be great to catch up. Let's plan on it. Oh—before I forget, how is Barbara?"

"She's doing fine. Such a capable girl. She's wondering what to do with her poli-sci degree from Columbia, talking about entering the foreign service. But it's a hell of a time to be doing that. I've made her an offer to come into the firm, and she's mulling it over."

It seemed that after what had happened with Adam, J.L. was putting all his stock in Barbara to ensure his legacy, but Tobias kept his thoughts to himself. "You think she's interested?"

"I don't know. I'd like to think she is. It would guarantee her financial future."

"Don't get me wrong, Josh, but don't you think she can do that on her own? Maybe you should let her cut her own path. Not everyone is suited for the corporate world."

"Let's see what she says. I promise not to push it on her."

"Tell me what you know about this Todd fellow. From what you've said, he and Barbara have taken quite a liking for each other."

"He's got his law degree and was practicing with Colbert and Jefferies before the war. He signed up for the Army and got involved with this intelligence thing—you know, codes, spies, and whatnot. I don't know much about it, except it's taken off since the beginning of the war. Todd wasn't there long before Bill poached him, and he went to the OSS."

"He seems like a good man. Barbara called me just yesterday, and we're having lunch. It's been a while, so I'm looking forward to it. The last time she wanted to talk to me, it was about the State Department. She knew I had friends there and wanted to know what I could tell her about the culture."

"I have a feeling it might be about Adam. I don't think she feels comfortable talking about him with me. She probably thinks I'm too subjective—and she's correct. She told me she saw him in town and had spoken to him, but she didn't elaborate."

"What do you think Adam will say if he hears you've offered this position to Barbara?"

"I don't know. When I told him I wouldn't bring him into the company, he took it hard. I think it led to this business with his girlfriend, Julie."

"Don't you think he might need professional help?"

"I do, but he refuses it. Ever since the skiing accident, he's taken a callous approach to life. He's become insensitive and even cruel. When he joined the Marines, I thought it might be a chance for him to straighten himself out, but he barely made it a week before they discharged him for insubordination. He's lucky they didn't court-martial him and pack him off to the brig."

"You could obtain a court order and have him confined. It's drastic, but it might be the only way to get him the help he needs."

J.L. knew Tobias was talking about having Adam committed. He loathed the proposition of committing his son to a mental institution and had little confidence in psychiatrists. He turned his desk chair around, away from Tobias, and stared out his office window.

"Honestly," he said as if speaking to himself, "I sometimes think it may have been better if he had died with his mother that day."

After leaving Barbara's apartment, Adam decided he'd blow off the rest of the day and went on a drunk, touring the seedy bars down by the piers. Hours later, he woke up in a dingy rent-by-the-hour hotel room. He couldn't recall her name, but his room key, wallet, and the woman were gone. All he remembered was that she was older, maybe in her forties, wore a pillbox hat, and called him "sugar lips."

I must have been sauced. That wallet had my last fifty bucks in it.

Still a little shaky, he dressed and went downstairs. He stopped at the desk and asked the clerk for the hotel address.

The fat, greasy man in a T-shirt looked up from his copy of the *Daily Racing Form*, pointed to the door, and said, "Number's on the building, Mack."

Adam felt like slugging him, but he didn't have the energy. He gave him the finger and walked out onto the street.

Once he knew where he was, he figured he had a forty-minute walk back to the hotel Pole had set him up in. He reached into his pants and, to his relief, found that he still had the key for that room.

Then he turned and walked back into the grimy hotel lobby. He explained to the fat man at the front desk that he had lost his key and had no idea where he'd misplaced it. The clerk gave him a duplicate and explained that his room would be billed two dollars to cover the cost of the missing key.

Adam took the duplicate, walked to the elevator, and took it to the fifth floor, where he splashed some water on his face before leaving the room. He then took the stairs down to a second-floor fire escape, shoved the steel door open, and descended the metal staircase to a dingy alleyway between the hotel and another building.

His head still throbbed with a dull ache, and he was sluggish from dehydration as he started on his way.

Adam returned to his original hotel and took the elevator to his room. At the door, he turned the key in the door lock and stepped into the cold, dark room. Reaching for the light switch, he flipped it on—and turned to see Fredrick

Pole sitting in the chair next to the desk, a gun in his hand, aimed directly at him.

"You missed our appointment," Pole said.

"I had something to do. Sorry."

"Sorry doesn't cut it, Mr. Wilson. The next time, I shall be forced to dismiss you."

When he looked at Pole and saw the expression on his face, Adam realized that the term *dismissal* carried a sense of finality. It was a face he'd seen many times in the mirror—more than a blank stare. In Pole's eyes, he saw the dead, unfeeling look of someone about to engage in an act of brutal violence.

"I had to see my sister. She was sick."

"Come now, Mr. Wilson. That sounds like an excuse a schoolchild might offer. I'm sure you can do better than that."

"All right, she wasn't sick. But I went to see her and tell her—" Adam stopped, knowing he couldn't tell Pole the nature of his visit—that he didn't know what was happening to his life and didn't understand this thing he was about to do. "I just wanted to see her," he finished.

"Are you in or are you out, Adam? You must assure me so we may proceed."

"I'm in, Mr. Pole, and I won't miss any more appointments." Adam swallowed hard. He didn't like the idea of kowtowing to anyone.

"Fine. With that out of the way, tell me now, what are your plans?"

Adam hadn't yet put a plan together, so he improvised. "He has a regular date with a hot blonde. Every Tuesday at two o'clock at The Plaza. It'll be easy enough to follow them to their room. I'll give them a couple of minutes to get comfortable, then jimmy the lock, open the door, and give Scrivner three slugs—two to take him down and one for the coup de grâce."

"What about the blonde? She'll see you."

"I'm way ahead of you." Adam reached into his pocket and pulled out a large handkerchief, which he quickly tied into a mask that covered his face from the nose down.

Compton—also known as Pole, a.k.a. Rainer Heydrich—paused, weighing Adam's crude assassination plan, then said, "I suppose that will work. When do you plan to—excuse the term—*execute* your plan?"

"Today's Thursday, so next Tuesday, the nineteenth."

Reaching into his pocket, Compton extracted a slip of paper and handed it to Adam. "Call this number at eight that morning and confirm that you're proceeding as planned. Don't disappoint me."

"What about the money?"

"I'll meet you here at four with the entire amount in hundred-dollar bills. Is that satisfactory?"

"Yeah, I guess that's all right."

"Once we've completed the transaction, we will part ways. If I require your services again, I'll contact you." He stood, went to the door, and opened it. "Very good. I'll be on my way." With his back to Adam, he said, "I'll say it one more time—do not disappoint me. It would be messy for both of us." Then he walked out the door, closing it behind him.

Adam dropped onto the bed and massaged his temples to clear his head.

What a fucking mess. From college boy to hired murderer, all in six months.

As Adam pondered his fate, Compton—now descending in the elevator—was already thinking.

Crude plan, but it should work well enough. I'd better go to The Plaza and familiarize myself with the hotel and the surrounding area. I'll need an escape route. Too bad for the girl—she'll have to go too. "JEALOUS LOVERS' QUARREL OVER WOMAN LEADS TO TRAGIC END"—that's what the papers will say, and Hansen will be satisfied. Two deaths served up as requested. Though I'll bet he'd never have guessed it would play out like this.

Now . . . what about the disguise?

EIGHT

THE BERMUDA TEAM left Ter Meer's house early on the morning of the fifteenth, retracing their steps across the countryside to the spot in the woods close to the Kowalski farm. They made good time and arrived a little before eight o'clock.

Although it was a bit far from Ter Meer's home, it was equidistant to the hydrierwerks plant to the west and their rendezvous location to the north, where they would meet the Liberator early Saturday morning. It was the perfect location.

Their campsite was comfortable—a small glade not far into the woods across the fields from the farm. They were next to a small stream, so they didn't have to travel far for water. Todd, Stafford, and Newley made camp while Hendricks set up the shortwave. When they were finished, they tucked in to catch up on their sleep for a few hours.

Todd awoke to someone shaking him into consciousness. It was Joe Hendricks. He had stayed on watch while the others slept. All four of them were awake now, and Joe led them from their camp to the edge of the forest abutting a field that Zemel had allowed to go fallow, the house sitting on the far side.

"Listen," he said.

They stood still, trying not to make any sound. In the

distance, they heard the low rumble of what had to be a military vehicle. It grew louder, and a minute later, they saw it—a German armored vehicle, a Panzerspähwagen 204, with a 45mm anti-tank cannon mounted on top, capable of firing fifteen rounds per minute. It held a crew of three and was towing a troop carrier with eight helmeted soldiers, seated in two rows of four, facing each other. An officer stood in the open hatch above the crew cab.

"What do you think is up, Mick?" asked Todd.

"Whatever it is, old son," Stafford replied, "it can't be good."

They watched as the armored vehicle stopped in front of the farmhouse. The troops, carrying Bergmann MP35 9mm submachine guns, jumped out of the carrier and stationed themselves around the building. The officer then climbed out of the Panzer wagon, followed by one of its crew. A closer look revealed him to be an *Unterfeldwebel, a* staff sergeant. The other soldiers almost obscured the short, skinny man with glasses. On his hip was a Luger 9mm Parabellum, and to Stafford's amusement, he carried a riding crop.

Four soldiers peeled off and kicked in the front door while the others watched the side and back for anyone who tried to escape.

Looking through a pair of binoculars, Newley asked Stafford, "Are we going to get involved in this? They're going to kill them."

Stafford turned to Todd. "He's right. Bloody Huns will execute them all."

Todd, stern-faced, said, "Right! Mick, you and Reg hook to the right. Joe and I will come around behind the armored car. On my signal, open fire on the soldiers on this side and the back of the farmhouse. We'll try to get the ones out front."

"What's the signal?"

"You'll know it. Go!"

As they spoke, the two soldiers who had gone inside the house ushered Jan and Pesha out, with Dovid helping Chasya, his arm around her. They lined them up in front of the house.

The sergeant walked up to them and demanded their papers. After reviewing them, he began his interrogation, speaking in a tinny, high-pitched voice.

Todd and Hendricks could make out his voice as they stealthily made their way around the field and down the road, hidden behind a hedgerow. It wasn't far from there to the main road that the armored car had arrived on. When they came out from around the hedgerow, they saw that the sergeant and his squad had their backs to them, so they scurried up the road and took cover behind the gray metal-plated car.

"Herr Wojcik, I see here on your work papers that you are a teacher from Krakow. What are you doing so far from home?" said the officious German sergeant, spittle escaping his tiny mouth as he spoke.

"We were visiting our friend, Mrs. Kowalski, and my wife fell ill," said Dovid.

"You are Mrs. Kowalski?" said the sergeant, turning to Pesha.

Shyly, Pesha answered in the affirmative.

Jan had seen Todd and Hendricks darting up the road and taking cover behind the Panzer wagon. He waited for the right moment to draw the pistol tucked into his waist-band behind his back, hidden under his jacket.

"Tell me, Mrs. Kowalski, how do you know Antoni and Misha Wojcik?"

Pesha fumbled for a lie. "We went to school together. Well, Misha and I."

The sergeant beamed, knowing she had fallen for the ruse. "I find that amazing since her papers say her name is Freyda." He unholstered his Luger. "Now tell me, who are these people? Tell me, or I will use my authority to execute you. Speak!"

At this moment, Todd pulled the pin on the M36 hand grenade and dropped it into the open hatch on top of the car. The explosive went off with not so much a boom but more of a hollow bang, the blast contained by the vehicle's armored shell.

Stafford and Newley let loose with their fully automatic Sten guns, the sound muted by their silencers. Stafford targeted the two soldiers at the side of the house, and Newley the other two in the back. They fell to the ground without a sound.

Jan drew his pistol from behind his back, put a bullet square into the center of the shocked sergeant's forehead, then turned and fired at one of the four soldiers, his bullet catching him in the shoulder.

Meanwhile, Todd and Hendricks advanced, unleashing controlled bursts of muted 9mm fire into the three remaining soldiers.

Then, all was quiet.

Dovid spoke as he clutched a tearful Chasya in his arms. "I thought our lives were at an end. God be praised."

As Todd looked around, assessing the situation, Stafford and Newley joined the group in front of the farmhouse. Seeing Stafford, Todd approached and said, "We have to get rid of the bodies and hide the vehicles somehow. They can't be found until after we've completed the mission."

"Seems like we've accomplished everything but the bleeding mission in our time here. I suppose that's war, eh, Captain?"

Looking over the human slaughter once more, Todd nodded his head. "Yeah, that's goddamned war."

Jan walked up to the two and pointed at the wounded soldier who lay bleeding on the ground, relieved of his weapons. "What do we do with him?"

"We have to execute him," said Stafford. "We can't leave him alive. If he gets a chance to talk, the farm woman's life will be good for naught."

"We can't shoot an unarmed man," Todd said. "War or no war, we're supposed to be better than them."

"Well then, what do you propose, old man? Take him with us?"

"I don't know yet. I'll think of something."

Pesha was kneeling next to the soldier, trying to dress his wound with a strip of her apron. She looked up at Todd as he came to her side.

"He's just a boy."

Todd looked down at the wounded soldier. He couldn't have been more than sixteen. With help from Reg Newley, they took him into the house and attended to his injury.

Once the boy was stabilized, they loaded the dead onto the carrier. Hendricks and Stafford drove the still-operational Panzer wagon with the carrier down the road and then across to the forest, leaving it in a depression behind the trees. Given the time they had, it was the best they could do.

When they returned, everyone but Chasya and Dovid was in the front room of the house. The young soldier was lying beside the fireplace, hands and feet bound, sobbing.

Newley commented to Stafford. "He was lucky. The bullet went straight through the upper bicep. Nothing broken, and the bleeding has stopped."

"It would have been better if he'd died," said Stafford, standing over the wounded soldier as Newley looked after his wound.

Newley looked up. "Pesha told me he's a local conscript, an ethnic Pole who willingly joined the Wehrmacht. According to the Jerries, that made him a German citizen and gave him all the benefits. He must have lied about his age."

"A collaborator, Reg," said Stafford. "All the more reason to be rid of him."

"Sir, he probably joined to protect his family. They've been persecuted before—and since the end of the last war, when a large part of Upper Silesia was ceded to the Polish. Not to have done so would have left his family open to further persecution—possibly death or deportation to one of the camps."

Stafford grunted, then turned and moved away.

Kneeling next to Newley, Pesha was still fussing over the boy. She had been mollycoddling him ever since she heard him asking for his mother in the local dialect.

"Mister soldier," she spoke to Newley in halting English, "I'll fetch him hot soup and bread." Then, after a pause, she asked, "Are you a doctor? Is he to be well?"

"Madam, I am trained as a medic, not quite a doctor. However, I can say the boy is going to be just fine, but it will take some time before he has full use of his arm."

Pesha smiled and hurried to the kitchen. Newley realized that the boy had found himself another mother. He was lucky.

NINE

On Friday morning at 0930 hours, Obersturmbannführer and Camp Commandant Rudolf Hoss and his immediate staff shivered on the steps before the commandant's office—the central building in a row of three administrative buildings just inside the camp gates. Hauptsturmführer Balsiger, Herr Doktor Crowning, and Pierre Ter Meer were in attendance.

Reichsführer Heinrich Himmler, his military entourage, and his security would enter the camp through the northeast gate by the Sola River on the road to Oswiecim. After arriving in Katowice by train earlier in the morning, his car, a 1933 Wanderer W11, would have been offloaded to drive him the sixty-three kilometers to the camp.

Hoss shifted his weight.

It's 0935. What the devil is keeping him?

His newly laundered pair of jodhpurs were giving him trouble. A Polish prisoner working in the officers' laundry had purposely soaked the pants of all the senior officers in water heavily dosed with ground rose hips—smuggled out of the kitchen by another prisoner. Once dried, fibrous hairs that enveloped the seeds remained in the fabric, producing a maddening itching sensation.

Hoss wasn't alone in his discomfort. Had he not been so preoccupied with his own itchiness, he might have noticed his entire senior staff fidgeting as well—each trying to relieve the itch without visibly scratching.

Ter Meer noticed. He watched the group twist and writhe ever so slightly, each man in his own way, as they struggled to maintain their rigid posture.

Finally, they heard the large Wanderer W11 booming along the road parallel to the camp. Just before it turned, Himmler rose from his seat and stood, keeping his left hand on the back of the front seat to keep his balance. Then, as the car passed through the gate, he affected the stiff-armed Hitler gruss as the car drove up to and stopped at the bottom of the stairs.

Seeing this, Obersturmbannführer Hoss fervently hoped they had prepared a suitable enough triumph for the Reichsführer.

Himmler stepped down from the car and again raised his right arm in the Hitler salute. "Heil Hitler!"

Instantly, the gathered mimicked the salute and chorused a resounding "Heil Hitler!"

Hoss descended the stairs, saluted again, and shook hands with Himmler.

"Welcome, Reichsführer. We are honored to have you with us. Please allow me to introduce my staff."

One by one, he presented his commanding officers, Balsiger being the last.

"And may I present Herr Doktor Hans Crowning, managing director of the Blechhammer Hydrierwerks, and Herr Pierre Ter Meer, operations director and representative of the American company that owns the facility."

Himmler looked surprised. "You mean to say the

Americans do not know that we have nationalized their factory for the greater good of the Reich?"

"Not as yet, Reichsführer. Herr Ter Meer has been invaluable in the plant's conversion to synthetic fuel. We have also benefited from secret American technology he obtained through his contacts in the company."

"Her Ter Meer," said Himmler, "you have no qualms related to your actions?"

"Reichsführer, I have always been a loyal German citizen and member of the NSDAP since 1933. My allegiance is to the Führer. I'm sure the Americans will become aware of the circumstances shortly, but there'll be nothing they can do."

Himmler smiled at the fact that American assets and technology had been redirected to support the Führer's vision.

"I understand I will be billeted in your home . . ." Glancing over at Hoss, he said, "And Rudolf tells me it is unique, and your kitchen is exemplary."

"Herr Ter Meer is hosting a dinner this evening in your honor," Hoss said.

Ter Meer feigned modesty, smiling and shifting his feet. "It will be an honor to have you as my guest. For tonight, however, I have engaged an excellent caterer to prepare a very special meal. I've used them before, and I'm confident you'll enjoy the fruits of their labors." He smiled again. "I look forward to your comments about the house and its design."

Ter Meer hoped that Himmler wouldn't recognize the Bauhaus influence in the house and many of the furnishings. The Nazis claimed that the movement was Cultural Bolshevism—a threat to the German body politic—and shut down the school in 1932. If questioned, Pierre planned to lie and say the design was inspired by the Gauforum in Weimar, created by Hermann Geissler—allegedly with Hitler's assistance.

Himmler turned to Doktor Crowning. "Herr Doktor, I am looking forward to touring your facility tomorrow. Reichsmarshall Göring would like to hear my impressions."

Crowning bowed slightly. "It will be my great honor, Reichsführer."

"And my pleasure. So then, on to the inspection. Rudolf, I expect you have all the statistics prepared?"

"Jawohl, Reichsführer. They will be waiting for you in the conference room. Hauptsturmführer Balsiger will report the numbers. You will be pleased—the admittance rate and labor productivity have increased, daily mortality has increased, and we've made significant improvements in the crematory." Hoss beamed as he reported the improvements.

"We shall see, we shall see," said Himmler. "Herr Ter Meer, my security officer, Oberleutnant Stamn, will need to visit your home. He will brief you on the standard security arrangements."

Wanting to ensure any security provisions had his imprimatur, Balsiger butted in. "I'll be pleased to accompany Oberleutnant Stamn after the briefing."

Ignoring his interruption, Ter Meer said, "Naturlich, Reichsführer. I'll call my assistant and tell her to expect the Oberleutnant." Then, not wanting to disregard Balsiger altogether, he added, "Hauptsturmführer Balsiger is familiar with the property. I trust he will know what additional needs may be required."

Hoss, somewhat perturbed by Balsiger's interruption,

said, "Hauptsturmführer Balsiger, I think the Reichsführer will be better served if you stay and explain the security aspects of the camp during our tour."

Balsiger, embarrassed and struggling to contain his anger, replied to his commanding officer, "Of course, Obersturmbannführer."

Himmler started into the building, followed by the gathering of officers. As they did, Ter Meer moved to one side. He wanted to make that phone call to Helga Blunt and be sure everything was in order—no foreign commandos and the shortwave safely stowed away in its new hiding place. After making the call, he would leave Auschwitz for the last time, although it would be ingrained in his memory for the rest of his life.

Stafford opened the farmhouse's front door, using the boot scraper before he entered. "Everything is tucked away out of sight," he said. "We should probably be going."

Todd, sitting at the living room table, turned toward him. "We have a problem. The woman has grown much worse. I'm sure this morning's exercise didn't help. If she doesn't receive medical attention soon, she'll die. I propose we take them with us—her, her husband, and Jan."

"Are you out of your mind? We can't do that! This isn't the bloody Red Cross! We've already got three bloody extra people with Ter Meer, his Frau Blunt, and a goddamn bloody Deutsches Reichsführer."

"We can't let her die."

"Have you considered how the extra payload would affect the plane's range? We'd be running on fumes on the last leg, and there's a good chance we'd be forced to ditch. No can do, old man. I'm afraid it's not in the cards."

"We can dump some of our excess gear, and I'm sure there's something else in the plane that it can do without. I'll stay if I have to."

Hendricks came through the door, and Newley came downstairs, both hearing the tail end of the argument.

"Poor woman's running a fever. I gave her something to help her sleep," Newley said.

"Mick," Todd said, "if we leave her here, she'll die."

Stafford looked around the room. It was apparent that Newley and Hendricks agreed with Todd.

"He's right, Commander," said Newley. "She may need to be put on a ventilator to help her breathe, and there's nothing like that here."

"It'd be nice to save a life amid this mayhem," said Hendricks.

Though it was a joint operation, he was technically the commanding officer since Ter Meer was a British asset—but he had no intention of pulling rank on the other three.

"If we do this," said Stafford, "you'd better be damn well bloody prepared to find yourselves hanging off the side of some mountain peak in the Balkans, if we survive at all."

Todd looked at Stafford. "Come now, Mick," he quipped, "you enjoy a brisk hike as much as the next man. If we come up short, it's just a good stretch of the legs."

No one said anything at first. Then, Stafford said, "Lieutenant Commander Newley, you'll take charge of the patient and assume full responsibility for her health. Is that clear?"

"Yes, sir!" replied Newley, coming to attention.

"Well then, we'll come back for them tomorrow. Now, let's get going. No dillydallying."

They made sure not to leave any sign of their presence.

Stafford looked at the wounded boy by the fireplace, then turned to Mrs. Kowalski. "You must promise not to unbind the boy until late Saturday morning. Do you understand?"

Still intimidated by the tall Englishman, she said, "I leave tied up 'til Saturday morning."

"That's correct. We'll take the German patrol car and the men and hide them as far away from your farm as possible. If anyone comes looking for them, say you haven't seen them, never did. Do you understand?"

She nodded her understanding, grateful to have them gone.

Todd stood and walked over to Jan. "Will your staying here be a problem if the krauts come looking for their patrol?"

"No, I don't think so. I can stay hidden."

"We'll swing back around here once our business is finished."

"I'll talk to Commander Stafford, but I don't think that will be a problem."

"Will you take us to America?"

"I'll try, but immigration quotas have shrunk recently. Congress pretty much shut the door—their response to their constituents saying they didn't want foreigners taking their jobs. The global refugee crisis scared the public. They forgot that we were all immigrants at one point."

"I understand you must have an American sponsor and five thousand American dollars to be allowed to immigrate.

I have relatives in New York City who immigrated thirty-six years ago. Back then, the family name was Babinski. The boy was adopted, and his sister married and took the name Abramowicz. Perhaps you could contact her."

"Jan," Todd said, thinking it couldn't possibly be the same Abramowicz, "the woman who immigrated to the States, was her first name Miriam?"

"Yes, she's my half sister. We had the same mother."

"And the half brother?"

"I'm ashamed to say I don't know his first name, but the family my uncle sent them to in New York was also connected with Poale Zion. The family name is Bach."

Barbara Wilson was supposed to meet Tobias Bach in the lobby of the Waldorf Astoria at nine. He'd insisted on taking her to Peacock Alley off the grand *art décoratif* lobby. Bach treated Barbara like his daughter, spoiling her in ways only a godfather could, with ten-dollar eggs Benedict and three-dollar champagne cocktails.

Tobias arrived first and was looking over his appointment book when Barbara snuck up behind him. In the lowest voice she could muster, she said, "Mr. Bach, I'm Jones with the FBI. Please come with me."

Without turning around, he replied, "Mr. Jones of the FBI, may I buy you breakfast first?" He turned to his god-daughter, feigning surprise, and said, "Barbara? What have you done with Mr. Jones? I so wanted to buy him breakfast."

Barbara hooked her arm around his and started to walk. "Well, I guess you're stuck with me."

Leaning against him as they walked toward the

restaurant, she felt the scratch of his tweed jacket on her cheek and smelled his aftershave, a familiar scent since she was a child. It always gave her a feeling of warmth and protection.

The waiter sat them at a table for two in a quiet corner of the restaurant, and as he handed them each a menu, Bach said, "If you would be so kind, we'll begin with two champagne cocktails, please."

The waiter nodded his understanding and left them to peruse their menus.

"A little early in the day, isn't it, Uncle Tobias?" *Uncle* was an affectionate moniker both she and her brother Adam had stuck him with when they were children.

"Not today. I know I'm here at your behest, but today, we must celebrate."

"What are we celebrating?"

"I've come to find I have another brother and sister. That is, a half brother and sister. They live in occupied Poland. Miriam has known for years and only just now told me."

"That's fantastic news, Uncle. We'll toast to your new-found family ties. What are their names?"

"My sister is Chasya, and she's married to a teacher. They live in Krakow. My brother Jan is a lawyer in Warsaw. Sadly, I also found out that my mother passed away some years ago from influenza. I could go on, but enough. You asked me here because you had something on your mind."

"Let's have that toast first. I'm so happy for you."

With spot-on timing, the waiter returned with two champagne flutes and set them on the table. Barbara and Tobias each ordered the Eggs Benedict.

Tobias cleared his throat, raised his glass, and said, "To

absent family." As he finished, he realized what he had said summoned Adam to mind as well as his newly discovered siblings. "I'm sorry, Barbara. That was insensitive. I wasn't thinking of Adam."

"I know, and don't worry." She clinked his glass with hers and repeated, "To absent family."

Barbara giggled to put Tobias at ease. "Well, Uncle Tobias, thank you for providing me with the perfect segue. I'm worried about Adam. I know we've all been saying that for the last couple of years, but this time, it's different. You see, he came to me for help. At least, I think that's why he came to see me.

"He showed up at my apartment out of the blue and said he was worried about the direction his life was taking and that the detective he's been working for asked him to do something." She paused, and a worried look crossed her face. "He said that if he did this thing, there was no going back."

"That does sound grave. He didn't say what this detective wanted him to do?"

"No, it was a struggle for him to say even that much. He went on about the old times—I think he meant before the accident. Then, when he was about to tell me what it was, he got up, said never mind, that he should never have come. As he was leaving, he stopped and gave me a peck on the cheek. He wasn't like himself. He was scared, Uncle Tobias."

"And you don't know who this detective is he's working for?"

"No, and that was the other curious thing. I bumped into Adam a few days ago, and I saw Anthony Scrivner walking along Fifth Avenue, toward the park."

"Anthony Scrivner?"

"Yes. In any case, that was when I saw Adam. He was walking behind Anthony and appeared to be following him. I was on the opposite side of the street. I let them get ahead of me and followed them up the street."

"You followed Adam, who was following Scrivner?"

"That's right. I wanted to see where this led. We kept walking toward the park, and then they—or rather Anthony—went left at Fifty-ninth Street. I saw Adam do the same, so I ran across the street, went to Fifty-ninth, and walked around the corner. That's when I saw that they had both stopped. Adam was watching Anthony as he stood in front of the Plaza Hotel, talking to a young blonde woman. After a brief time, Anthony took the woman by the arm and walked in."

"The hotel, I gather. And you spoke to Adam?"

"Yes, we caught up a little. He said he was back in town and that he'd been hired by this detective agency. I asked if that was why he was following Anthony, and he said yes, but he wasn't told who hired the agency. I gave him my number and told him to call. You know the rest."

"It sounds plausible—I mean, working for a detective agency and following someone suspected of having an affair. But what he told you in your apartment worries me. Not sharing the details of what this detective supposedly asked him to do. Well, whatever it might be, it sounds unsavory at best, and dangerous at worst."

"For Adam?"

"Or for Scrivner."

Barbara searched her memory for what it could be and

kept coming back to the most compelling answer. "You think he might do Anthony harm?"

"What else could it be unless it's got nothing to do with Anthony? But I don't think that's the case. Can you call Adam?"

"No, he said he just moved into a new place, and the phone wasn't hooked up yet."

"That presents a problem. We can't find out what he's up to if we can't find him."

Tobias thought about what resources he could bring to bear. He was the president of one of the city's largest banks. Audit firms, lawyers, and financial consultants were the only assets he could come up with. Then he thought about the lawyers.

"Barbara, your friend Richard might be able to help. He's in the intelligence business, and come to think of it, my sister Miriam might be helpful too."

"Your sister?"

"Yes, this week has been full of revelations. It seems my stepmother—and now Miriam—runs a New York branch of a Polish Zionist organization and has been supplying arms to the Polish resistance. She might have connections here in the city that can help us. But what about Richard?"

"I don't know much about his branch of the service, just that his office is in the Plaza. We could ask Daddy. He knows the director, Bill Donovan."

Tobias smiled at the mention of Bill's name. "One thing's for certain. We know where Anthony Scrivner is. We should keep tabs on him."

"I can do that. I think I did rather well the other day,

tailing the two of them. If our suspicion is correct, it will lead us to Adam."

"No, Barbara. It's too dangerous. You might get hurt."

"Adam's my brother. He wouldn't hurt me."

"I'm not thinking of Adam. There's still this detective wandering around who we don't know anything about."

"I'll be careful. And it's only until we get other people on the trail."

The waiter came with their breakfast. It looked marvelous—everything one would expect from a ten-dollar Eggs Benedict.

"Well then, you can talk to your father, and I'll have a chat with Miriam. I'll call you afterward."

Barbara looked across the table at Tobias as they began to eat their breakfast. Still young at forty-eight, he was handsome and successful. She wondered why he wasn't married, but quickly set the question aside, telling herself to skip it. She had enough mystery to deal with.

⁘

It was still foggy and cold on Friday morning when Todd and Hendricks returned to Ter Meer's house. Stafford and Newley weren't far behind. They'd split up to reconnoiter Pławniowice, the village where the truck that Ter Meer had arranged for was stashed.

Todd and Hendricks entered through the side door and walked down a short hall with rooms on either side. One was a storeroom containing household supplies, the shelves on one wall serving as a pantry filled with cooking essentials—flour, sugar, cooking oil, salt, peppercorns, everything in bulk. The second room was the staff lavatory.

At the end of the hall, they passed through the swinging door that opened into the kitchen, where they found Ter Meer alone, sitting at a table in the corner.

Seeing them enter, he said, "Himmler's security detail came here yesterday, and they'll return at three this afternoon ahead of his arrival."

Ter Meer hadn't been present for the security sweep, but Helga told him Oberleutnant Stamn had been very thorough, but not so much that he found the shortwave she and Ter Meer had moved behind a slop sink in the laundry. Making a final declaration that everything was in order—or *alles in Ordnung*—Oberleutnant Stamn departed with his men, but not without a promise to return.

Helga Blunt was finding the company of the German military, and especially the SS, increasingly vile and repellent. She thought more and more about how wonderful it would be to leave all this behind.

Now, Ter Meer, Todd, and Hendricks sat together at the kitchen table, reviewing the plan again, pointing out steps where something could go wrong, and debating ideas that could mitigate them. After an hour of sometimes heated discussion, they were satisfied with a final version, which was remarkably similar to the original.

"Dinner should be finished by nine," said Ter Meer. "I'm told Himmler is not one for after-dinner discourse over glasses of port, so I expect everyone will leave shortly after that."

"Perfect," Todd added. "Stafford and Newley will bring the truck at nine thirty, so that should give us plenty of time to prepare Herr Himmler and stow his adjutant."

Ter Meer stood to start some water boiling for a pot of

tea when he noticed Oberleutnant Stamn standing in the open doorway to the dining room, his Luger P08 leveled at him. From the look on Stamn's face, Ter Meer could guess he'd been there for some time—and had heard enough.

"Herr Ter Meer, my English is not very good, but it is good enough to understand what you and the other gentlemen were speaking about." He turned to Todd and Hendricks. "You two," he barked, "stand up and keep your hands away from those gun belts!"

Todd and Hendricks did as he asked.

"Herr Ter Meer, I want you to slowly remove their guns from their holsters and place them on the floor in front of me." Ter Meer did as he was told and slowly walked toward the Oberleutnant. He bent down and deposited the weapons on the floor in front of him.

"Oberleutnant Stamn," Ter Meer said, "I think there's some misunderstanding."

As he spoke, he spied Frau Blunt in the dining room a few paces behind Stamn.

"*Scheisskopft*, do you take me for a fool? I overheard your exact plan for the kidnapping of Reichsführer Himmler, the destruction of the synthetic fuel facility, and how you plan to rendezvous with a plane and make your escape."

Frau Blunt inched closer as he spoke.

Knowing they were compromised, Ter Meer said anything to keep Stamn's eyes on him. "Well, we thought the Reichsführer might enjoy a trip to Great Britain this time of year. It's really quite lovely."

Stamn's face went red, and he started screaming in German. He was raising his weapon when Helga, almost a foot taller than him, reached around, knocked the gun out of his hand, and encircled his neck with her left forearm. Stamn's gun joined the others on the floor as she maintained her vicelike grip on his throat.

Hendricks and Todd jumped up from the table and grabbed Stamn's arms while Ter Meer retrieved all three guns from the floor.

"That's good enough, Frau Blunt. We have him," said Ter Meer.

She said nothing but continued to squeeze as Stamn's face turned a deeper red.

"Helga, we've got him," Ter Meer said. "You can let go."

Stamn began to lose consciousness.

Todd and Hendricks tried to wrest her arms away from his throat, but she was too strong.

Finally, she released her grip, and he fell limply to the ground. He wasn't breathing. She'd crushed his windpipe along with his larynx.

Hendricks got down on his knees to examine Stamn. He gently lifted his head using both his hands, turning it to the right and then the left.

He looked up at the others. "He's dead. I've seen this before. His spine has been dislocated at C1 or C2. I can't be sure. You can ask Newley. He's the doctor."

Ter Meer looked at Helga. Her expression was blank, her eyes glazed and fixed in an empty stare. He guessed her actions were the result of the rage she'd bottled up—the anger she had suppressed since seeing the horrors at Auschwitz, since seeing that child murdered before her eyes. It had all exploded at once, and Stamn had simply been the wrong man in the wrong place.

"Helga, you're all right. It's over now. Come, sit down

and rest." Ter Meer moved beside her, gently took her arm, and guided her to a chair by the kitchen table.

Once she was seated, he returned to Todd and Hendricks and said, "We've got to get the body out of here."

"We can't just dump it," said Todd. "When he doesn't report, alarm bells will sound."

Then Hendricks said, "Leave it to me. I have an idea. But first, we have to make sure he came here alone." With that, the lieutenant left the kitchen to check the house.

Todd looked at Helga. "Is she going to be okay?" he asked Ter Meer.

"I think so. She's witnessed some horrifying acts perpetrated by the SS in the camp. It shattered her perception of a glorious Germany. Give her some time. I think she'll come around. She's a strong woman."

"You're telling me. As much as I tried, I couldn't loosen her grip on that guy."

"That's not what I meant by strong."

"I know, Pierre. I didn't mean to be flippant. And I hope you're right—I trust your opinion, and she seems to have her heart in the right place."

Hendricks returned and confirmed that there wasn't anyone else there. Just one staff car, apparently Stamn's, was parked in front.

"We can put him in the car," he said, "and I'll put on his hat and coat while I drive him a good distance away from here. I'll stop by a gully or a bridge, put him back in his hat and coat, smash him in the head with a rock, put him in the driver's seat, and push the car down the embankment, making sure it's visible to passing motorists. They'll think it was an accident."

Todd and Ter Meer looked at each other and shrugged.

"Let's do it," said Todd.

They took him out to the staff car and placed him in the boot. After that, Hendricks put on Stamn's coat and hat and drove off, looking every bit like an SS officer.

When they returned to the house, Frau Blunt was no longer at the kitchen table. Ter Meer found her sitting on one of the sofas in the living room.

"Helga?"

"Yes, Herr Ter Meer."

"You did nothing wrong."

"Nothing wrong? Don't you see? I've become one of them, a murderer."

Ter Meer sat down beside her and placed his hands on hers. "You just reacted as any human being would after what you've seen. You're not to blame."

She turned and looked at him with tears in her eyes. "I want to leave this place and never come back. Not here, not to Germany."

There was nothing Ter Meer could do but say, "We'll leave this evening."

❧

Dinner began at seven. Dr. Crowning, Balsiger, the Reichsführer and his adjutant Oberleutnant Kilmer, and Hoss and his adjutant were seated in the large dining room in Ter Meer's home. As host, Ter Meer sat at the head of the table, with Himmler to his immediate right as the guest of honor. Only Oberleutnant Stamn was not in attendance. He'd been found that afternoon, the apparent victim of an auto accident.

Looking at the vacant chair, left empty in his honor, Balsiger spoke. Alluding to Stamn, he said, "It is a great loss to the nation, and I'm sure for you, Reichsführer, to lose such a man."

"Yes," Himmler replied. "He had a promising career ahead of him. He served well and had fought bravely in France before joining my detail. He survived so many battles only to die in a car crash. Oberleutnant Kilmer will temporarily assume his position until I've chosen a suitable replacement."

"A great loss," Crowning said. "May we have a toast in his honor?"

"Of course, Herr Doktor," said Himmler, raising his glass. "Gentlemen, I give Oberleutnant Dieter Stamn as dedicated a warrior as the Reich has ever seen. *Der Tod ist ihm zum Schlaf geworden, aus dem er zu neuem Leben erwacht.*" (*Death has become his sleep,*
from which he awakens to new life.)

They all drank, but some did so with affected solemnity.

After drinking, Himmler raised a brow. "This is an excellent wine, Herr Ter Meer."

"I'm happy to hear you say that. It's a '37 Riesling, a Qualitätswein from the Mosel region."

"You seem to have exceptional taste—the wine, your art collection, and of course, your home that seems to have been inspired by . . ."

Ter Meer steeled himself, thinking Himmler recognized the Bauhaus influence.

". . . Geissler. Modern and so distinctly German in nature."

"I hope you will be impressed with the hydrierwerks tomorrow," said Ter Meer. "It's quite an achievement."

"I'm certain I will. The initial production figures are impressive. I look forward to a primer on the technology."

"Reichsführer, would you care to comment on your tour of the Auschwitz main camp today?" asked Commandant Hoss.

"Commendable, but after hearing my brief today on the results of the Wannsee Conference, you have to agree that much more needs to be done. We have now codified the Führer's goal to annihilate eleven million Jews. That number is representative of all of Europe, including the neutral countries and, eventually, Great Britain." Himmler paused momentarily. Then, in a commanding voice, he declared, "Der Führer's edict must move forward! Heil Hitler!"

All at once, the officers leaped to their feet, shot their right arms forward, and cried, "Heil Hitler!"

Dr. Crowning and Ter Meer followed with a passive "Heil," Ter Meer thinking, *There can't be two ounces of brains between the lot of them.*

They sat just in time for the soup dish, *Leberknödelsuppe*, to be served—balls of beef liver, egg, breadcrumbs, and marjoram floating in a clear beef stock. It was followed by beef rouladen, a warm bacon and celery seed potato salad, and sautéed green beans. Dessert was a German blueberry cheesecake—*Kokosmakronen*—and coconut and chocolate macaroons, accompanied by a snifter of brandy.

As predicted, once dinner was over, each officer bid the Reichsführer good evening, and except for his adjutant, Kilmer, they departed. Dr. Crowning stayed behind briefly to discuss the next morning's plant tour, but in a few minutes, he was gone as well.

As Ter Meer, Kilmer, and Himmler stood in the living room, Helga entered the room from the kitchen to greet Himmler. As she joined the group, Ter Meer introduced her.

"Frau Blunt," said Himmler, "I understand you are Herr Ter Meer's personal assistant." Himmler had been briefed and knew full well she was an Abwehr plant.

"That is correct, Reichsführer. I see to his needs and occasionally assist Hauptsturmführer Balsiger."

Then, out of nowhere, Todd and Hendricks emerged from opposite sides of the room, semiautomatic Sten guns raised and ready.

"Be so kind as to put your hands behind your heads," ordered Todd in German.

Himmler and Kilmer did as they were told. Himmler noticed that neither Blunt nor Ter Meer did so.

"What is the meaning of this?" cried Himmler.

Ter Meer stepped forward. "I should think it's rather obvious, Herr Reichsführer. You and Oberleutnant Kilmer have just been taken prisoner."

"Fool," scoffed Himmler. "Don't you know my security people are just outside, and Balsiger has the perimeter surrounded?"

"Yes," Todd replied, "and anyone trying to get in would have a difficult time doing it, don't you think? But we're already in—the trick will be to get out. But I'm sure you'll lend your assistance."

Himmler shot a hateful sneer at Helga and said, "You'll hang for treason, you cow."

"Is that any way to speak to your traveling companion?"

Blunt said. When he seemed confused by her reply, she said, "We are going on a long journey together, and I will have my arm around you the entire time. And while we travel together, I'll have this with me." She produced a long, narrow dagger. "The point is sharp, as are both edges. I could easily gut you like the pig you are with this, but I won't. That is, as long as you stay quiet and do as you are told. *Klar?*"

"You wouldn't dare."

"Then allow me to demonstrate." Blunt pushed him onto the couch and then straddled him, entrapping his torso between her formidable thighs. "Lieutenant, if you please?"

Hendricks fetched the hot water and the tube of shaving cream they had set aside in advance.

"The water's grown tepid," Blunt said to Himmler. "You don't mind now, do you?"

Himmler tried to free his arms, but it was useless. As Helga applied the shaving lotion to his upper lip, he spat at her, missing badly. She reached behind her, put her hand between his legs, grasped his testicles, and applied pressure. "You do want to cooperate. You wouldn't want to vex me now, would you?" She squeezed a bit harder, and he yelped, quickly nodding.

As this was happening, Oberleutnant Kilmer kept still, simmering with rage. His face flushed with anger and indignation. His commander, a man he idolized, was being mocked and made to look like a buffoon. He finally reached his breaking point, crying, "*Hör Auf!* Mein Reichsführer. Heinrich," and charging toward the couch with murder on his mind.

Hendricks intercepted him, landing a straight right

punch with such force that he spun left and crashed head-first into an end table.

"Time for this one to go to bed," said Todd. "Give me a hand, Joe."

Todd lifted him by the arms, and Hendricks took him by the feet, and they carried him upstairs to one of the spare bedrooms, where they bound and gagged him and left him in the closet.

Ter Meer couldn't help but be amused by the proceedings. He smiled and left to get the white jackets he had brought from the plant.

When Todd and Hendricks came back downstairs, Ter Meer returned with what they hoped would pass for catering uniforms.

Frau Blunt released her grip on Himmler, rose from the couch, stood back, and admired her handiwork. She decided that a few finishing touches were in order for him to be completely unrecognizable. Holding the razor-sharp knife a few inches from his face, she said, "Reichsführer, you must hold still. I wouldn't want to slip and injure you." With a look registering pure hatred, he grudgingly complied. Blunt removed his glasses and sheared the outer inch of both eyebrows with two quick strokes of the blade.

The four of them assessed the finished work. Helga had transformed Himmler's facial features, and without his glasses, he no longer resembled his former self.

With a different pair of pants, a white jacket open at the top to reveal a white T-shirt, and Ter Meer's gardening shoes, the second most powerful man in Germany would pass for an ordinary Silesian dishwasher.

A kilometer away, Stafford and Newley were in the truck

retrieved from the village, rumbling up to the checkpoint on the road leading to Ter Meer's house. The commander slowed the truck and came to a halt next to a bored-looking German sergeant. He wasn't alone—behind him was a troop transport with six soldiers sitting inside, trying to keep warm. Newley rolled down the passenger side window, and the sergeant pointed his flashlight first at Newley's face, then at Stafford's.

Yawning before he spoke, the sergeant commanded, "Your papers, please, and state your business."

Stafford handed his forged papers to Newley, who in turn passed them to the sergeant along with his own.

In broken German, Stafford said, "We are here to pick up the caterers from Herr Ter Meer's dinner party. They are finished for the evening and are no longer needed. We've come to drive them back to the village."

"The catering crew left thirty minutes ago."

"That was the cook and his staff. They live in a different village. We're here for the rest of the crew—kitchen assistants, servers, and dishwashers."

The sergeant told them to turn off the engine and wait. He and one of the soldiers went around to the back of the truck, pulled back the canvas tarp, and flashed their lights inside, revealing an empty truck bed, save for the benches on either side.

The sergeant then came to the driver's side and tapped the window, motioning Stafford to roll it down. He looked at Stafford, glanced down again at their papers, then back to Stafford and said, "You can move along." He handed their papers back through the window.

Stafford turned over the engine and put the truck in gear, but the sergeant stepped in front of the truck.

"Halt!" he said in a commanding voice.

Stafford and Newley reached under the blanket between them, placing their hands on the automatic pistols.

The sergeant motioned his corporal to come over, and they exchanged words.

Stafford was calculating the odds of their survival if they had to engage a squad of German soldiers in a firefight when the corporal, his submachine gun leveled, moved to Newley's side of the cab.

"The sergeant says you don't have to stop on the way out. Move on," he said.

Newley nodded, and Stafford put the truck in gear and drove away.

They turned onto the drive and entered the grounds surrounding the house. Stafford maneuvered the truck into the reserved space near the side door that led to the kitchen. Himmler's security detail encircled the house, spaced equidistantly from each other, one of them standing ten yards away from where the truck was parked.

The side door to Ter Meer's house opened, and five people, all dressed in white catering uniforms, filed out and calmly walked toward the back of the truck. Helga Blunt pressed her dagger firmly into the small of Himmler's back.

"Stop there," said the nearest guard. Stopping in front of the five jacketed caterers, he asked, "Have you any coffee left over from the dinner?"

Blunt pressed the blade into Himmler almost hard enough to break the skin. He stiffened but said nothing.

She smiled benevolently at the soldier and said, "I'm

sorry, but everything is washed and put away for the evening. We have some dirty linens," she said, holding up a large bag that contained Todd, Hendricks, and Himmler's uniforms.

The soldier's eyes were on her as she spoke. He shrugged at her reply and said, "Schade." Then, with a quizzical look, he peered down at the man standing in front of her. He looked straight into Himmler's face and said, "What a funny-looking fellow. Tell me, what does he do?"

Helga quickly responded, "He washes dishes. He's a bit challenged if you understand my meaning."

The soldier did and smiled. He put his hand on Himmler's shoulder, leaned in, and said, "You go home and rest now, funny little man." He chuckled, turned, and returned to his station.

The five climbed into the back of the truck and took their seats. The truck's engine came to life, and they slowly rolled away.

The private plane landed at the Washington-Hoover Airport south of the Pentagon in Virginia. Washington-Hoover was a short-lived airport that had only existed since the mid-thirties and was about to be permanently closed, replaced by the new National Airport at Gravelly Point, once the home of George Washington's stepson.

The plane, a Waco E series biplane built in 1939, taxied along the apron to its assigned parking spot, where it stopped and the engines powered down. Its iconic pilot climbed down to the tarmac, opened the cargo compartment, and pulled out a small soft-sided suitcase.

He walked to the small terminal, intending to hail a cab to take the short hop to his hotel in Arlington. Inside the terminal, people remarked as he walked past them. You didn't have to have a flying background to recognize him, one of the most famous people in America.

He exited the terminal and walked to the cab stand. It wasn't that busy, and the cabbies leaned against their cars. He went to the first cab in line.

The cabbie stood up straight upon seeing him and said, "Where to, Mr. Lindbergh?" with a bright smile.

"Alexandria. King Street and North Washington, please."

"Yes, Mr. Lindbergh. I'll have you there in a jiffy." Excited, the cabbie reflected that he had driven his share of politicians and mucky mucks, but this was the first time he had a real live American hero in his cab.

He dropped Lindbergh off at his hotel on King Street, where Lindbergh checked in and took a quick shower before heading out again, this time to Arlington Cemetery.

He caught another cab to the parking lot next to the cemetery's administration building. From there, he made his way up the hill to the amphitheater and the Tomb of the Unknown Soldier.

It was getting on three in the afternoon—just in time for his rendezvous. To his surprise, Bill Donovan was already sitting on the bench at the end of the path leading to the memorial.

Lindbergh walked up and sat next to him on the bench. "I see you made it on time, General."

Looking off into the distance, Donovan said, "I came early to pay my respects to a few old comrades." Then, turning to Lindbergh, he said, "So this is the spot."

Lindbergh looked across the lawn to the tomb. "This is the spot, all right."

Donovan had received intelligence from Stephenson in MI6 that German agents in the United States were working to flip an American national to participate in a plot to assassinate the commander in chief. They believed the intelligence to be accurate, but they didn't know who that American national could be—until Lindbergh telephoned Donovan on a mutual friend's advice and told him his story.

Lindbergh said he'd received a mysterious message from someone who quoted a phrase no one else could have known—the inscription on a dagger Hermann Göring had presented him during his trip to Germany in the thirties. He was provided information on where and when to meet, along with a passphrase he would hear and his response.

Donovan had instructed Lindbergh to go to the rendezvous and hear what the man with the code name Cassius had to say. If he attempted to suborn him, he should play along.

That night, after he and Cassius parted ways, Lindbergh called Donovan and gave him details of their meeting. They had been in regular contact since then, so Donovan knew the details of their Rockaway Beach meeting.

"I was surprised when you called me. I was supposed to be meeting a Mr. Todd today."

"He's off taking care of other business," said Donovan as he assessed Lindbergh. This was the first time he had met him in person. He didn't like his politics—trying his best to keep the States out of the war and all but promoting Hitler's anti-Semitic agenda. But he had failed, and the US was in the fight. As distasteful as his politics were, Donovan knew he wasn't a traitor, and he had come through on this.

Looking out over the cemetery, Lindbergh reflected on all the battles fought and the men killed defending the country. Then he remembered why he was there and asked, "What did you think of the poison pen?"

"Thanks for reminding me." Donovan reached into his overcoat pocket and produced the box that Lindbergh had given Todd after his last meeting with Compton. "It's rather ingenious. We've taken the darts out and analyzed them. What he said about these particular capsules is true—they're harmless. But I'm told this radioactive material he spoke of is as deadly as it is hard to come by. The science of it worries us, and it could portend something even more sinister." He handed the case over to Lindbergh.

Lindbergh took the box and put it in his breast pocket. "So we go through with it as he planned?"

"We have to," said Donovan. "We have to lead him on as long as possible. He slipped the tail we put on him after your meeting at the beach, so he's still out there. If he doesn't make contact again, we have to be prepared to take him down here, before or during the ceremony."

"Compton said he wanted me to come here and familiarize myself with the scene so I'd understand where I should position myself for the shot."

"Then you should do so and tell him you've seen the setup and know what to do. You said he indicated when the pen set with the live ammo should arrive?"

"He said in the next couple of weeks. That would mean they're likely to arrive this coming week."

"All you can do at this point is continue playing along.

I'll stay in touch, but Todd may contact you as well. He's supposed to be back in the next few days."

"Thanks, General. Are you going to be here on the thirtieth?"

"I will, along with the Secret Service, several FBI agents, and a few men of my own."

Lindbergh stood. "Well, until then, General."

Donovan got up, and they shook hands.

"I know you don't agree with my opinions on what the US should and shouldn't do," said Lindbergh, "but I'm grateful to have made your acquaintance."

Donovan smiled. "To paraphrase Dickens, it is a far, far better thing you do now." Lindbergh smiled, and the two men parted ways.

⚬

Stafford drove the truck along the national road in the light of the full moon and turned off onto the dirt track that led to their encampment near the Kowalski farm. Once he found a spot obscured by some trees, he killed the engine and turned off the headlamps. They all piled out of the truck—Himmler with some assistance from Hendricks.

Todd took off his white jacket and tossed it aside. "Let's get our gear," he said. "We've got a little over four hours to get to the Blechhammer, plant the explosives, and get to the rendezvous. Joe, you've got everything in hand?"

Hendricks had already exchanged his white jacket for combat fatigues. He picked up the stashed satchel of explosives and detonators and slung it onto his back. "Give me five, and I'll be ready to roll out."

Pointing toward Himmler, who was now in handcuffs,

compliments of Ter Meer, Stafford approached Todd and said, "What are we going to do with him?"

"Leave him here. We have to come back this way to get to the rendezvous. We'll pick him up then."

Himmler heard this and became quite animated. "You can't leave me here. I assume you will bind me, and if you don't come back, I could rot here in this godforsaken forest."

"Don't worry, Reichsführer," Hendricks said, "we'll be there and back in an hour or two. No sweat."

Himmler grew increasingly anxious. "What if you don't come back?" he blurted, his voice rising with desperation. "You can't go. Don't leave me here."

He had everyone's attention now.

Todd looked down at him. "Why not?" he asked.

Himmler, his voice tight with fear, said, "Because you will be killed."

"What do you mean?"

A smug look crossed Himmler's eyes. "Nobody knows this, not even Doktor Crowning." He turned toward Ter Meer and said, "Or you, traitor!" A tight smile curled on his thin lips. "We've known for some time that you were coming to destroy the facility. One of your fellow Americans passed this information to an Abwehr spy stationed in New York. There is a special contingent of the Einsatzgruppen posted along the grounds perimeter. They have remained hidden—until now."

"It must have been Hansen," said Ter Meer.

"You know who it was?" asked Todd.

"He contacted me almost a year ago," Ter Meer replied. "Saw the handwriting on the wall and thought he could profit from it. He collaborated with all the Nazis' requests—and he knew the SS was eliminating anti-Nazi employees."

"And what were you doing?" yelled Todd, gripping him by the shirt collar.

Ter Meer swiped his right arm upward, knocking Todd's hand away. Matching Todd's volume, he said, "My job! I was undercover. I saw many things that turned my stomach. When I could do something, I did. But there were just as many times when I could not stop what was happening. You want my fucking job?"

Todd backed off, then said, "Why didn't you report it?"

Ter Meer looked at Stafford. "I did."

"Don't look at me—I wasn't your handler. I'm sure your man did the same thing I would've done if you were one of my Joes—filed it in the record." He turned to Todd. "Captain, you've got to understand that this was before our so-called special relationship with you Yanks. When we did start sharing intelligence, an enormous backlog of intel was sent your way—reams of it, including everything regarding Blechhammer. It's probably buried at the bottom of a pile on somebody's desk at one of your numerous intelligence bureaus—Army, Navy, FBI, wherever the hell it was sent."

They were silent for a while, then Todd said, "Okay, Mick, and I apologize, Pierre. I guess I got a step up. Neither of you did anything wrong."

"What do we do now, and what's the Einsatzgruppen?" asked Newley, relieved that the tension seemed to have subsided.

"For lack of a better description," said Stafford, "they're a Nazi murder squad. As their Waffen troops advance, they follow behind them, sweeping through cities and villages and murdering suspected resistance—Jews, Roma, lawyers, and communists—ever since Adolph turned on the Soviets last June. They're all SS, *Sicherheitsdienst*, their security service. With help from the Waffen and collaborators, they've killed tens of thousands of people."

"And what do we do next?" Newley asked again.

"This is no longer a stealth operation," Todd said. "They know we're coming. As I understand it, Commander, they're not meant to be regular combat troops. So what kind of weapons do they carry?"

"I say, old man, you're not thinking of a frontal assault?"

"What choice do we have? If we try to sneak in, they'll pick us off, one by one. Again, what sort of weaponry do they have?"

"Rifles, pistols, submachine guns—whatever they need for their executions."

"Then I have an idea that might work. It will get us onto the plant grounds and to the railway siding with those liquid hydrogen tanks." Todd paused, then added to no one in particular, "We'll have to discuss how we get out."

There were sixty Einsatzgruppen men assigned to watch over the hydrierwerks. All were armed with 9mm Lugers and 8mm semiautomatic Gewehr 43 semiautomatic rifles. A smattering of them had Mauser Karabiner 98K sniper rifles with Zeiss Zielvier 4× telescopic sights.

Todd was relieved that there was no light artillery, which meant they stood a chance in a standoff. The SS had no need for heavier weapons when all they did was murder unarmed and defenseless men, women, and children.

✦

Sixty men were evenly distributed around the plant's perimeter in pairs. They alternated, taking turns sleeping or fetching food and relieving themselves. They did not wear their standard uniform but were dressed in camouflage and had been hiding in the tall grass and trees for weeks.

Since they were defending and not attacking, they faced away from the plant, looking for and expecting a stealthy advance of similarly camouflaged saboteurs.

Two of the SS men were chatting as they shivered in the long grass.

"Helmut, I'm sure anyone coming at us will smell us from fifty meters out," one of them said.

"Up close, you smell fifty times worse," the other replied.

The first man laughed and said, "The first thing I'm going to do once we're finished here is jump into Adolf's canal. I feel things crawling all over me."

He referred to the new canal between the Oder River and Gliwice, built to replace the old Klodica canal. At its inauguration in 1939, Rudolph Hess dedicated it to Hitler. It ran past Blechhammer North, the newer construction at the facility that housed the advanced processing capabilities for synthetic fuels.

"*Ruhe!*"

"*You* be quiet. You're not infested with these damned bugs."

"No, I mean be quiet because I hear something."

The two were posted at the facility's northwestern periphery. Something that sounded like a tank was approaching them from the south, by the main gate. They took up their rifles and readied themselves.

A Panzer wagon with two German soldiers keeping pace on either side moved at a slow but steady speed toward the main gate, its glaring lights illuminating the ground ahead of it. The top hatch was open, and an officer stood there, his hands holding onto the rim as the car proceeded. A troop carrier with an additional two soldiers was hitched to the vehicle.

The faint crackle of the model KLF field radio broke the silence. The men's commanding officer, Untersturmführer Bierhals, instructed them to hold their fire.

Bierhals had just turned twenty-four, and this was his first command assignment. His men knew his commission was a cushy position secured by his father, a major general in the Waffen SS, and he desperately wanted to prove himself worthy in their eyes.

Bierhals looked through his field glasses at the officer standing in the vehicle. *A late-night visit?* It couldn't be—but he could swear it was Reichsführer Himmler.

And it was—thanks to Helga bringing his uniform and glasses with her from the house, and an improvised return of his mustache and eyebrows with the help of some black face paint from the team's camouflage kit.

Frau Blunt was driving the Panzer wagon, and Hendricks kept his gun pressed against Himmler's spine. Todd and Stafford walked beside the vehicle, and Newley and Ter Meer, dressed in German uniform, rode in the troop carrier behind it.

Ghastly as it was, they had retrieved the armored car and troop carrier from its hiding place in the forest and stripped the uniforms from the ripe bodies of the dead soldiers. They hoped the bloodstains wouldn't be noticed in the moonlight.

They stopped at the swinging gate next to the solitary sentry's kiosk. Himmler said to the guard, "Private, I've come to perform a spot inspection of the facility before tomorrow's formal visit. Open the gate."

The guard jumped to attention, not expecting anybody to interrupt his night, much less Heinrich Himmler.

"Yes, my Führer. I mean, Reichsführer," the guard said as he stepped to the gate, removed the locking pin, and swung the gate open. He faced Himmler and saluted. "Heil Hitler!"

The Panzer wagon, along with its carrier, rolled through the gate, with Stafford and Todd continuing on foot. They went directly to Blechhammer North and its adjacent rail spur with the two tank cars of liquid hydrogen. When they reached the spur, they turned and stopped the car, now positioned in profile to the guard at the gate. Ter Meer and Newley jumped out of the carrier and ran to the front of the vehicle to join Stafford and Todd, while Frau Blunt coaxed Himmler out of the car.

Keeping Himmler in front of them, they walked as a group ten meters in one direction, then turned and strode twenty meters back before returning to the vehicle. During all this back-and-forth, while all eyes were focused on Himmler and his entourage, Joe Hendricks quietly slipped out of the Panzer wagon. He was dressed in black, his face smeared with the same camouflage paint used to restore Himmler's mustache and brows. The twenty-five kilos of RDX explosive and PETN detonators were strapped to his back.

Himmler returned to the Panzer wagon, with Todd joining him in the crew cab this time. Stafford, Newley, and Ter Meer climbed into the troop carrier. They started to drive back to the gate, having delivered their clandestine payload, when suddenly, a man appeared from nowhere and ran across the yard to a point directly in their path.

It was Untersturmführer Bierhals, smiling in anticipation of personally greeting the Reichsführer before he left. Todd instructed Frau Blunt to drive past him without stopping, but keeping a slow, steady speed.

Bierhals fantasized about telling his father he'd met the Reichsführer himself. Indeed, his men would think more of him if he were seen shaking hands with the second most powerful man in the world. But the car didn't seem to slow down as it approached him.

Todd gave Himmler five words to say as they passed.

Himmler looked down to the left at Bierhals as they went by, saying, "Deutschland uber alles! Heil Hitler!"

Bierhals' fantasy collapsed. He would have no story to tell his father, and now his men would talk about how Himmler had disregarded him on his exit from the facility. But as the troop carrier rolled past him, he looked closer at the soldiers riding in it.

None of the soldiers made eye contact with him. That was normal as they were on duty and he was a superior officer, but he couldn't help but notice how their uniforms were so ill-fitting, with sleeves riding high on their forearms and their helmets so small as to be ridiculous. Still, this did not raise any alarm with the Untersturmführer. Not until he noticed the bloodstained exit wound on one soldier, his back facing him.

Bierhals turned and ran toward his redoubt and the radio to raise the alarm. This man was impersonating the Reichsführer. Though he had blithely dismissed it before, he noticed as the man passed that his mustache seemed painted on.

According to the plan, Hendricks would rig the explosives to detonate the excess hydrogen in the railcars. He would give himself five minutes to get to the canal, descend the embankment, and swim with the current to the next lock, a half mile farther east. Dovid, Chasya, and Jan had been left there earlier to wait with the truck. If everything went according to plan, they would all meet there, abandon the Panzer wagon, and take the truck to the extraction point to meet the plane.

Todd, Stafford, and the rest were almost on top of the gate when the facility's alarm siren started to sound.

"Pick up speed and ram the gate," Todd told Helga. "We're not stopping."

Bullets pinged off the car's sides as the Einsatzgruppen tried in vain to stop it. Ter Meer, Newley, and Stafford were on the floor of the open carrier, avoiding fire as best they could.

Helga Blunt put her foot to the floor, but the Panzer could only manage forty-two miles per hour at top speed. The gate, however, was no obstacle for the armored car, and they smashed through it and kept going. The solitary gate guard raised his gun but hesitated and didn't shoot. After all, it was Heinrich Himmler.

They barreled down the road, heading toward the canal lock.

"Captain, there's an impediment," said Helga.

Todd bent down and looked through the driver's

retractable front hatch. A half mile ahead, a large supply truck had turned sideways on the road, blocking them.

"There are gullies on either side of the road, Captain. I don't think ramming it will do any good."

He turned around and saw Himmler lying on the floor, his hands covering his head. Just beyond him, he saw what he was looking for—the ammunition magazine. The ammunition came five to a clip. He grabbed two, thinking that would be the most rounds he'd be able to fire before they got to the supply truck. He opened the top-loading breach and rammed the first clip into the gun, hoping that if he hit the truck's gas tank, the explosive might budge it enough so they could get past.

But before he could get the first round off, an explosion erupted—so loud and forceful that the shockwave nearly lifted the Panzer wagon off the road. After the initial blast and repercussions, a wave of heat rolled over and through the crew cab.

Todd allowed himself a moment of satisfaction—they had met their main objective, and the hydrierwerks had been destroyed. He prayed Hendricks had made it out safely. Refocusing, he sighted the truck's gas tank, just behind and below the cab. He let one round go and watched for impact. It hit the truck bed, high and on the outside, tearing nearly halfway through it.

They were getting closer, so he decided to fire three rounds in quick succession. He adjusted his aim and fired. The first hit midway up on the cab, ripping through the driver's door and blowing out the front windshield. The second hit the undercarriage between the cab and the trailer.

The third—bingo! The gas tank exploded, separating the trailer from the now-decimated cab.

Todd reached down, touched Helga's shoulder, and shouted, "Make for the gap, Frau Blunt! Full speed!"

Blunt did as she was directed, aiming the four-and-a-half-ton armored car straight for the breach created by the cannon fire. She hit it dead-on, sending the cab into the gulley by the road and turning the trailer aside. The obstruction now cleared, they continued down the road toward the lock.

Joe Hendricks was sitting on the bank of the canal. He had made it down the embankment in time to escape the direct shock of the detonation and the fireball of the explosion. Unfortunately, he hadn't counted on the chunks of metal machinery that flew out of the blast at three thousand feet per second. A piece of what had once been part of the reactor housing tore through his upper right shoulder. He felt something like a punch, but when he craned his neck to look at it, he saw that the skin was gone. He couldn't tell much more than that. It was bleeding but not profusely. He felt himself going into shock, so he lay down on the bank, propping his feet up on a rock.

He wondered what to do next. If he didn't move, the Germans would soon find him, but with his arm nearly blown off, he couldn't swim.

Come on, Joe. You can't just sit here. So what if you can't swim? You can float.

The fear that he might drown entered his mind, but he quickly dismissed it and slowly slipped himself off the bank and into the water.

The Panzer wagon, reaching its destination, pulled

alongside the canal, and everyone got out. It wasn't far to the lock, and they started walking toward it after Todd, Stafford, and Newley unhinged the troop carrier and pushed that and the armored car into a stand of trees bordering the canal. Their truck was parked close to the lock keeper's house. No traffic was moving on the canal at this hour, and all was quiet.

When they saw the others arriving, Jan, Dovid, and Chasya emerged from the bushes where they were hiding. Now, they only had to collect Hendricks, and they could be on their way.

Todd and Newley descended the stairway that took them to the upstream side of the lock. They didn't see Hendricks right away, but then Newley caught sight of something floating toward them in the middle of the canal. It was Hendricks, and he appeared to be injured. Todd took off his coat, dove in, and swam to his side.

"Joe, Joe," he said, hoping for a response.

He got one arm around his torso to keep his head above the water, then started a one-armed front crawl and made for the shore.

Noticing the severe injury to Hendricks' shoulder, Newley helped Todd pull him ashore and then rushed for his medical kit. When he came back, Todd had covered him with his coat.

He looked over to Newley and said, "He's breathing."

Newley cleaned the wound. "This is pretty bad," he said. "We've got to get him to a hospital."

"That's eleven hours away at best. Will he make it?"

"Maybe, if we keep him warm and sedated. He's lucky— the bleeding's mostly from torn muscle and bursa. I'm more worried about infection. I gave him a shot of penicillin, but we'll need to keep the wound clean and dressed."

Stafford and Jan came down, and together, they lifted Hendricks and carried him up the stairs and to the truck.

Todd had just told the others, "Let's get going," when the sound of automatic rifles rang out, and bullets ricocheted off the pavement. A badly burned Untersturmführer Bierhals had gathered what was left of his Einsatzgruppen squad—six men—and pursued the Panzer wagon, albeit on foot. They had made it as far as the lock when they heard people speaking English.

"Englanders!" Bierhals said in broken English. "Surrender, and we will let you live."

Hearing this, Himmler broke out in a dead run in that direction, shouting in German not to shoot. "Nicht schliessen! Nicht schliessen! Ich bin—"

But before he could get "Reichsführer Himmler" out, a bullet struck him in the face. The shot came from the side, so it entered one cheek and exited the other, taking several teeth with it. He spun around, his head the axis of his spin, bounced off the side of the truck, and went down.

Assuming Himmler was dead, Todd jumped in the truck, turned over the engine, and slammed it into first gear. Bullets continued to rake the truck, but fortunately, no one was hit as they turned onto the bridge east of the lock, taking them north over the canal and out of Bierhals' range.

It was now a quarter to two. If everything went to schedule, the Liberator would be landing in a little over an hour at the designated coordinates. Todd was angry they had lost Himmler, but at least he was dead. That was something command would be surprised to hear.

Just before 3:00 A.M., they pulled into one side of a long, flat clearing—three-quarters of a mile long and about five hundred feet wide. Like clockwork, the B-24 came in low, just above the trees, to make a perfect three-point landing. The plane taxied far enough to ensure ample runway for the takeoff, then turned around and stopped, its engines on high idle.

Todd sped the truck down the length of the clearing and stopped by the plane. The belly hatch opened, and the navigator dropped out, waving people over.

Helga and Ter Meer ran to the plane, and the navigator helped them up and in. They were followed by Dovid and Jan carrying Chasya. Last came Stafford, Newley, and Todd, who carefully bore Hendricks to the plane. Not two minutes later, they were airborne.

Once they got to altitude, Todd checked on Hendricks. He was awake but groggy from the morphine Newley had administered.

"How're ya feeling, buddy?"

"Good, Cap. That was one hell of an explosion."

"We were a couple thousand feet away, and it nearly threw our jalopy off the road. I can't imagine what it would have been like where you were."

"Violent," said Hendricks.

Todd put his hand on Hendricks' good shoulder and said, "You try to get some shuteye. We'll get you to the hospital as quickly as we can."

Todd turned around to see both Jan and Dovid crying. Chasya had died somewhere between the lock and getting to the rendezvous.

TEN

"WHAT THE HELL happened?" General William Donovan was livid. The Nazi ring under surveillance by the FBI had been rounded up and arrested in four predawn raids along Florida's Atlantic coast. The arrests took place between St. Augustine and Jacksonville. A total of eight agents were apprehended.

Without editorializing, Allen Dulles looked at his notes and gave Donovan the facts as he had understood them from his contacts in the FBI. "Well, Bill, it seems this man, Willis B. Semlow, was recently promoted to special agent in charge of the Jacksonville field office. He's only been in place since last week. Semlow was briefed on the ongoing six-month surveillance of these eight individuals and the intelligence collected so far. He's quoted as saying, 'Watching these krauts doesn't win any medals. It's time to do something bold and decisive.' He then put the plan to arrest them in motion."

"Why weren't we informed? Hell, we provided the intel that told who they were and where."

"Apparently, Semlow purposely kept the raids a secret so he could announce them on Deputy Director Tolson's birthday."

Donovan stood up and began to pace. "We'll be that much more in the dark."

"Bill, they did capture them with a significant stockpile of arms and explosives. They were planning on sabotaging something, but we don't know what. Maybe we'll get it out of them."

"They'll have plenty of motivation. Conviction on a count of spying during wartime brings the death penalty." He bent over the intercom and flipped a switch to connect him with his new assistant, Julia McWilliams.

"Can I help you, General Donovan?"

"Julia, please bring me the file on Operation Bermuda."

"Right away, sir."

"What about the ring on Long Island?" Allen asked.

"Hoover had no choice," Donovan replied. "He had to bring them in before they scattered to the wind."

Allen nodded. "Well then, we can't count on further intel from shadowing them either."

"You're thinking about Cormorant, specifically?" *Cormorant* was the code name they had assigned to the FDR assassination plot.

He gave a low, almost murmured response as if speaking to himself. "Yes." Then he turned to Dulles. "We should check to see if the agent who contacted Lindbergh is one of the Long Island crew they corralled. If he was, you must ask yourself whether the assassination is scrubbed."

Ms. McWilliams came into the office with the dossier Donovan had requested. She had a pleasant demeanor and spoke with a lilting mid-Atlantic accent that reflected her Branson education.

Donovan took the folder from her and said, "Thank you, Julia. May I ask one more favor?"

"Sure thing, boss . . . uh, General."

Donovan laughed. "Boss is fine. Would you call the FBI and tell them we need photographs of the Nazis they recently arrested in Florida and on Long Island?"

"Will do!" she replied and left.

"Even if Lindbergh does identify one as Cassius," said Dulles, "it doesn't mean they're no longer going through with the attempt."

"I know, and it would mean there's another cell we haven't discovered."

"Unless he's a loner," Dulles said. "In which case, he'll be difficult to unearth."

"There are only two weeks left before Decoration Day, Allen."

Dulles knew his boss's personality wouldn't allow him to sit still. He had to act. And he was right—with only two weeks to go, the best they could do would be to catch Cassius beforehand. Even though they knew how the assassination was supposed to be carried out, they couldn't assume there wasn't a backup plan. FDR had already refused to cancel his appearance, and hundreds of people would be on hand. They couldn't keep eyes on all of them.

"Allen put a tail on Lindbergh in case Cassius approaches him without arranging the contact in advance."

"You know, Bill, keeping tabs on American citizens is Hoover's job. If he found out you were spying on a US citizen, he'd go straight to the White House."

"Not that he hasn't done that plenty of times before. And it's not spying—it's protection."

"You could just tell Lindbergh you're watching him."

"No, it's better he isn't aware."

"This is the guy I want to stake out Lindbergh." Donovan

slid the Bermuda dossier across the desk to Dulles. It was open to Todd's CV. "I told Lindbergh he was going to be his contact with the OSS some time ago. He was surprised when I was the one to meet him at Arlington."

"Todd's in Europe," Dulles said.

"Yes, but he gets back next week. Put someone else on it for the short term."

"Don't you think he'll need a rest?"

"Time and tide, Allen, time and tide. We'll meet him at the airport."

⋦

It was eight A.M. Sunday morning. Anthony Scrivner left his apartment at the Beresford via the lobby on Central Park West and walked north, turning left on West Eighty-first Street. He was headed for Mickey's, a quaint breakfast and lunch restaurant on Columbus Avenue. He sat at a corner table, ordered coffee, and unfolded his Sunday *Times*, turning directly to the theater section.

Barbara Wilson recorded Scrivner's movements in her small spiral-bound notebook. This was her second day tailing him, and so far, no sign of Adam. As she stood outside the restaurant, cold and enviously eyeing Scrivner's hot cup of coffee, she decided there was nothing glamorous about playing the role of a private detective.

Scrivner looked up from his paper and spotted her standing on the other side of the window. He smiled broadly and waved her in. Barbara's apartment was only nine blocks away, so she thought she should be able to convince him that her presence was purely coincidental.

Barbara spoke first as she approached his table. "Anthony, what a coincidence. What brings you to this part of town?"

"Breakfast." He laughed. "My apartment's only two blocks away."

"Is that a fact? I'm only a few blocks away myself."

"Isn't it more like ten blocks? Your dad and I shared a cab once. I was on my way home, and I dropped him off."

Barbara didn't respond. Instead, she queried him, seeming to be interested. "The theater section. I didn't know you were a theatergoer."

"Normally, I'm not, but my investment broker talked me into buying a few shares in this new Broadway show. It opened last weekend—*The Life of Reilly*, at the Broadhurst. Have you heard of it?"

"No, I haven't. Is it any good?"

"Apparently not. It closed after five performances."

"Oh, I'm sorry."

"It's okay. It wasn't much money. I'll write it off, and that brings my theater career to an end." He laughed again, then said, "I seem to be seeing a lot of you these days."

"Oh?"

"Yes, I was coming out of Bergdorf Goodman yesterday, and I could have sworn I saw you across the street." His tone had become accusatory.

"Oh yes, I was meeting a girlfriend yesterday in that part of town."

Sitting directly opposite her, Scrivner leaned into the table and said, "Barbara, time for honesty. You've been following me, haven't you?"

Barbara knew he had her dead to rights. She decided to come clean. "Yes, in a way."

"In a way?"

"Well, I have no idea where Adam is or how to contact him. But since I saw him following you the other day, I figured if I followed you, sooner or later, he might show up."

"Are you talking about the other week when I saw him down by the Plaza?" Scrivner didn't mention Ms. Simpson.

"Yes, I saw him follow you up Fifth Avenue, so I followed him. I talked to him, and he admitted he was trailing you, but he didn't tell me why," she lied. "In any case, he didn't have a phone and didn't tell me where he lived. Then he visited me a few days later, and I could tell he was in trouble."

Anthony thought he could guess why he was shadowing him. *Does my wife suspect something?* Speaking aloud, he said, "You say he's in trouble?"

"He wanted to tell me about it, then changed his mind and left. I haven't seen him since."

"I'm sorry to hear that, Barbara, but I can't have you following me all day."

"But it seems like the only way I can find him."

"All the same, it's not right. Now that I know he might be tailing me, I'll watch for him. If I see him, I promise I'll let you know."

"All right. I guess this brings my sleuthing career to an end."

"C'est la vie," said Scrivner. Then he asked, "May I buy you breakfast?"

"No, thank you. I've already had it. I'll get out of your hair," she said, standing.

"Okay then, I'll see you in the office."

"No, I've decided not to take Daddy's offer. I can't see myself behind a desk."

"The job's more than that, but I see what you mean. Good luck, and I hope to see you sometime soon."

Barbara picked up her purse with the black spiral-bound notebook and left Scrivner to his paper and breakfast. She'd have to tell Tobias she had flunked out as a gumshoe.

◈

Bradley Compton also had breakfast that morning and, after reflecting on how he had fallen out of his exercise regimen, decided to walk the mile and a half from the restaurant back to his apartment. As he turned the corner and walked toward the entrance, he saw an older gentleman walking toward him, wearing a charcoal overcoat and sporting a thick mane of gray hair. He immediately recognized him as his superior, responsible for all Abwehr activities in the eastern United States. He recognized him but was never supposed to meet him. Only the most extreme circumstances could warrant his being here.

The man, looking straight ahead and not at Compton, continued to walk toward him, and as he passed by, Compton distinctly heard him say the three words "Sequence Delta Romeo." Compton knew the message those three words conveyed. One or more of the members of their network on the Eastern Seaboard had been compromised.

A chill ran through him. The Delta Romeo protocol dictated he cut and run, arrange for passage out of the country, go to Mexico City, and take refuge in a designated safe house.

Scheisse! What could it be?

He was furious. Everything had been going so well. Geist was primed and ready to go, and he had planned to see him once more in the next few days. The last time before Reichsführer Himmler's Operation Eastern Storm would commence. It would be hailed as the single greatest act in the war. By murdering that crypto-Jew, Roosevelt, the alliance would be badly damaged, and he, Rainer Heydrich, would be hailed as one of Germany's greatest heroes.

Mein Gott, this cannot happen!

He ran into his apartment building and took the elevator to the eighth floor. Sprinting down the hallway, he had his keys out when he reached the door. He burst into his apartment, went to the hall closet, took two pieces of tan Pacraft Bridgeport luggage, and placed them on his bed.

One already contained his SE88/5 shortwave. He opened the other and reached in toward the back, releasing two hidden locking tabs and removing the false bottom. Hidden beneath were his forged American, Canadian, and Mexican passports, a Sauer 38H semiautomatic, and five eight-round clips. He added five thousand American dollars that he retrieved from his dresser along with his code book.

He replaced the false bottom and packed clothes to last him three days. When he finished, he put on his jacket and overcoat, returned to the dresser, and pulled it out from the wall. He took his M33 SS dagger, which had been taped to the back of the dresser, and slipped it into the custom-made pocket in his overcoat.

As he walked out of the door to his apartment, never to return, he resolved not to run to Mexico. He would stay and complete the mission. But first, he had to understand the reasons for invoking Delta Romeo. He'd have to find someplace to set up his wireless and receive this evening's transmission.

∽

After her encounter with Anthony Scrivner, Barbara was a little embarrassed by her lack of skill as a detective. She decided she would take in the Met. By the time she walked through the park and up Fifth Avenue, it should just about be opening. It was a beautiful day, after all.

I'll spend a couple of hours at the Met and then take a pleasant walk by the lake. I'll stop by the market and get something special for dinner—maybe I'll make a veal scallopini? Yes, that and a salad and a nice bottle of Pouilly Fuisse to go with it.

She got home around three and took a hot shower, committed to spending the rest of the day relaxing. Richard was due sometime tomorrow if his schedule held, and she had plans for a special night.

After donning her silk pajamas, she put some jazz on the record player, opened her French Chardonnay, and started to prepare dinner.

She was making the salad when the doorbell rang.

Could Richard be home a day early?

Hurrying to the door, she discovered it wasn't Richard, as she had hoped. Realizing she was in her PJs, she slid behind the open door. Peering around it, she said, "Hello, may I help you?"

"Hello. Sorry to bother you, but I'm a friend of your brother. That is, he works for me. My name is Pole, Fredrick Pole."

"Oh, hello, Mr. Pole. I'm afraid Adam isn't here. I haven't

seen him in a couple of days," she said, wishing he would go away. Something about the man made her skin crawl. He had invited her brother to do something that scared him—scared him enough to seek her help.

"Ms. Wilson, may I come in for a moment? I have news about Adam that's rather important."

"Well, I suppose so, but give me a moment. I'm not fully dressed." She left him in the open doorway, went to her room, and put on her robe. The door to her apartment was closed, and Pole was inside when she returned.

"I sincerely regret disturbing you, Ms. Wilson, but you see, I've been put out of my lodgings and will require the use of yours for a few days."

She started for the door. "I think you should leave, Mr. Pole."

He grabbed her arm as she passed by him, pulling her back from the door, swinging her around, and throwing her onto the couch. He took his Sauer 38 out of his coat pocket and pointed it in her direction.

"I'm afraid I must insist. I won't harm you. Not as long as you stay quiet and cooperate." He was, of course, lying. He had every intention of eliminating her upon his departure.

"What was it you asked my brother to do?"

"Oh, he shared that with you. A colleague asked me to do him a favor in exchange for certain information. In turn, I employed your brother to perform that favor."

"You asked him to murder Anthony Scrivner, didn't you?"

"Why, yes. Adam has been quite open with you, hasn't he?" As he said this, he produced a pair of handcuffs, pulled her up from the couch, cuffed one wrist, then spun her around and cuffed the other so that both wrists were bound behind her back.

"You're not a detective. Who are you? What's this all about?"

"Let's just say I'm a man on a mission."

Pole put away his gun and walked to the door. He opened it and went out to retrieve his luggage from the hallway. When he came back in, he shut the door and locked it, then picked up the two cases and placed them next to the dining table.

"Now, if you don't mind, I have to go out for a while, and I'm afraid I'll have to bind your legs and place you in the bedroom for the duration."

He went over to the couch and yanked the lamp cord out of its plug. Then he reached into his coat, pulled out the razor-sharp SS dagger, and cut the line from the lamp's base. He set the dagger down on the end table and tied her ankles together with the cord.

Dread filled Barbara Wilson as she saw the dagger, its ebony hilt inlaid with an eagle clutching a swastika in its talons. The truth was now impossible to deny—he would never let her live. This man was going to kill her.

Pole finished his trussing, lifted Barbara from the couch, carried her into the bedroom, and placed her on the bed. Then, he ran a second lamp cord through her two cuffed hands and secured her to the bedstead.

"There now, you should be comfortable during my absence."

As a finishing touch, he walked to her dresser, took a

chemise, tore a long strip of fabric from it, and used that to gag her. He left the room, closing the door behind him.

Compton reflected on how this was the perfect place to lay low for a day or two until he got out of town. Finding her address in the telephone directory had been easy enough, and it had no connection to him.

He walked over to the telephone in the living room, picked up the receiver, and dialed a number. After a few rings, someone picked up on the other end of the line.

"I have to see you. It's somewhat urgent," said Pole. The man on the line said something, to which he replied, "That's fine. Say in half an hour." A pause, and then, "Good, see you there." He hung up the telephone.

Pole looked at his watch. It was six o'clock—plenty of time to make his appointment and return for the ten-thirty shortwave transmission.

He saw the bottle of scotch on the bar and poured himself a tot. *Plenty of time for this as well.*

Then he grabbed his hat, walked to the door, turned off the light, and exited, leaving the door unlocked.

∽

At that same time, the Bermuda team, along with Ter Meer and the others, finally landed in England. It took twenty-two hours of flying first to the secret Allied airfield

in northwestern Turkey, then to Lisbon, and finally to the RAF base in Andover, Hampshire, on the eastern end of Salisbury Plain.

Hendricks and Newley had deplaned in Turkey and were transported to a hospital in Istanbul. Stafford would continue on to London, and Todd, Jan, and Dovid would transfer to a Douglas C-54 Skymaster for the flight to the Army base at Mitchell Field, Long Island.

Todd was visibly tired. The last thirty-eight hours had taken a lot out of him. They were all in a small Quonset hut, waiting for vehicles to take them in separate directions. Stafford would write his final report from home before returning to his office in Whitehall Court.

Ter Meer had to remain at the base. His MI6 handler was driving down from London to debrief him.

"Pierre, where do you go from here?" said Todd as he approached.

"I have friends in London—people who used to attend the same parties before the war. I'll stay with them until I can arrange accommodations."

"Any regrets about leaving your home behind?"

"Doesn't that American song say, 'Home is where you hang your hat'? I believe that's true. Nevertheless, I do regret having to leave the artwork behind. I can replace the furniture, but the art is singular, irreplaceable. Worst of all, that ape, Göring, will probably loot it."

"I'm sorry, Pierre. Maybe you'll be able to retrieve them after the war."

"Not likely. I'm afraid art tends to disappear. You never know, however. The odd piece may show up at auction someday." Ter Meer sighed heavily, then said, "You know they've arrested Helga?"

"I'm not surprised. She's a German national and a member of the Abwehr. But I'm sure they'll be lenient once they've read what she's done for the war effort. She's an amazing woman to have realized what Hitler was all about and gotten out."

"I am going to make it my duty to get that woman released."

Todd smiled at his German friend. "And I'll do all I can to help you."

"I'd like to visit New York someday."

"When you do," said Todd, "you'll be my guest."

Someone called out Ter Meer's name. He turned to see a man dressed in a British uniform with the insignia of a commander.

"I am Pierre Ter Meer." He turned back to Todd. "Good-bye for now, Captain."

The two men shook hands, and Ter Meer crossed the room to the man who had called him. Todd couldn't hear what they discussed, but he saw Ter Meer smile, pick up his jacket, and leave.

Stafford was inquiring about his transport with a young lieutenant. When he finished, he walked over to Todd, warming himself by the coal-fired potbelly stove.

"Captain, I sincerely hope your man Hendricks recovers from his injury. He's a courageous man to have done what he did. He was lucky the explosion didn't kill him outright."

"Joe's a tough egg from what I can tell. He'll recover, but I think that shoulder will trouble him for the rest of his life."

"And what about you, Captain? Have you got someone waiting for you back home?"

"I think so . . ."

Stafford smiled. "You think so?"

Todd laughed. "Well, we've only been seeing each other for a few months. Her name's Barbara, and she's the bee's knees."

"I thought we British had the market cornered on

colloquialisms, but you Yanks always surprise me," Stafford said with a chuckle. "Your Bill Donovan is a great one for that."

"You've met General Donovan?"

"Yes, when he visited England. He's well-liked there. Rumor had it that we lobbied Roosevelt to have him replace Kennedy as ambassador. Never happened, however. On another occasion, I visited the States and met him there. I was part of a team sent to see how we could coordinate with your intelligence apparatus. It's all very complicated. You Americans have dozens of intelligence agencies while we have only the one."

"Yes, and we're not known for interagency cooperation. Territorial, I guess you'd say."

"We have a bit of that as well. The crypto boys tend to hold their information close to the vest."

A British sergeant entered the hut. "Captain Todd and company," he announced, "your flight is ready for you to board."

Todd acknowledged the sergeant, then turned to Stafford and said, "Well, Mick, I guess this is it. It's been both a pleasure and an honor serving with you."

"Todd, about that . . ."

"About what?"

"Just that the SIS higher-ups always want to keep things very hush-hush. You know, under wraps."

"I suppose so."

"Well, the fact is, I am a naval commander, but Mick isn't my real name, nor Stafford. Sorry for the deceit, old son."

"I see," said Todd, arching his brow. "Then what is your real name?"

"Fleming. Ian Fleming."

He shook Todd's hand as both an introduction and farewell.

⤞

Every Sunday evening, George Hansen could be found in the living room of his duplex apartment on the eighteenth floor of 730 Park Avenue. After he had finished dinner and his wife had retired to their bedroom, he would go to the living room to claim his chair by the fireplace and switch on the WCBS six o'clock news with Edward R. Murrow.

This Sunday evening, the phone at the other end of the room rang, interrupting his routine. Perturbed, he rose to answer it and was surprised to learn it was Compton. He wanted to meet and said it was urgent.

Reluctantly, Hansen went to the entry hall closet, took out his overcoat and hat, left his apartment, and walked down the hall to the elevator. As he descended, he wondered what it was that was so urgent. He hadn't yet secured the formula for the new solid rocket propellant. Still, he had discovered they would use nitramine rather than ammonium perchlorate in the composite.

If Compton presses me on delivery, I can give him that detail. It might be enough to satisfy him for now.

The elevator doors opened into the lobby, and he left the building, heading north on Park for a block and a half. He then turned left on East Seventy-second, crossing Madison and Fifth Avenues to reach Terrace Drive, which ran through the park.

Hansen had suggested Bethesda Fountain—which was only a quarter mile into the park along Terrace Drive—as a meeting place. Since there was very little traffic, he jaywalked across the street, turned before the Mall, and headed toward the fountain. He could see it silhouetted against the city lights, the Angel of Waters holding a lily and the four cherubs—temperance, purity, health, and peace—just below her. He spotted Compton on the far side and walked over to meet him.

"Hello, Bradley. What, may I ask, is so urgent?"

"Good evening, George. I've received some news that required me to rethink my various tasks, such as our quid pro quo proposition. Let's sit on the bench. It's been a long day."

They went to a bench across from the fountain next to the footpath that led back to Terrace Drive. As they walked, Compton glanced about. No one else was nearby except for a couple sitting on a bench on the other side of the fountain. Hansen sat first, then Compton to his left.

"I apologize, George, but I'm afraid I can no longer hold up my part of the bargain."

Hansen had given some thought to what he might do if Compton didn't eliminate Adam Wilson and Scrivner for him. He would have to make other arrangements. "Isn't there anything you can do? I'm close to getting the complete formulation for the propellant."

"I'm sorry. It's been a pleasure." He put his right hand on Hansen's left shoulder and then, using his left, drew his dagger across Hansen's throat, severing the carotid artery.

Compton stood, keeping his hand on Hansen's shoulder until he was sure the body wouldn't fall to one side. He wiped the dagger clean on Hansen's pant leg, put it back in his overcoat, and took the path back to Terrace Drive and Barbara Wilson's apartment.

When he checked in on her, Barbara was still bound and secured to the bed. He walked over to her and removed the gag.

"I can't imagine you're very comfortable, and I suppose you need to use the powder room. Just to show you I'm a gentleman, I'll allow you to do that. But afterward, it's right back to bed for you, young lady."

He loosened her bindings and led her to the bathroom. Standing in the doorway, he kept an eye on her.

Barbara scowled. "Gentleman? I don't think so."

Compton gave her a smile. "Gentleman, yes. Stupid, no."

When she had finished in the bathroom, he led her back to the bed, where he bound her legs. He had started to handcuff her when the doorbell rang.

His head snapped up as he turned and looked out the bedroom door to the living room. Then he turned back to her and hurriedly cuffed both wrists. Forgetting to secure her to the bedstead, he ran back into the living room.

He put his ear to the door and listened, but didn't hear anything. Glancing down, he saw a piece of paper jutting out from the bottom of the door. He listened once more—still nothing. He bent down and picked up the slip of paper. It was a laundry receipt. Gun in hand, he cautiously opened the door an inch and peered out. Releasing his held breath, Compton smiled to himself, then plucked the laundry bag off the doorknob and closed the door.

ELEVEN

THE WEATHER OVER the Atlantic had been merciful, allowing the C-54 Skymaster to touch down at Mitchell Field at 3:00 P.M. Todd had wired Donovan a quick summary of the Bermuda operation results and requested that he pass on a message to Miriam Abramowicz to let her know when and where they'd be arriving.

Two pilot-green Plymouth P14 military staff cars were parked on the tarmac. Bill Donovan and Allen Dulles stood next to one, and Miriam Abramowicz, her brother Tobias, and their rabbi were next to the other. Donovan had arranged for them to be picked up and driven to the airbase. A third vehicle, a hearse, was parked a little further away.

The plane wheeled to its parking spot, stopped, and shut down the engines. After a while, the two rear cargo doors swung open to either side. The ground crew helped deploy a folding airstair for the passengers as a forklift sat to one side, waiting to offload cargo.

Todd was the first to disembark, wearing a bomber jacket a crew member had given him for the flight. He sported a three-day beard and was ready for a hot bath.

Dovid and Jan deplaned next and waited as the crew placed Chasya's body, secured on a stretcher, at the edge of the bay. The rabbi approached, introduced himself, and offered condolences. The crew gently lowered the stretcher to two funeral home employees. Dovid said he would go with them to ensure that Chasya wasn't left unattended. The rabbi assured him there would be shemira to watch over her as was the custom, but Dovid thanked him and insisted on going with her.

Miriam and Tobias introduced themselves to Dovid and Jan. With tears in their eyes, they hugged Dovid and then Jan.

Miriam wiped the tears from her face. "I brought the rabbi," she said, "and everything has been arranged. The funeral service and burial will be at our family garden in the cemetery tomorrow."

"I wish you could have met her," said Dovid, having a hard time getting the words out. "She was the kindest woman I've ever known."

Miriam hugged him again and watched him walk with the rabbi to the hearse.

Jan looked at Tobias standing next to Miriam, and a smile came over his face. "Brother! Sister!"

Another round of hugs followed.

Tobias said, "We have so much to talk about. I have so many questions. It's hard to believe I have a brother."

Miriam hooked her arm in Jan's, and Tobias put his arm around him as they walked to the car, laughing and talking to each other. Todd smiled, grateful to see signs of joy that might lift some of their grief at Chasya's passing.

And then Todd was alone, standing by the plane as the forklift started unloading its cargo.

He recognized Bill Donovan as one of the two men walking toward him. Beside him was Allen Dulles. Todd had met Dulles more than a few times and had grown to admire him.

Donovan reached out his hand. "Welcome home, Richard, and congratulations on a successful mission."

Todd grasped his hand and shook it. "Thank you, sir. It ended up being more than we expected. We had to leave Lieutenant Hendricks in a doctor's care in Turkey." He put his hand out and said, "Hello, Allen. How are you keeping?"

"Let's get back to the city," said Donovan. "You can fill us in on the details along the way."

The three got into the limousine and returned to New York. As much as Todd wanted to brief the general on the operation—and the fact that they had captured Heinrich Himmler—he was asleep within ten minutes. He was exhausted and hadn't experienced the level of comfort the limo offered since he'd left the States.

⁂

Bradley Compton was looking across Central Park through the window of Barbara Wilson's apartment. Glancing left, he could see past the reservoir to Harlem Meer and the park's northern border. In front of him, he could make out the top of the carousel shrouded by trees and, beyond, the Hotel Pierre with its terrace overlooking the park. New York and Central Park, in all their splendor, awed him.

Of all the cities in Germany, Berlin seemed the closest match, yet New York was three times its size. For the first time, he considered the possibility that Germany might not win this war, and that infuriated him.

He was adamant about what he should do, thinking only a change in leadership could alter the course of the war.

With that change would come new thinking. Right-minded people like Lindbergh could bring about an armistice with Germany and let the war play out in Europe on its own terms. This wasn't America's war. The Japanese could go to hell—they had attacked America and deserved America's wrath.

I have to act. Roosevelt must die. It's Monday, and I have one more loose end to tie up. Adam Wilson will be found dead in his sister's apartment—killed by her hand as she tries to protect herself from the crazed madman her brother has become. She'll suffer a fatal wound in the gunfire that follows.

Fortunately, he'd gotten out of his apartment when he did. After his farewell to George Hansen and before the scheduled shortwave transmission, he had just enough time to swing by. He'd noticed what he assumed to be two FBI agents sitting in a parked car directly across from the building entrance. But no one would think to look for him here.

The shortwave message he received that night in Barbara's apartment confirmed the Sequence Delta Romeo protocol. The prior Thursday, eight agents operating along the coast of Florida had been captured. It was reasonable to assume that one of them had talked while facing death by electrocution. Although they weren't working with Compton, they knew of his presence in New York. Then, the day after, closer to home, the four Long Island agents were arrested. It was a near clean sweep of the Atlantic coast network.

Compton had escaped only because he was a lone agent and not communicating with the others, but they knew his alias. The superior who had passed him the message wasn't German—he was born in Gary, Indiana. This man's name was perhaps the closest-guarded secret of the war. A German agent recruited by the Abwehr in 1930, he now lived in Washington, D.C., and held a prominent position in the office of the Secretary of War. None of the twelve captured agents knew of his existence.

Compton dared not go out during daytime hours, so he had to get Adam Wilson to come to him. Simple enough, he thought. He merely telephoned and left a phone message with the front desk of Adam's hotel—*Urgent that I see you. Please come immediately, Barbara.*

As for Lindbergh, he was a gamble. He'd forgo the meeting he'd considered for Wednesday of this week. In his mind, Geist was too big a risk to the success of Eastern Storm. He would wait to see if Roosevelt's presence at the ceremony was canceled and the wreath laid by some other dignitary.

If not, and Geist balks, I'll be there to do the job myself.

He made that clear to his superiors in that evening's transmission.

❧

Adam Wilson didn't descend to the lobby of his hotel until three in the afternoon. His head ached with the dull, flat pain of a mammoth hangover, the result of an almost two-day bender that hadn't ended until two this morning.

The desk clerk spotted him walking through the lobby and managed to intercept him at the door. "Mr. Wilson, message for you," he said, extending his arm and handing him the missive.

Wilson, still foggy, grunted, "Thanks," and took the note to some chairs in the vestibule that separated the lobby from the entrance. He sat in one to read the message.

It was from Barbara. She said she needed to see him right away and that it was urgent. He wondered what could be so urgent. He couldn't think of anything, but then something crossed his mind—maybe the old man was sick or dying or dead. None of the three possibilities sparked any great sense of urgency in him, so he decided to go see what Barbara was talking about after he got something to eat and sobered up.

He was about to walk out onto the street when he was struck with a sudden impulse and went back to his room. There, he fished his gun out of his suitcase—a Smith and Wesson Model 10 snub-nose .38 he had purchased from a pawnshop along with a box of .38 Special cartridges shortly after accepting Pole's job offer. He checked to be sure it was loaded and then slipped the gun into his coat pocket.

Returning to the lobby, he thought he should call Barbara and tell her he'd received her message. He stepped into one of the phone booths next to the front desk, sat down, and dialed her number.

The phone rang two or three times, and then someone picked up the receiver.

Adam said, "Hello, Barbara." But the other end of the line remained silent. "Hello?" Then he heard the distinctive click of the phone disconnecting.

He decided to ring the number he had for Pole.

"Mr. Pole is not available. This is his answering service. May I take a message?"

Adam replied, "No, that's all right. I'll call back later."

"May I ask who's calling? I'll leave him a message you rang," the agent quickly added.

"Tell him Adam Wilson called."

"Is there a number where Mr. Pole may reach you?"

"No, just tell him I called and will call back."

Adam cradled the receiver and left the phone booth, having no idea that the answering service had been an FBI agent. He stepped outside and hailed a cab. Deciding that food could wait, he gave the driver his sister's address.

The FBI agent who had answered the phone also disconnected. He took his headphones off and shut off the recording machine.

"Who was it?" his partner asked.

"He said his name was Adam Wilson. He didn't leave a message other than saying he would call back."

His partner turned to another man and said, "See what you can find out about an Adam Wilson."

"There's got to be fifty Adam Wilsons in New York," said the junior agent.

"Then give me details on all of them."

With the information provided by one of the Nazi agents detained by the FBI in Florida, they had located and raided Bradley Compton's uptown apartment. They found a small box with some bogus business cards Compton had printed. They also discovered that the phone number on the cards was an answering service.

Further inquiries with the service found that Compton had arranged a separate service for a number assigned to Fredrick Pole. The FBI had both numbers rerouted to the field office downtown, and they'd been monitoring the lines ever since. This was the first and only call they had received for either number.

"I think we'd better let the OSS know we've finally gotten something on one of the lines."

"Good call. Pass it along."

⁂

Todd woke up as they were pulling into the parking garage.

"Sleep well? I didn't have the heart to wake you up," said Donovan.

"That nap helped, but I could sleep for a week," Todd said, yawning.

"We won't keep you long, Richard. Just a quick debrief, and we'll get you a cab home."

They entered the thirty-seventh-floor office of the OSS, where Ms. McWilliams was waiting with a message from the FBI. Dulles took it and began to read it as they made their way to Donovan's office.

Once there, they sat down—Donovan behind his desk, and Todd and Dulles in front of him. Julia came in with a cup of coffee, cream, and sugar on the side. "I thought you could use this after your long flight, Mr. Todd."

"Thank you. Maybe four of them in a row, please," he said, smiling.

"Julia, stay and have a seat. I need you to take notes on the debrief," said Donovan.

She left and quickly returned with her notebook. Todd sat up straight in his chair and took a sip of his coffee.

"This information from the Bureau says that one of the spies cracked under interrogation and gave them the name of another agent here in New York," Dulles said. "They located and raided his apartment, but he had already fled."

Dulles went on to tell them that they had found the business card with the answering service number, discovered another account with a different name, and had been monitoring both numbers.

"I just got a call from the FBI," Ms. McWilliams said, handing a copy to Dulles. "They said a message came about an hour ago."

"What does the message say?" asked Donovan.

Dulles read it aloud. "It's from an Adam Wilson. No message other than he'd call again later." He reached over the desk to hand Donovan the note.

"Adam Wilson?" Todd exclaimed. "It's got to be a coincidence."

"Isn't that J.L.'s son's name?" said Donovan.

"Allen, what was the name that went with that second number?" Todd asked.

"Pole. Frederik Pole."

Todd pondered the name, but it meant nothing to him. Then he asked, "General, may I use your phone? I want to ask Adam's sister if she's heard anything further from him. The boy's been in trouble."

"Go ahead," said Donovan, sliding the telephone across his desk.

Todd dialed Barbara's number.

On the other end, Compton debated whether to answer the phone. If it was Adam again, he should answer and hang up as before. He thought that would ensure his visit and reckoned he could do it without raising too much suspicion if it happened to be anyone else. Resolved, Compton went to the bar and lifted the receiver.

Barbara Wilson heard the phone ringing for a second time. After the first call, she'd heard him replacing the phone in its cradle without saying a word and gathered he had chosen not to speak with that caller.

Desperate, she thought that if he picked up again, this might be her only chance to tell someone something was wrong.

She wriggled across the bed, dropped to the floor, and inchwormed to the door Pole had left ajar when he dropped the laundry on the bed earlier. As she squirmed through the doorway, she saw the man not three feet away—his back to her, the phone at his ear. This was her chance.

Cautiously, she moved closer behind him, and with as much force as she could muster, she kicked him in the back of both legs, forcing him to lose his balance temporarily. He succeeded in holding on to the receiver but grabbed the bar's edge to steady himself and tipped the glasses on the bar to the floor, breaking one. Regaining his balance, he quickly hung up the phone.

Alarmed, Todd put the receiver down and said, "I think something's wrong at Barbara's. I heard something like glass breaking, and then the line went dead."

He stood, apologized, and asked the general if there was a car he could borrow.

"I'll take you," Dulles said. "I'm parked in front of the building."

"Thanks. Let's go," said Todd, and he headed for the door.

"Wait a moment." Dulles briefly disappeared to his office and returned with two High Standard .22s with silencers. Holding one out to Todd, he said, "Best be prepared."

∽

Enraged, Compton looked down and hissed, "Stupid bitch!" He kicked Barbara Wilson in the side before planting his foot on her neck. "Do something like that again, and I'll torture your brother before your very eyes." Then, taking his foot off her neck, he stepped over her prone figure, grabbed her right arm, and dragged her back into the bedroom, leaving her on the floor and shutting the door as he went back to the living room.

He walked about the room, turning out all lights except the one next to the front door, which he unlocked. Pulling a chair to the far side of the room by the window, he sat down in the darkness with his .38 Sauer semiautomatic and waited for Adam.

Thirty minutes passed before he heard footsteps in the hallway.

Adam paused at the door. He didn't ring the bell or knock. Instead, he tried the door and found it to be unlocked.

At that same time, Richard Todd and Allen Dulles, downstairs, entered the elevator and pressed the button for the twentieth floor.

Wilson hesitated in the hallway. The fact that someone had answered the phone earlier and hung up on him—and now he found the apartment door unlocked—heightened his suspicion. He took his revolver out of his coat pocket and backed up as far as he could in the hallway. Although the door was unlocked, he didn't dare ease it open, as he suspected foul play. He charged through the door into the living room, diving to the floor as a muzzle flash lit the room and a shot was fired. He rolled toward the bar and took cover.

Compton, too, dropped out of his chair to the floor, firing a second time and hitting the corner of the bar, wood splintering off at the point of impact.

Wilson returned fire without any idea where his opponent was, hitting one of the windows and shattering it.

"Adam, why don't you stand up, and we'll talk this through," said Compton, dropping his affected American accent and speaking in his native Saxon timbre.

"You first!" said Adam, taking another wild shot in the direction of his voice.

The elevator doors opened, and both Todd and Dulles heard Wilson's last gunshot. Cautiously, they advanced down the hallway, staying flat against the wall adjacent to the open door.

"Stand up, Adam, and I'll tell you where your sister is. She's waiting for you. Waiting for you to save her."

Todd peered around the doorjamb and yelled, "Government agents! Drop your weapons!"

Compton fired at Todd, missing him as Adam stood and rushed him. He shot again, hitting Adam square in the chest.

Todd and Dulles darted into the room, shooting as they did. Compton ducked to the side, opened one of the windows, squeezed off two more rounds, and jumped out.

Dulles, gun leveled in front of him, walked guardedly to the open window.

Todd went to Wilson's side, kneeling and turning him over onto his back. Then he realized he hadn't seen Barbara—she'd escaped his thoughts during all the commotion. He stood and looked at the closed bedroom door, a sense of dread swelling in the pit of his stomach.

He ran to the door and opened it. There, on the floor, was Barbara, bound and gagged but alive, her eyes pleading with him to untie her. He pulled the gag from her mouth.

"Richard," she said, "thank God! I heard all the gunshots. Are you all right?"

"I'm fine, darling. Are you hurt?"

"Just my pride. I'll be okay once I get some blood back in my feet."

He loosened the binds on her wrists and ankles, and she managed to stand with his help.

"I heard Adam. Where is he?"

Todd put his arm around her shoulder and led her back to the living room.

When she saw Adam lying on the floor, grievously wounded, she dropped to his side and started to cry. "Adam . . . Adam."

Adam's eyes opened. He looked up, and a smile came to his face upon seeing his sister. Blood seeped from his mouth, and he coughed, expelling more as he did.

"Hi, Sis. How're tricks?"

"You'll be okay," said Barbara. "We'll get you to a hospital."

"I think that might be a waste of cab fare." His eyes rolled up into his head as he whispered, "I guess I screwed up ag . . ." He didn't finish the sentence.

She bent over, embracing him and sobbing. "Oh, Adam, Adam."

Dulles walked back from the window and stood next to Todd. "He jumped to the apartment terrace one floor down. He got away. How's the kid?"

"He's gone," said Todd.

Dulles bowed his head as two uniformed police officers appeared at the door.

"Police! Drop your weapons and stay where you are."

Todd bent over and put his gun on the floor. "Federal agents. This man has been shot."

Keeping their guns trained on Todd and Dulles, the officers moved farther into the apartment.

"You two, move to one side. You got any identification?" one of them asked.

Todd reached into his breast pocket and brought out his wallet. He flipped it open, revealing his identification card, and handed it to the officer.

The policeman looked at it and said, "OSS? What branch of the government is that?"

"Office of Strategic Services, sir. We report to the Joint Chiefs of Staff, and they report to the president."

The officer looked down at Barbara, sitting upright on the floor and holding her brother's hand. "Ma'am, could you please state your name?"

She looked blankly at the officer and said, "My name is Barbara Wilson, and I live here." Turning back to Adam, she said, "This is my brother, Adam."

"We'll get an ambulance here as quickly as we can, ma'am." Then he looked over to Todd and Dulles and said, "Okay then, tell me what this is all about? Mr. . . . ." He looked again at the ID. "Mr. Todd."

"We're after a suspected German spy. He escaped through that window," said Todd, gesturing toward the window.

Then he saw the piece of luggage next to the table. Picking it up, he set it on the table, then flipped the latches on either side and opened it. Inside was the Nazi agent's shortwave receiver and transmitter. Todd was amazed at how small and compact it was—it couldn't have weighed more than ten pounds. He knew Donovan would want it reverse-engineered and made available to agents in the field.

He returned to Barbara and helped her up. "C'mon, honey, let's get you out of here. You can stay with me tonight."

She buried her head in his shoulder, sobbing. "Oh, Richard."

"I'll wrap things up here," Dulles told Todd. "You get her out of here."

"Thanks, Allen. I'll talk to you in the morning."

TWELVE

"Hansen? Murdered? I can't believe it. And J.L.'s son was shot to death in his sister's apartment? I don't know what this world is coming to."

Anthony Scrivner was standing in a coffee nook on the thirtieth floor of the Union Chemical building, talking to Sophie Campbell, J.L.'s assistant.

Sophie was dabbing the tears from her eyes, although it felt like a hopeless exercise. She hadn't stopped crying since arriving at work a little over an hour ago. She worked with George Hansen and had known Adam since he was a boy.

"I don't know if I can face him when he gets in. That is, if he comes in at all. I don't think he should. Don't you think so, Mr. Scrivner?"

"Yes. I mean, no. He should stay at home. He must be devastated. Barbara, as well."

The elevator doors opened, and to their amazement, J. Leland Wilson, accompanied by Tobias Bach and another man they didn't recognize, stepped out.

Sophie dabbed her eyes again and hurried down the hall toward his office.

As she approached J.L., she said, "Mr. Wilson, I . . . I mean, I . . . oh my goodness' sake." She broke down again, sobbing uncontrollably.

"There, there, Sophie. I understand," he said, putting

his arm around her shoulder. "Why don't you go home? Take the day off. I'll be fine."

Sophie looked up at him, eyes filled with tears, then threw her arms around him.

"Now, now. You get your things. Anthony will take you downstairs and get you a cab." He turned to Scrivner. "Anthony, would you do that, please?"

"Certainly. Come with me, Sophie. Let's get your purse."

J.L., Tobias, and Bill Donovan continued to J.L.'s office. Once inside, they sat around the coffee table by the window.

"Thank you, old friends, for coming to see me today." J.L. let out a heavy sigh. "I wish our reunion could have been under different circumstances."

By coincidence, both Donovan and Bach had entered the lobby of the building at the same time. Both men had heard the news and felt they should see their old friend and comrade.

"Tobias, Bill, how long has it been since we were in the same room together?"

"The way I remember it," said Bach, "we were in Calais. I was shipping out on a transport back home to the US, and you, Bill, were on a separate boat to England. Joshua, you were headed to your new posting in Paris. It was a long time ago."

"A lot of water under the bridge," said J.L., going blank for a few seconds.

"Josh, I came to offer my condolences but also to tell you some of the details surrounding Adam's death," said Donovan.

"Something you're involved in?"

"That seems to be the case. We think we know the man

who shot Adam. He's an undercover agent with the German Abwehr, their counterespionage group, although they're all under the SS these days. We don't know his real identity, but his code name is Cassius."

J.L. remembered what Todd had mentioned when they first met. "How is Adam mixed up with that?"

"We're not entirely sure, but Cassius hired Adam under the pretense that he was some sort of private detective. What's more, we think he was also responsible for George Hansen's death yesterday."

"My God, Hansen?" said Wilson. "Why?"

"While on his mission in Poland, Richard Todd collected intelligence that George Hansen had been feeding the Germans your company's secrets for high-yield synthetic fuel processing. He's been working with the Nazis for over a year—since before they took over the plant—and was colluding with Pierre Ter Meer. What Hansen didn't know was that Pierre was working for MI6."

"Then why didn't Ter Meer tell us about him?"

"He told his MI6 minders, but we weren't in the war then and weren't sharing intel with the British on their operations. That all changed when Hitler declared war on the US. After that, a huge glut of intel came our way from the Brits, and some of it got lost in the shuffle," Donovan said. "In any case, we believe this Cassius was eliminating his American contacts to cover his tracks. We know why Hansen was involved, but we don't know how Adam was connected."

"But why hold Barbara hostage?"

"We think it had something to do with the recent arrest of two groups of Nazi saboteurs. Even though they weren't working with Cassius, they had peripheral knowledge of his existence. He was already on the run when one of the captured men gave up his alias and told us he was somewhere in New York. Because we were already aware of this, it didn't take us long to track him down, but he was gone when we raided his apartment. He knew about Barbara through his connection to Adam and thought—correctly, as it seems— that no one would ever think to look for him at her place. And it was the perfect trap to draw Adam in."

"How did you already know about this agent?" Tobias asked.

"We've known about him for a couple of months, thanks to an American he attempted to enlist. You see, apart from handling Hansen, he was here with one specific task in mind. His primary objective in coming to America was to assassinate Franklin Delano Roosevelt."

The blond man at the bus station looked very ordinary— not unusually tall or short, thirty or thereabouts, medium build. He wore sneakers, beige pants, a white shirt under a well-worn cloth jacket, sunglasses, and a baseball cap. Nothing about him stood out.

After Compton— née Heydrich, aka Pole— finished changing in the bus station washroom, he didn't return the suitcase to the locker he had rented the day after fleeing his apartment. He left it behind and went to the interstate to see if he could hitch a ride south.

I should have put the shortwave back in the locker Sunday night after relaying the transmission to Berlin. Now I'm on my own, without a means to communicate. At least I clarified that I'll be staying to see the mission through.

He knew he had also made a mistake in killing Wilson. Though he wanted everything tied up neatly, in retrospect, it was a bad decision. Undoubtedly, the boy could have identified him, but Adam had no idea who he was or what he was there for.

So now I'm on the run, and two government agents and the Wilson woman can identify me. I should have just cut the boy loose.

Though Compton had plenty of money and false identification papers, he knew that the FBI would soon be circulating composite drawings to state and local law enforcement. He would have to assume a better disguise— but that wasn't a problem. He knew how to blend in and disappear.

Two disguises are all I need. When I'm finished here, I'll escape the country and return to the Motherland, triumphant.

⁘

At 8:00 A.M. on Friday, May 21, Richard Todd and Allen Dulles sat in General Donovan's office again. This time, they were joined by Frank Conroy, director of the Secret Service.

Donovan gestured toward Conroy. "I've asked Frank to join us today. The president refuses to cancel his appearance on the thirtieth, and it's Frank's job to protect him. We need to give him all the help we can."

"Much appreciated, Bill," said Conroy. "I'm sorry to say that after four and a half days of every state and federal agency trying to find this guy, we're still no closer than when we started. We have to assume he's a threat to the president. Still nothing new from Lindbergh?"

"No, sir," Todd replied. "Cassius hasn't contacted him. We think he decided Lindbergh was too much of a risk—and of course, he was right."

"Frank," said Donovan, "If Cassius is still gunning for the president, I assume you've done everything possible to increase the security presence."

"I've got six cars escorting FDR's Sunshine Special from the White House to the cemetery—it's armor-plated with bulletproof windows and run-flat tires. Twelve agents will accompany the president from the parking lot to the Tomb of the Unknown Soldier. The Army's third division has assigned an additional platoon to cover the perimeter of the cemetery, and of course, there are the sentinels that guard the tomb twenty-four hours a day."

"Hoover's got twenty agents patrolling the grounds," added Dulles. "Attendees are by invitation only, and his men will check everyone as they enter. It sounds like it's sewn up tight as a drum."

"The best we can do is to have those people who can identify Cassius in attendance," Donovan said. "Allen and Richard caught only a glimpse of him, so the best chance of spotting him would be for Lindbergh and Barbara Wilson to be present."

Todd, looking uneasy, said, "I'll talk to Barbara about that. Has Lindbergh agreed?"

"Yes, he's willing to play along. No need to ask Barbara. We briefed her on the situation, hoping she would be willing to go there and see if she might spot him. She volunteered without us having to ask."

"Does he still have the pen?" asked Dulles.

"Yes, although none of the poison capsules. He handed over the two poison rounds to us after he received them through the post. They're with the FBI's ballistics lab at Quantico. But he still has the original six practice capsules. He'll surrender the pen once we get past the Decoration Day ceremony. Who knows, Cassius may still contact him."

"Even with all the precautions in place," Conroy said, "it's too dangerous. We know how he intended to do this, but now . . ." He thought for a moment, then said, "If he has a backup plan half as cunning as his original plan, we're in trouble."

"We've been brainstorming various scenarios in an attempt to be prepared," Dulles said, "but nothing like a pen that shoots deadly radioactive isotopes over thirty feet. We think that whatever he tries, it will have to be at close range. We've mapped all the possible firing angles for a high-powered rifle shot and staked out the most likely locations he would use. Everyone attending will be searched for weapons, bombs, and the like at the entrance to the cemetery."

"Do we have the names of those expected to be present—politicians, military, and civilians?" asked Todd.

"Yes," said Conroy. "We'll make copies of the list available to you."

"It's certainly possible that one of the attendees is our would-be assassin. Allen and I will go through the list and see if we can identify any potential suspects."

They were interrupted by Ms. McWilliams opening the door to Donovan's office. "Anything I can get you, boss?"

"I think these gentlemen would like some coffee,"

Donovan said after glancing around and taking in the expressions on their faces. "Thank you, Julia."

As she shut the door, Conroy said, "One thing we should note."

"What's that, Frank?"

"I mean, we're grateful for him coming forward and his assistance, but if Lindbergh is going to be there for the ceremony . . ."

Donovan knew it was going to be something about his politics. Roosevelt didn't hide his disregard very carefully.

"It's just that I'm pretty sure FDR . . ." Conroy hesitated again.

"What about Roosevelt?" Donovan queried.

"Well, he suspects Lindbergh of being a crypto-Nazi."

They all looked at each other and broke out in laughter.

❧

"Thank you, young man. Sure, it's very kind of you."

The old one-armed man, his voice carrying a bit of an Irish brogue, spoke to the gentleman who'd offered to carry his grocery bag up the steps to the Georgetown entrance of the veterans home.

"My privilege, sir. Always an honor to help a fellow veteran."

"Then won't you come in, boyo. There's always coffee and biscuits in the downstairs parlor."

"Thank you. I think I'll take you up on that," said the young man.

They walked through the entrance to the home and into a clean, well-lit front parlor. Scattered about were several chairs and small tables, occupied by other veterans, some quite old and sitting alone, and some with visiting friends or family.

Off to one side, against the wall, was a buffet with cups, saucers, a pot of coffee, cream, sugar, and a plate of what looked like sliced banana bread.

"Ah, to be sure, we're in luck. Something special today." Then, helping himself, he said, "I am fond of banana bread. How about you?"

"One of my favorites, sir."

"See here, boyo. You don't have to keep calling me *sir*. My name's Liam Fitzgerald—Private Liam Fitzgerald—late of the First Marine Battalion, Huntington's Battalion." Glimpsing down and to his left, he said, "I lost this in June of '98 at the battle of Cuzco Well in Cuba."

"I'm sorry," said the young man.

"Sure now, there's no need for that. You see, they gave me a medal. Fair exchange for my arm."

"You're courageous, sir. But I'm surprised you don't wear it. After all, you fought for your country. The most honorable thing a man can do is fight—and maybe die—for his country."

Fitzgerald laughed and leaned forward. "Here now," he whispered, "no bastard ever won a war by dying for his country. To be sure, he won it by making the other poor fecking bastard die for *his*." They both laughed, and then he said, "But I don't know your name, young man. Tell me, what's your story?"

"My name is Pole, sir. Sorry, Liam. I'm Fredrick Pole, and I'd be happy to tell you my story."

✍

At New York's Grand Central Terminal, Tobias Bach and J. Leland Wilson boarded the Marylander for the three-and-a-half-hour trip to Washington, D.C.'s Union Station. They were to meet Bill Donovan, who had driven down the day before with Allen Dulles. It was Thursday, just two days away from the Decoration Day ceremonies that would see the president laying a wreath at the Tomb of the Unknown.

"Barbara's coming down, isn't she?" asked Bach, settling into his seat for the long ride.

"Yes, she and Richard are driving. I think it's faster than the train. At least once, you get out of the city. Are you sure you didn't want to stay in town to get to know your brother better?"

"We'll have time. He and I spent time talking after Chasya's funeral. He's quite a fellow, and from what he tells me, things are much grimmer in Poland than what's been reported. The refugee problem is critical, and it's not being addressed."

"You can blame Secretary of State Cordell Hull for that," said Wilson. "The State Department has been doing everything it can to prevent the Jews from immigrating. He cites security risks, but I think he's bowing to the short-sighted, xenophobic, or even anti-Semitic opinions of some of the public. The president has to step in."

"You're a good man, Josh. But even if the US allowed them to immigrate, they'd have to get here first. Jan says the Nazis are stopping them in every country they've occupied and the ones where they wield political or military influence. It's a desperate situation."

Wilson turned to Bach. "Tobias, don't you wish we were

young again? I don't like war, but I envy Todd and people like your brother for what they can do on the ground."

"From that perspective, yes, but if it meant being as thick-headed as I was back then, no thanks." That got a chuckle out of Wilson.

"Well, here's to the young and thick-headed. God bless them."

Later that evening, they met Bill Donovan at the Old Ebbitt Grill. They had booked a private dining room upstairs. Over the course of the war, the ten-man squad had lost three of its members.

Bach and Wilson arrived at the restaurant at seven. It was busy as usual, teeming with Washington's great and small illuminati, pundits, and elected officials. Its proximity to the Treasury Building across Fifteenth Street NW and the White House just beyond made it a popular dining venue and watering hole. Upon entering, the two walked to the back of the restaurant and up the stairs to the second-floor dining room.

Bill Donovan, already seated, stood to greet them.

Bach shook his hand. "Good evening, Bill. How was the drive down?"

"Uneventful and, as such, calming and restorative."

"Thank heaven for that. How many are we this evening?" asked Wilson.

"There'll be three more, and with us, that makes six. Oh, seven. I invited Allen Dulles. Werner couldn't make it. He's in California, and it was too far to travel."

"All the originals," said Wilson. "That's good news." The seven were the only survivors from a squad of ten. Three were killed while seeing action in Europe.

"Still no news about Cassius, Bill?" asked Bach.

"None. I've received daily briefs from the FBI, the Secret Service, and various police agencies in New York, Maryland, and D.C. None of them has turned up anything. We'll be meeting all the groups at Fort Myer in the morning. I'll ask Julia to send the particulars to your hotel. Where are you staying?"

"The Mayflower on Connecticut," said Wilson.

"Then, better still, Allen and I will pick you up in the morning, and we'll drive over together."

After all the original comrades in arms were assembled, and after all the conviviality that goes with good food, old friends, and excellent wine, Donovan rose to propose a toast. He tapped his wine glass to get everyone's attention.

"Gentlemen, twenty-four years ago, we sailed home after fighting the war to end all wars, and now we find ourselves once again locked in a battle against despotism and authoritarian rule. The freedom of our families and loved ones is in peril from an evil the likes of which this world has never seen. We must never forget the ones who sacrificed their lives so that we may engage this threat. Never shall we allow the memory of those three that remained behind to fade." He raised his glass and solemnly spoke their names. "To Burke, Perez, and MacGyver!"

And the squad responded, "Burke, Perez, MacGyver!"

❧

That same day, Richard Todd and Barbara Wilson checked into the separate rooms Sophie had booked for them at the Washington hotel. Along with Allen Dulles, they were staying at the Mayflower, compliments of her father.

A bellhop was retrieving their luggage from the front entrance, where they had also dropped the car. Barbara turned to Todd and said, "Richard, I'll just put my things away and freshen up a bit. Want to meet back in the lobby in, say, half an hour?"

"Sure, we can go get lunch. I have to stop by my office at OSS headquarters on Navy Hill. The Secret Service dropped off a list of attendees for Saturday's ceremony. It'll take only a minute."

"Then you'll show me around D.C.?"

"Whatever your heart desires. After that, we can have dinner at Matin's Inn in Georgetown. It's my favorite spot. It's not fancy, but it's cozy with good food. The atmosphere is quiet there, and we can hear each other talk."

Barbara looked sideways at Todd. "Talk? Why? Is there anything special on your mind?"

Todd took a deep breath, then exhaled. "I just want to be sure you can hear me, and I can hear you. That's not so strange, is it?"

"I suppose not. Well, we'd better get going. I want to see the White House, the Capitol, the Jefferson and Lincoln memorials, and . . ." She stopped and asked excitedly, "Will we have time to tour the Smithsonian?"

"I don't know—that's a lot for one afternoon. But we'll try if that's what you want."

Friday morning, Todd met J.L. Wilson for breakfast in the hotel restaurant.

"Good morning, Mr. Wilson. I see you're an early riser as well."

"A holdover from my paper route days. I threw the morning *Times*, guaranteed delivery by 6:30. But Richard, remember—you can call me J.L. We know each other well enough." He lowered his voice and in a conspiratorial tone asked, "Everything went well at dinner last night?"

Todd smiled. "She said yes. I took her to a little tavern on Wisconsin and popped the question sitting in one of the booths over dinner."

Wilson shook hands with him. "That's wonderful. I'm happy for you both."

Tobias Bach came into the restaurant with a newspaper tucked under his arm. He joined them, saying, "Good morning," and then took a seat to Todd's left, across from Wilson.

"Tobias," echoed Wilson and Todd.

"Page one of *The Washington Post* has a big story on Decoration Day and the history of the Unknown Soldier. Did you know there were four unknowns and that the one interred at Arlington was chosen from the four identical caskets in the city hall of Chalons-en-Champagne by a fellow wounded soldier, Sergeant Edward Younger, by placing a spray of white roses on one of the caskets? He chose the second casket from the right. As a vet, I'm ashamed to say I didn't know that."

"Tobias, given your service in France during the war, I don't think you should be ashamed of anything," said Wilson. "Besides, I have news you'll want to hear. Todd, here, and Barbara are engaged to be married."

Tobias turned to Todd and grabbed his hand. Pumping it vigorously, he said, "Congratulations, Richard! That's fantastic news. As her godfather—and if Josh hasn't already done it—I'll talk to you about how you're expected to behave over the next sixty years."

Todd stared at him, not sure whether he was serious or not. Then both Bach and Wilson let out a roar of laughter, Wilson slapping Todd on the back at the same time.

"I guess I know what I'm in for from you two," Todd said with a smile. He reached into his pocket, took out a page of notepaper, and unfolded it. "I got the attendee list yesterday and went over it when I got back to my room last night. I think I have an idea about how to approach this."

"Let's hear it," said Bach.

"I noticed that, with a few exceptions, nearly everyone who will be at the ceremony tomorrow is readily recognizable—you know, the Joint Chiefs, senators, congressmen, and dignitaries. So I thought it likely that if our man is with the invitees, he would be part of one of the few less recognizable groups. He certainly wouldn't come as an individual—too easy to spot."

"That makes sense," said Wilson.

"There'll be members of three veteran groups attending. They're from all over the country, so even their fellow vets won't be familiar with them all."

"I can guess what the groups are."

"Right. There'll be veterans from the Civil War, the Spanish-American War, and World War One—ten from each, Medal of Honor recipients from each of the services. I'll bet dollars to donuts that if he's in disguise, he'll be in one of those groups."

"I think you've got something there," said Bach.

"Thanks. I'm meeting Donovan at Fort Myer next to the cemetery this morning and will run it by him."

"We're going as well. Bill and Dulles are picking us up on their way over."

"Great. I'll meet you there. I want to have breakfast with Barbara first."

Wilson laughed. "Well then, son, you're off to a good start."

THIRTEEN

Saturday morning, Rainer Heydrich—also known as Fredrick Pole and Bradley Compton—visited Liam Fitzgerald at the retirement home for breakfast as promised.

"Good morning, Liam. How are you this morning? Ready for your big day?"

Liam Fitzgerald was making every effort to stand upright and fill out the uniform that now hung at least two sizes too large for his shrunken frame. "I couldn't be better, boyo," he said in an exuberant voice, masking the embarrassment he felt for the loose uniform.

Still, Private First-Class Liam Fitzgerald cut a proud figure in his lovingly preserved uniform, the left sleeve pinned neatly at the shoulder and his Medal of Honor gleaming as if it had been placed around his neck just yesterday.

"Big day? I don't know about that. The reason I was invited—to see the president, that is—is because I'm one of the ten servicemen still living who received the Medal of Honor from the war—and the only Marine among them."

Compton stood straight and put his hand on Liam's shoulder. "Nonsense, Liam. You're the right man to represent all the other brave men who fought for their country and died in that war." He looked the man in the eye and said, "Private Fitzgerald, it's your privilege and your duty."

Then, he held up a bag. "I've brought a bottle of potcheen to celebrate afterward." Compton was surprised by how much he meant what he was saying. He respected Liam for his service.

"You're a good man, Fredrick," Liam responded with tears in his eyes. "Thank you, boyo."

"Now, you're supposed to assemble with others an hour before the ceremony at Memorial Gate, right?" He had promised to drive Liam to the cemetery since he had no family and had stolen a car earlier in the morning for this purpose.

"To be sure, that's correct, Fredrick. The Spanish War Veterans Society people said there'd be a sign in the parking lot and to meet and assemble there. They'll drive us up to the amphitheater in a bus." Liam fumbled in his pocket with his one hand and produced the letter. Still unsure of himself, he was grateful for Compton's assistance.

"Then we should probably think about leaving."

Liam noticed a sudden look of surprise on Compton's face. "What is it, boyo? Is there something wrong?"

"It's just that you have a stain on your shirt collar. Let's go to your room and see if we can get it out."

Worried and a bit confused, the old native of Kilkenny, Ireland, agreed, and Compton helped him up the steps to his second-floor room.

Once there, Compton went to the sink in the bathroom, took the hand towel, and wet it. Coming out of the bathroom, he said, "Here, let's get that coat off and see what we can do about that spot." He helped Fitzgerald slip off his coat. "Turn around, and let's have a look."

Liam did as he was told. Setting down the towel,

Compton reached into his pocket and brought out a garotte of half-inch braided rope. He pulled it taught and brought it over Liam's head and around his throat.

As he tightened it and began to strangle the decorated veteran, he whispered in his ear. "History shall record your name, friend Liam. I'll ensure you are not forgotten for what you do now." Then he twisted the rope as hard as possible. "For the greater glory of the Third Reich! Sleep, my friend."

Rainer Heydrich saw Himmler's plan coming together. In 1941, after the Japanese bombed Pearl Harbor, Hitler declared war on the United States—believing President Roosevelt to be part of an international Jewish conspiracy against the German race. Himmler proposed that with Roosevelt's death, America would cease to support the war in Europe—a war many Americans wanted no part of in the first place. Thus, Operation Eastern Storm was born. America responded with its declaration of war on the same day.

Rainer Heydrich—under aliases like Fredrick Pole and Bradley Compton—was chosen to lead the mission and was sent to America at the end of 1941.

Compton had long considered the when and how of Roosevelt's assassination. Now, the time had finally come to finalize the plan and put it into action.

While waiting for the right time to come, he kept himself busy. Suborning Hansen and obtaining the technical secrets of Union Chemical had proven very successful. But allowing himself to become embroiled in Hansen's plot to replace J.L. Wilson as CEO of Union Chemical was a mistake he regretted.

He had successfully turned the American hero Lindbergh into a willing soldier of the Reich, which was the original plan. But fate had intervened, and the Abwehr's East Coast network of agents had been compromised. Compton now believed that Lindbergh was no longer reliable, suspecting that he, too, had been compromised—or was maybe even working as a double agent.

Sequence Delta Romeo—the order to flee to Mexico—had been initiated, but Compton had disregarded it. He was too close to fulfilling Himmler's ambition. He was a capable spy—and he had a contingency plan.

Liam Fitzgerald was that contingency plan. He had known that the ceremony made it a point to invite veterans of past wars, so he waited to see which veterans would be invited to the May ceremony. In January, the names were publicized in the national papers. This year, it would be surviving Medal of Honor conferees.

He found as much information as he could get on them, quickly setting aside most of them for being too tall or too short, or because they were members of an inferior race. He then researched the personal histories of the few that were left. Liam Fitzgerald became the obvious choice. He had no family, but more importantly, out of the one hundred and twelve service members awarded the Medal of Honor, there had been fifteen Marines. He was the last alive and, conveniently, the least recognizable to the others.

Compton disrobed Fitzgerald and hid his body in the bathtub, pulling the shower curtain closed and shutting the door. Opening the bag that allegedly held a bottle of potcheen, he took out what he believed would transform him into a man forty years his senior—makeup, a prosthetic nose, and a bottle of a vile liquid that, when ingested, would color his skin a jaundiced yellow, boosting the effectiveness of his practiced cosmetic talent. The prosthetic nose wasn't huge, but it transformed his aquiline feature into something a tad more bulbous.

Compton had affected these changes twice before, and they were convincing even in full sunlight. Still, he counted on the likelihood that people wouldn't pay much attention to any single individual in the assemblage of elderly veterans. He also knew that people were naturally averse to dwelling on the features of the aged, as it reminded them of their inevitable fate.

When he finished rendering the physical characteristics of his disguise, Compton put on the uniform. This was Fitzgerald's last qualification—that he and Compton fit the same clothes. He hid his left arm inside the jacket and assessed himself in the mirror, and he was pleased that it wasn't noticeable. Having one arm confined would be less than advantageous, but he would make do.

Having completed his transformation, he reached again into the bag and removed the one item that would contribute the most to the success of his plan to assassinate FDR—a device designed to ensure the president's death and allow him to escape without being detected. Inside the small black leather case was a replica of a Montblanc Meisterstuck 4810 and two small capsules.

During the operation's planning phase, he wisely demanded a second device in case the first was lost, destroyed, or rendered unusable. He had received his two capsules in the regular mail delivery just days before being forced underground.

He took the pen and capsules out of the case, loaded

one capsule into the pen, and then put the pen and the second capsule into his right jacket pocket.

Compton took one final look in the mirror. He looked the part now in the private's dress blue jacket with the white belt, brass buttons, and stitched red trim. Picking up the patterned cap, he adjusted the brass eagle, globe, and anchor device at its center and placed it on his head.

A little large, but it fits.

He slipped the Sauer 38 into his waistband at the small of his back, buttoned the jacket, and was ready to go. At the door, he paused, turned back, took the Medal of Honor off the bed, and left.

§

At Arlington Cemetery, Barbara Wilson stood on the steps of the amphitheater, wearing what she considered to be a disguise—a dark blue dress suit, sunglasses, and a floppy blue hat. She aimed to remain inconspicuous so that if Pole were present, he wouldn't recognize her unless he got very close.

Todd came up behind her and whispered, "Hello, Mata Hari."

"Very funny, Mr. Wisenheimer. I'm doing as you suggested—paying special attention to the veteran groups. They're not all here yet. The Spanish-American War vets haven't arrived."

The ceremony was scheduled to begin in thirty minutes with the president's arrival. It would open with a brief prayer led by Admiral William Leahy, chair of the Joint Chiefs of Staff, followed by thirty seconds of silence. After that, the color guard would be posted, and the president—accompanied by a member of the color guard carrying the wreath on a stand—would approach the tomb. The wreath would be handed to the president, who would place it in front of the tomb and salute. The ceremony would close with a member of the Marine band playing Taps.

Donovan, Dulles, J.L. Wilson, Bach, Frank Conroy of the Secret Service, and J. Edgar Hoover were standing on the steps in front of the amphitheater's neoclassical Beaux-Arts facade, among other dignitaries, politicians, and ranking officers of the military. The press was clustered off the plaza's southwestern path. Donovan and Dulles were scanning the scene, watching for any suspicious movements.

The last group of veterans—those from the Spanish-American War—arrived and were directed to the south side of the plaza. The Civil War veterans, many of them frail, were seated before the amphitheater steps. Veterans of World War One took their position on the plaza's north side, so that together with the Spanish-American veterans, they flanked the tomb. Compton took his place toward the end of his row of vets, where he would have a clear line of sight to the president. The tomb stood in the middle of the plaza.

He looked across to the other side of the plaza and the north path that led to the back of the amphitheater, eyeing the position where he had instructed Lindbergh to stand for his attack on the president. The aviator was nowhere in sight.

A hush came over the gathering as people caught sight of FDR, aided by Admiral Leahy, at the top of the northern path. Roosevelt walked with a cane in his right hand, his left arm linked through Leahy's for support. Although he was paralyzed from the waist down, no one could see the ten pounds of leather and steel leg braces that locked his knees in place as he appeared to walk, swiveling his torso to swing his legs forward. His disability—infantile paralysis, or polio—had first been diagnosed in 1921 when he was thirty-nine. Although many people were aware of it, it was rarely spoken of. Together, they slowly approached the center of the plaza and stopped directly before the tomb.

Compton readied himself, reaching into his right pocket and grasping the pen. Having practiced the movement for hours, he used his fingers to rotate the back end of the pen.

He saw FDR say something to Admiral Leahy, and then the two of them looked his way, FDR smiling. Then, to Compton's surprise, they started to walk toward his group, which for FDR took some effort. Compton looked around and saw the soldier beside him smiling brightly as they approached. FDR had recognized him.

What perfect luck. I can't miss at this range.

He watched as they came closer.

A little more . . .

FDR was now only a couple of yards away from him.

I'll do it when he reaches out to shake hands. I'll have a clean shot.

Roosevelt reached the line of Spanish-American War veterans. He looked ready to embrace the soldier, which would be even better. But then Compton felt something stabbing into his lower back.

"Hello, Bradley. I thought you would be here."

Charles Lindbergh stood behind him with his Montblanc Meisterstuck jammed into Compton's back.

"Don't take your hand out of your pocket. Just let the president have his word with the soldier and leave."

Compton said nothing.

Todd, Donovan, and Dulles, their eyes following the president, saw Lindbergh standing behind the soldiers. Without speaking, all three started moving to the side and down the steps.

Roosevelt took the soldier's hand and said, "My goodness, dear Bucky, I'm glad to see you again. How have you been?" He turned to Admiral Leahy. "Bucky Holt worked with me in the Navy Department during the First World War. The Navy wouldn't let him return to sea after being wounded in Cuba." FDR was now standing directly in front of his old acquaintance. He placed his hand on his shoulder.

"I'm fine, Mr. Roosevelt. God bless you and what you've done for the country."

"God bless you, Bucky. You'll have to come by for lunch. Yes, please come. My secretary will get in touch." He stood smiling for a moment, then said, "Until then, my friend."

Compton was too close to let the opportunity slip through his hands. In a swift motion, he drew the pen from his pocket, wanting to get the shot off before the president could move away. But Lindberg's reflexes matched his—he deflected Compton's hand as soon as it emerged from his pocket, and both of their pens fell to the ground.

They dove after them. Compton grasped his pen, tore open his jacket, and lunged forward at the president and Admiral Leahy, nearly knocking Leahy to the ground. Wrapping his left arm tight around Roosevelt's upper body, he pressed the deadly device to the president's neck with his right hand. Todd and six Secret Service agents had their guns drawn, all with a bead on Compton, but the president was so close that none dared take the shot.

Compton, realizing there was no escape, resigned himself to a soldier's stoic death.

Everyone on the plaza was silent. Compton prepared himself.

Calmly, Lindbergh spoke up. "Bradley, the only thing you will do with that pen today is sign your confession."

"What are you saying, Charles? I am completing my mission."

Lindbergh held up the Meisterstuck in his hand and said, "This is your pen, Bradley. You've got mine, and it's only as dangerous as any other pen you'd buy at the five and dime. Look at the barrel—it's got my mark on it."

Heydrich glanced at the pen and saw the "LL" etched on the barrel.

Lindbergh took the opportunity and threw a lightning-fast cross punch, landing it directly on Heydrich's nose. Caught off guard, Heydrich, his head reeling to the right, let go of his grip on the president and was immediately swarmed by the Secret Service, who not too gently wrestled him to the ground and cuffed him.

Leahy got to his feet, supporting the president with his arm. "Franklin, are you all right?"

Tilting his head backward in a silent laugh, FDR replied, "Couldn't be better, Bill. That was the most excitement I've had in a long time."

Then, turning to Lindbergh, he said, "Charles, I vehemently oppose your politics—and frankly, I've suspected you of having Nazi leanings. But I want to thank you. I may have occupied my spot on these sacred grounds sooner than I imagined."

He reached out his hand, and Lindbergh took it.

"Now," the president said, "let us pay our respects to those known and unknown who have served our country."

The ceremony went on as planned.

❧

Afterward, Donovan, Todd, and Dulles sat with Lindbergh on the same bench where Lindbergh and Donovan had spoken weeks before.

"How did you spot him?" Donovan asked Lindbergh.

"Well, when I arrived, I decided to station myself opposite the location where I'd been told to stand, a little further off the path so I wouldn't be spotted. When the president arrived, and the veterans came to attention, I noticed that the one-armed man toward the end of the line gave a queer little shake of his leg as he did so. Bradley did that same thing at our first meeting, and it happened again when we met at the beach. I think he was suppressing the heel click some of the Nazi officers of Prussian descent perform with their salutes."

"And you made him drop his pen and exchange it for yours?" asked Todd.

"That was just luck," Lindbergh replied with a sheepish grin. "We both reached for a pen, and it worked out. I'm just glad I checked the one I picked up and saw it wasn't the one I brought. So what happens to Bradley now?"

"He'll be tried by a military tribunal here in Washington for the crimes of espionage and murder during wartime," Donovan said. "If he's found guilty, capital punishment in D.C. is death in the electric chair."

"That's if the prosecutor in New York waives extradition,"

Dulles added, "and I think he will. If not, he'll be tried twice. Either way, he'll get the chair."

They all went silent until Donovan broke the silence. "Normally, I abstain, but if anyone is interested, I'll stand a round of drinks."

The affirmative response was unanimous.

"Colonel Lindbergh, could you use a lift?" asked Donovan.

"Yes, I could. Thank you, General."

❧

Donovan, Dulles, Lindbergh, and Todd drove into town together, dropping off Todd along the way. He promised to rejoin them shortly and bring Barbara, J.L., and Tobias with him.

Donovan and Dulles were staying at the Willard, and since it was convenient, they had decided to meet in its iconic Round Robin Bar. When Todd and the others arrived, they found Donovan, Lindbergh, and Dulles seated to one side of the bar on a tufted leather bench, against a mahogany-paneled wall. They'd commandeered three small two-person tables and pushed them together.

It was a cozy scene that became even cozier with the addition of the four newcomers. Once everyone was seated and their drinks had arrived, Donovan proposed a toast, and they all drank to it. This was followed by several other toasts requiring fresh rounds of cocktails. And so it went, on into the evening.

Warmed by the cheer of close friends, new acquaintances, and his bride-to-be, Todd couldn't help but reflect on the whirlwind of activity over the last month—the people, the emotions, and everything that had happened. Family and friendship were at the core of it all. J.L. had lost one son and gained another. Tobias had connected with the family he never knew existed. And Donovan, along with his brothers from World War I, remained dedicated to the memory of their fallen comrades.

Todd knew he would always hold dear those people who had fought bravely and sacrificed to free people from tyranny and protect the dignity of human life—Hendricks, Fleming, Newley, Ter Meer, Helga, and all the men and women of the OSS. They were his newfound family.

Barbara put her head on his shoulder and said, "Penny for your thoughts."

Todd smiled and looked into her eyes. "I was just thinking that two girls would do as well as two boys. What do you think?"

"I think two of each would be better."

Epilogue

WILLIAM DONOVAN DIRECTED the OSS until the war's end, when President Truman disbanded it. Shortly after the war, he suggested to Truman that a permanent intelligence agency was essential for America's safety and for protection from foreign intrigue, notably from the Russians. Truman balked at the suggestion, and popular opinion was that it would become an American Gestapo. With the onset of the Cold War, however, Truman reconsidered. In 1947, Congress passed the National Security Act, creating the Central Intelligence Agency (CIA)—formed along the lines Donovan had proposed.

Stricken with dementia, Donovan died in 1959. President Eisenhower visited him just before his death, and afterward, the president was heard remarking to a friend that Donovan was "the last hero."

Allen Dulles would become the fifth Director of the CIA, followed by three other former OSS members—Richard Helms, William Colby, and William Casey.

In January 1942, shortly after the bombing of Pearl Harbor, Charles Augustus Lindbergh sought to be recommissioned in the Army Air Forces. Because of his political rhetoric of past years, his request was contested by Secretary of War Henry L. Stimson.

Lindbergh went on to contribute to the war effort by

working as a consultant to military aircraft companies, including troubleshooting the flaws of the B-24 Liberator. In 1944, as a civilian, he flew over fifty combat missions against the Japanese. In 1954, on the recommendation of President Eisenhower, he was commissioned as a brigadier general in the US Air Force Reserve. Later in 1954, he won a Pulitzer Prize for his autobiography *The Spirit of St. Louis.* After a long and varied career as an engineer, environmentalist, and champion of native tribal causes, he died of cancer on the island of Maui in 1974.

In April 1945, realizing the war was lost, Heinrich Luitpold Himmler secretly asked the vice president of the Swedish Red Cross to communicate his willingness to surrender to General Dwight D. Eisenhower on the western front. When Hitler was informed, in late April, he stripped Himmler of all his posts and ordered his arrest.

Himmler went on the run, only to be captured shortly afterward by the British. Using a cyanide capsule he concealed in a false tooth, he committed suicide on May 23 and was buried in an unmarked grave near Luneburg, Germany. The exact location of the grave remains unknown.

Afterword

This book is prefaced with George Santayana's familiar quote stating that if we don't remember the past, we are doomed to repeat it. In just the one locale mentioned in the book, 1.1 million people were brutally murdered during the camp's five years of operation. Humbly, I suggest that remembering this atrocity—and the hundreds of others like it—isn't enough. We should not only remember, but also reflect and understand that our own parents, siblings, or children could just as easily have been caught up in this crime against humanity. So yes—remember, reflect, take a moment, and even if only briefly, allow yourself to be horrified.

Acknowledgments

In writing this book, I am deeply grateful to the individuals who contributed to its completion.

James Werner and Gregory Han for review and comments on early drafts, and Robert Donovan and Daniel Purnell for their support and encouragement.

Honorable mention to my classmate, John Scudder, Lieutenant Colonel, United States Army (retired).

All of the above, except John, have been my poker buddies for the past fifty years, and as such, I am appreciative of the kind and consistent financial backing they've provided.

Finally, and most importantly, I'd like to thank my editor, Lori Draft, for her professionalism and expertise. I've heard it stated many times before, and with this second collaboration, I'm convinced it's true: the editor is always right.

Author Bio: James Ryan

James Ryan is a retired business executive living in Northern California. "The Himmler Gambits" is his second novel.